CURSED
ONCE MORE

CURSED ONCE MORE

THE SEQUEL TO *WITH THIS CURSE*

AMANDA DEWEES

Cursed Once More

ISBN-10: 1514200422

ISBN-13: 978-1514200421

Cover design by Victoria Cooper Art

Interior layout and design by Plaid Hat Books, LLC

Sign up for the author's newsletter at www.AmandaDeWees.com.

Acknowledgments

One of the best parts of writing a book is getting to spend more time with some of the wonderful people who helped me bring my previous ones into the world. For *Cursed Once More* I was delighted to once again draw upon the wisdom of plot whisperer Maurice Cobbs; critique partners Lisa Blackwell, Martha Crockett, and Susan Goggins (Raven Hart); and beta readers Peyton Smith-Hopman and Joani Van Demark.

I'm fortunate to be able to welcome some new companions in adventure, as well. My gratitude goes to Abby Dowling-Baker, beta reader and medieval literature advisor; Paige Rohe, brainstormer and cheerer-on; Charles R. Rutledge, fisticuffs consultant; and Rita Thompson, who drew my attention to a news article about the excavation of European graves that revived my interest in vampire lore.

Finally, writing would not be nearly as much fun without Thursday nights at Dr. Bombay's Underwater Tea Party and the writerly comradeship and enthusiastic support of Lindsey Mitchell, Diana Plattner, and Caitlyn Mitchell Trautwein. Thanks, ladies! Next week the scones are on me.

About the Author

Atlanta author Amanda DeWees received her PhD in English from the University of Georgia and wrote her dissertation on 19th-century vampire literature—the perfect training, although she didn't know it at the time, for writing Victorian gothic romance novels. Learn more about her and her books at amandadewees.com.

Books by Amanda DeWees

Cursed Once More
The Last Serenade
Nocturne for a Widow
Sea of Secrets
With This Curse

The Ash Grove Chronicles:

The Shadow and the Rose
Casting Shadows
Among the Shadows

CHAPTER ONE
Cornwall, September 1873

In eight months of marriage, I had not yet grown accustomed to the pleasure of being awakened each morning by my husband. Sometimes he woke me tenderly, sometimes passionately, and sometimes in a manner that made me dissolve into laughter even before my eyes were properly open. On this day he woke me with a kiss—or perhaps I should say an abundance of kisses.

"It is morning, my love." His voice in my ear was low and intimate, and his rough cheek grazed my face.

"So it is," I said, opening my eyes. "My favorite time of the day."

He smiled at me, his arresting pale blue eyes dwelling on mine. Icy blue, they are—the only cold thing about Atticus. His chestnut hair was rumpled above his broad, high brow, and the beginning of ginger beard darkened his jaw, emphasizing the wide, expressive mouth. He was a remarkably handsome man, my husband, with his strong noble profile and lean body, and often I was amazed anew at my great good fortune in being married to such a man—for his character was every bit as fine as his exterior.

"My favorite time of the day is the end of it," he said, his husky voice warm with suppressed laughter. "When we retire. Ought I to be troubled that it isn't your favorite as well?"

"I am quite partial to that time too," I admitted. "As I believe you can attest."

"Yes, I have observed a degree of enthusiasm on your part." His expression was so knowing that I felt my cheeks warm and had to drop my eyes. Even after being wedded more than half a year, my husband could still make me blush—and took great pleasure in doing so. Some day, I was resolved, I would return the favor.

"Morning is when I know that it hasn't all been a dream," I explained, returning to the point.

"That what hasn't?" He wound a lock of my curly hair around his forefinger in a favorite habit of his.

Happiness was still so new to me that it was not easy to put into words. "This," I said, gesturing at the opulence of my bedroom, with the lacquered Japanese furnishings and the rich, heavy draperies that wrapped us in quiet and kept out the worst of the cold. "You," I said, gazing once more at my husband, Atticus Blackwood, Baron Telford, the finest man I had ever known. "Us," I concluded.

My eloquence was rewarded with a lingering kiss. "Believe me, my love," he said at length, "waking to you every morning is sweeter than any dream." Then he must have seen something change in my eyes, for he said more soberly, "But I know your dreams are not always so sweet. Perhaps you favor morning because that's when you know that any unpleasant visions that visited you in your sleep were no more than phantoms." When I did not answer, he asked softly, "Did you have the nightmare again?"

"It wasn't so bad," I said, but he could tell I was lying, for he took me in his arms and held me tightly. I rested my head against his chest, feeling the reassuring thud of his heart.

"I wish I could chase it away for you," he whispered against my hair.

"You do. When I wake and I'm with you, I know all is well." It was just that my sleeping self did not seem to be as certain on this point.

Ever since the dreadful night seven months ago when Atticus's life was threatened by his murderous twin brother, Richard—thought to have died years before in the Crimean War—I had dreamed that I was once again traversing the underground passage that linked Gravesend Hall to the cove where they had confronted one another. That night, in search of Atticus, I had traveled that path without light and without knowledge of what lay before me, with no certainty that I would even be able to find my way out of the labyrinth. At the end of that passage I had found Richard attempting to force Atticus to give up his life as Baron Telford . . . or simply his life. The struggle left Richard dead by his own pistol. But events could so easily have gone the other way that I still shuddered at the thought of how close I had come to losing my husband.

In my nightmares all the terror of that night came back to me, magnified in the way of dreams, so that in my sleep I was once more taking that strange sightless journey, fearing for my husband's life and even his sanity as I groped through what felt like endless miles of narrow stone corridors. When I relived that night in my sleep, it felt as if all the weight of Gravesend itself were pressing down upon me, threatening to smother me in the darkness, to bury me alive. I would awake taking great gulps of the blessed air, feeling the comforting warm strength of my husband's body next to mine, and I would hold tightly to him as my breathing gradually slowed and fell into rhythm with his. Sometimes my panic woke him, and he would talk soothingly to me until I slept again—or find a way to make the wakefulness sweeter than sleep.

The dream did not come often, though, and for that I was thankful. It seemed now to be the only imperfection in our life together. Atticus and I were absorbed in pursuing his plan to establish charitable institutions for fallen women and their children. The second of the Blackwood Homes was already under construction, and just days earlier we had hit upon a scheme that delighted us: we would turn Gravesend Hall itself into a school. The manor was far too big a house for us, but it would

3

be ideal to house children and offer them rooms for study and play. We had decided to relocate to the lodge, which by normal standards was still capacious and luxurious.

Considering the simplicity we would gain, I would not be sorry to reduce the number of servants in our household. Those staying on at the new school would find their work less exacting than maintaining an aristocratic showplace. I considered that all of us would benefit from the change. The knowledge that before the winter was out Atticus and I would be settled in our cozier new home filled me with anticipation.

In the meantime, however, the grand routine of our Gravesend days continued, and with the coming of autumn came a return to the lighting of the fires in our rooms every morning before we rose. Like many luxuries, it came with a disadvantage—in this case, a loss of privacy. I seized upon the change of subject.

"Letty will be in soon to light the fire," I reminded Atticus. "If you don't wish to be seen, you had better go."

"I doubt she'll be shocked by my presence," he murmured, drawing me closer. "Considering that the only mornings I'm not in your bed are the ones when you are in mine . . ."

I had to concede the truth of this. "But she's so young," I said. "Seeing her master in a state of undress is certain to embarrass her."

"Then we ought to move to my bed."

"But that means that one of the manservants may catch a glimpse of me before I am dressed, and I should not like that, and I should think *you* would not like that."

"True enough." He placed a kiss on the end of my nose. "How is it that I never realized how complicated the running of my own household was until I married you?"

"I sometimes wonder the same thing. To think that you never noticed that the servants were turning their faces to the wall in your presence before I put a stop to it!"

Despite my teasing tone, he looked abashed. "I did notice from time to time, and I thought it odd . . . but I supposed it was their preference." My face must have conveyed my skepticism, for he hastened to defend himself. "How was I to know otherwise? I never had anything to do with the managing of the staff. I supposed that there must be some kind of tradition . . .

perhaps having to do with not being distracted from their work by the sight of dashing auburn-haired gentlemen . . ."

He began to laugh before he could finish the thought, and I shook my head at him tolerantly. "You certainly can be a disruptive influence," I said. "Which brings me back to the subject of Letty."

"Very well, then, if you're afraid my presence here will distress the tender innocent . . ."

"Thank you, Atticus."

". . . I'll hide under the bedclothes."

I swatted him lightly on the shoulder. "That is not what I meant."

"If I am to be chased from my wife's bed merely to protect the modesty of the servants, there is something very wrong with our household's priorities." His voice was half grumble, half caress. "Perhaps we should do away altogether with having a servant light the fire before we rise."

"That means the room will be frigid," I pointed out.

"We are quite warm where we are, are we not?" A roguish quirk of his eyebrows. "If you are cold, perhaps I need to hold you closer."

There was much to be said for this line of reasoning, but I strove to keep my mind on practicalities. "A charming thought, husband—but we shall wish to leave the bed at some point."

"Shall we?" He brushed his lips along the line of my jaw, and my eyes closed involuntarily at the sweetness of his touch. "Truly?"

"Well . . . we shall *need* to, whether we truly wish to or not." Even to my own ears my voice lacked conviction.

Sensing that I was weakening, he pursued his argument in ways that quite distracted me from thoughts of anything that lay beyond our bed. The discussion was so absorbing, and Atticus so persuasive, that I quite lost sight of my original point. Before I knew it the sound of light footsteps was approaching, and Atticus had barely concealed himself under the bedclothes when the door opened to admit Letty.

"Good morning, your ladyship," she said, her eyes widening as she spied the great lump in the bedclothes that was my husband. I could feel my cheeks burning again with blushes, especially when Atticus, unseen though he was, found ways to make his presence felt. I smothered an exclamation when I felt the touch of his lips in an unexpected place.

"Good morning, Letty," I said with determined nonchalance. "Is everything well with you this morning?"

"Quite well, madam. Did you—er—sleep well?"

"Yes, thank you. You may draw the curtains."

In the bright light that poured into the room I could see her more clearly as she went briskly about her routine, resolutely averting her eyes from the bed.

I sometimes wondered what the servants said of my marriage. Having once been a chambermaid at Gravesend, I had a good idea of how interested those below stairs would be in the lives of those they served. And my marriage to Atticus Blackwood, now Baron Telford, had come about under such strange circumstances that they would have been cause for comment in most any quarter, whether below stairs or above.

In my girlhood my widowed mother had been Gravesend's housekeeper. I had been sent away in shame after it was discovered that I had been meeting in secret with Richard, at that time a paragon in my eyes, and my first love. During the long years after first his apparent death and then my mother's actual passing, I had earned my living as a seamstress, eventually attaining a post with actress Sybil Ingram. After years of this life, Atticus had succeeded in tracing me despite my assumed name and offered me a marriage of convenience, promising me my freedom upon the death of his invalid father.

Grudgingly and only because my employment with Sybil Ingram was at an end had I accepted this arrangement, never imagining that it would become a union of love. Over the years I had spent alone, as I had grieved for Richard and resented the circumstances that had forced us apart, my heart had hardened into a small shriveled thing no bigger than a walnut. It had been a strange, slow, even painful process for this withered organ to swell, to expand, to beat again with love. Atticus had won me over with his kindness, his tenderness, and his devotion—for, just as I had held Richard in my heart ever since leaving Gravesend, so Atticus had held me in his. He had loved me . . . and I grew to love him so much that I hardly recognized myself as the wary, resentful woman I had once been.

A fire was now going on the hearth, and Letty stood awaiting further orders. "Shall I tell Henriette that you are ready to dress, your ladyship?" she asked.

An urgent tumult of the bedclothes suggested that Atticus was shaking his head emphatically.

"No, thank you, Letty," I said. "I'll ring when I need her."

"Very good, madam." She bobbed a curtsey and departed, to our mutual relief.

As soon as the door had shut behind her, my husband's head popped out from beneath the counterpane, as if he were some exotic (and extraordinarily handsome) tortoise.

"I still say we can do without Letty in the mornings," he pronounced. "Once we move into the lodge, let us rearrange the servants' duties. I can light our fire of a morning."

An impish riposte suggested itself to me at this moment, but I quelled it. "You wouldn't mind?"

"I shall consider it my duty as a husband to provide warmth for my bride," he said. "With utmost courage I shall brave the chill air, undaunted, springing forth to face the task—"

He flung back the bedclothes, preparing to suit action to words, but I caught his arm to detain him.

"That would be delightful," I said, "but there's no need just yet. What were you saying before we were interrupted? Something about our not wanting to leave our comfortable bed?"

Instantly he turned back to me and took me in his arms. "Why, yes," he said softly. "I do believe I had more to say on that subject."

The intensity of his brilliant blue gaze made me momentarily shy, and I dropped my eyes. The livid scars on his bad leg, conspicuous in the morning light, caught my attention. I had wept the first time I had seen those scars and the misshapen ankle of his club foot. Not because it diminished him in any way—the opposite, indeed, for he had overcome this disadvantage through strength of character, and without letting himself become bitter or hard. No, I had wept because the sight brought rushing to my mind all the pain he had endured for so many years: both the physical agony of the brace and surgeries to correct the condition, and the torment of spirit that he endured from his brother and parents, who felt that his condition made him inferior to Richard.

7

With time, though, I had gained the ability to look upon his club foot with something closer to equanimity. Atticus, seeing my distress, had gently pointed out that he might not be the same man had he not endured these things—the man whom I had come to love so dearly. And the thought of his not being this person was too horrible to be borne.

Now, to banish the idea, I turned my face up to his and kissed him. This was not a moment for sadness. This moment was about me and my husband and our future together—a future that, I suspected, would soon contain the most wonderful promise that a wife could present to her husband.

But that, too, was a thought for later. For now, the two of us were our own complete universe.

***

When we finally did dress and descend for breakfast, the morning was well advanced. Mrs. Threll, the housekeeper, was accustomed by now to our tendency to rise late, and she made certain that we did not have to wait long for our meal. As Atticus settled in with his correspondence—of which, thanks to the Blackwood Homes and forthcoming school, there was now a great deal—I poured our tea and hugged to myself the knowledge that I might soon be sharing with him.

I was not yet certain of it, however, so before I spoke to Atticus I planned to seek the counsel of my niece. This might seem like a turnabout, as Genevieve—known in the family as Vivi—was only half my age and had been married for an even shorter time. But Vivi had the advantage of me in one important respect: she was already expecting her first child. That afternoon she and her husband, George, would join Atticus and me for tea, and I knew that I would be able to draw her apart from the men at some point for a private conversation.

So absorbed was I in this happy train of thought that I did not at once notice the letter lying next to my place at the table. The handwriting was unknown to me, and I did not often receive letters except from the ladies of our social set. Such letters were not frequent, as Atticus and I had become less popular after the scandal of his father's murder and Richard's death had become known. Neither of us found this a cause for mourning, since our true friends had stood by us, but it made the appearance of this letter all the more curious.

The seal was the single initial B. I slid a knife under the envelope flap and removed the letter, which was written in a masculine scrawl on paper rather thinner than what I was accustomed to from those in my husband's circle.

My dear niece, it began.

Shocked, I glanced to the end to seek the signature. *Horace Burleigh, Esq., Thurnley Hall.*

I must have made some sound, for Atticus looked up from his work. "Is something wrong, my love?"

"I—no. No, not at all. Don't let me disturb your reading."

When he returned to his documents, I took up the letter again. My mother's name before her marriage had been Burleigh, that much I knew. But never had I dreamed I would hear from any of that branch of the family again. Had she not been turned out of her home, disowned by her family, because of her marriage to my father? Indeed, she had grown bitter with resentment against her kinfolk for refusing to help us when my father's death had left us alone and unprovided for. Had they taken us in, my mother would not have worked herself to a thread for all those years and might not then have succumbed to the illness that had killed her.

My thoughts were a tumult of anger and grief as I began to read the letter.

> *My dear niece,*
> *How overjoyed I was to learn of your existence! During a recent visit to London I caught sight of you and your illustrious husband, and I noticed at once your remarkable resemblance to my late, beloved sister, Miriam. When I made inquiries, I learned of your identity. Imagine my delight to discover that my sister had been blessed with a daughter. And not just any daughter, but a baroness! You have made me very proud by doing so well for yourself. I understand that the properties linked to the Telford estate are*

extensive and endow the title with a rich income, and you must be enjoying your new wealth and status among your new peers after the years of obscurity and privation. It is to your credit that you were able to weigh the advantages of a match with the present baron against his deformity.

Doubtless you are curious about the family you were never permitted to know, and you are surely as eager as I to re-forge the sacred bonds of kinship. You must have sorely felt the lack of family when you married and upon the tragic death of your father-in-law. Grieve no more, my dear, for now you have a paternal figure to help you through the strange new world in which you find yourself.

I entreat you and the baron to do me the honor of paying a visit to Thurnley Hall at your earliest convenience so that we may begin to make up for lost time.

Your devoted uncle,
Horace Burleigh, Esq.
Thurnley Hall

I dropped the letter as if it were a slug. How transparent the man was. He had been content to ignore my mother's very existence until her child was of some use to him. Now that I was married to a man of wealth and stature, my mother's brother was eager to batten upon us like a parasite.

"My dear?" Once again my husband's attention was on me, and his brilliant eyes were full of concern. "Are you certain nothing is distressing you?"

I realized that I was breathing quickly with anger and the hand holding the letter was clenching it too tightly. Forcing myself to relax my grip, I took a breath and smiled. "Nothing of consequence," I said. I would not expose my husband to the letter's ugly assumptions about our marriage. Indeed, I was of a mind to throw the thing into the fire, but instead I slipped it into the pocket of my pearl-gray morning dress. I did not want to draw further interest from Atticus, and it would do no harm to keep it for the time being. "What does the day have in store for you, my dear?"

"The dismantling of the folly is scheduled to begin tomorrow," he said. "I thought we might pay it a final visit before lunch, if you like. Make a sentimental journey, as Mr. Sterne would say."

The folly, a mock Gothic ruin consisting of a partial tower and two fragmentary walls, was an extravagant feature of the estate that dated from the previous century. The butler, Birch, had pointed out that it might be a hazard to young boys, who would be tempted (or dared) to climb to the top of the tower, where they might easily fall. The entire structure was unsafe, he said, due to the years of exposure to the elements, and Atticus and I agreed that it would be safer to have it torn down before Gravesend welcomed its first students.

I would not be sorry to see the folly go. It held a bittersweet place in my girlhood memories, having been one of the places that Richard and I would rendezvous during our secret romance. Indeed, a particularly sweet memory of an idyll there had sustained me over the long, desolate years after I had been ejected from Gravesend and lost Richard forever. In my memory of that perfect, golden afternoon with him, he had been the ideal sweetheart, showing a tenderness and consideration for me that I had not previously seen in him.

This was for the very good reason that Richard was not the man who met with me that day. He, in fact, had been trysting with another young woman, and in order to protect me from learning that sordid fact, Atticus had taken his brother's place in his rendezvous with me.

The discovery, which followed not long after our marriage, had devastated me at first. Atticus had deceived me, I felt; he had stolen from me my most beautiful memory of Richard, had thrown into doubt the love that I had cherished, miser-like, for all the years of my solitude. In that first flush of anger and pain I had refused to listen when he told me that the tenderness he had shown me had not been assumed. He had loved me—secretly— all the time that I had eyes only for Richard.

"You find it too painful a prospect?" Atticus queried now, when I did not answer. "The last thing I wish is to cause you distress."

I smiled ruefully. "It is painful only because it reminds me of my own foolishness. No, I would like to see it once more, in your company." I wanted to put completely behind me the girl I had been, with her blind stubbornness and youthful willfulness. The girl who had cherished an infatuation with a scoundrel.

For that matter, I wanted to put the ugly letter out of my thoughts. And it was easy enough to forget in the company of my husband. After its initial chill the day had become unseasonably warm, so much so that we dawdled on our way, walking hand in hand through the gardens and up the hill. The rise was gentle enough that Atticus hardly relied at all on his walking stick, a fine ebony one with an ivory handle carved in the shape of an eagle's head. When we crested the rise we stopped to survey the scene, as a breeze stirred the string tied between stakes to mark the area off limits. Time had brought a more authentic air of age to the crumbling tower and the two partial walls that extended from it. Stones loosened by age and weather had broken away and lay in the grass. It was a wise decision to dismantle it . . . and a kind one. I knew, though my husband had never said so, that he felt the presence of the mock ruin cast a shadow over my life at Gravesend.

That kind of consideration was so integral to his character that, for the thousandth time, I reproached myself for having been so blind to his nature when I was a girl. "This place is well named," I said. "That is exactly what it was—folly—for me to cherish the memory of being here with Richard for so many years."

I leaned against Atticus, and he wrapped his arms around me. I felt secure, resting against his support and his love. It was a feeling no one had ever given me but him.

His voice, like his embrace, was peaceful and reassuring. "Even though you didn't know it at the time, it was the memory of me that you held in your heart."

"True enough," I allowed. "I wish I had known then that it was you and not Richard who was here with me that day."

That won a hearty laugh. "You would have slapped my face and never let me near you again—and never in a thousand years would you have agreed to marry me, no matter what the circumstances."

The truth of this embarrassed me. "I didn't really know you," I said in my own defense. "My only impressions were the picture Richard painted of you, and he was . . . not kind."

"That doesn't surprise me. And my impressions of you were slightly askew, for that matter."

"That's right—after I let you unbutton my bodice that day, no wonder you thought I had borne him a child. I must have seemed quite a strumpet."

Again his voice, warm and husky, put my mind at ease. "Never did I think that of you. I admit that I assumed you were . . . well . . ."

"You assumed I was his mistress. Well, I can hardly blame you. And yet you are the only one I ever permitted that liberty."

"I am?"

I laughed at the surprise in his voice. "I might not have known it was you that day, but I knew somehow that I could trust the man I was with. That I could lower my guard and you would not take advantage of me. I never felt that with him." The memory made me shake my head. "It seems to me that I was a very foolhardy girl, and not a particularly virtuous one. I am astonished that you could love me."

"How could I not?" he returned. "You had such courage and ardor, such vibrancy. Everything was always more vivid in your presence, more brilliant and concentrated, sharpened to facets like a diamond."

Moved, I turned within the circle of his arms to look up into his face as he continued. "It didn't matter to the way I felt about you whether you were Richard's mistress," he said simply. "It did not diminish you or make me honor you any the less."

I put my hand to his cheek as if to reassure myself that he was real. "No other man would have felt so," I said. "Indeed, I would have thought less of myself." The respect my husband held for me sometimes astonished me—always humbled me. At the time when he proposed to me he had believed Genevieve to be my daughter by Richard, yet, rather than consigning both of us to an ignominious existence, he had worked to reunite us (as he thought) by marrying me and bringing Vivi to Gravesend. "You are the only person I have ever met who truly believes that a woman does not surrender all right to human dignity if she gives her heart and body outside of wedlock," I marveled.

Under my gaze he smiled, and the crinkles at the outer corners of his eyes appeared, as they did when he was amused.

"You make me sound quite the paragon. But I confess I did envy Richard what I thought he had enjoyed. Both your devotion and your favors."

His chestnut hair stirred in the breeze, for he wore no hat; he looked younger, more boyish when he was bareheaded. "I'm glad there was nothing of that sort between Richard and me," I told him. "Nothing that could cast a shadow between you and me. I'm glad you were the first man I lay with—the first and only."

He drew me close and kissed me softly, and the kiss seemed to be one with the rustling of the wind in the trees and the warmth of the sunlight on our faces, elemental and pure and deep as the earth itself.

We stood thus for a long time. Presently he said, "Despite everything, it makes me a little sad to say goodbye to the first place where I kissed you."

I could not bear for him to be sad, even a little. "But there are so many places, now, where you have kissed me," I said lightly. "Such as here"—I put a finger to my cheek—"and here"—to my lips—"and here . . ."

I was rewarded when he laughed, and any trace of sorrow in his eyes vanished. "Perhaps we need to say goodbye to this place properly," he said, and now there was mischief in his voice. "A kind of reverse christening." I frowned, uncomprehending, and he asked, "What would happen if I laid you down in the grass and kissed you right now?"

I could not help laughing at the idea. "I'm no longer a girl of seventeen, Atticus."

"My point exactly. Now you need have no fear of losing your virtue—or your position."

"Just what are you suggesting?"

He bent his head to whisper in my ear. "I thought we might finish what we began that day."

I could feel my cheeks growing warm: once again my husband had made me blush. "But it isn't proper," I objected, uncertain whether he was in earnest. Was this a jest? He did enjoy baiting me.

My protest was not very forceful, and he dismissed it easily. "We two are the only souls here, so we decide what is proper," he said, his voice silky and intimate. "And I think there is nothing more proper in a husband than to show his wife how much he adores her."

But in such a fashion! "Here in the out of doors there is no privacy." It astonished me that I needed to point this out. "Anyone might come upon us."

"Not now that the place is cordoned off and Birch has ordered all the servants to keep away until its destruction." There was devilry in his expression, but also the steadfast love that assured me that I was always safe in his hands . . . and in his arms.

I wrestled with indecision. True, the idea was shocking—or should have been. But it was surprisingly difficult to summon up indignation. What he had said was true, after all, about a husband demonstrating his love for his wife. And a wife could not be reproached for returning connubial affection, surely, even in a setting that was . . . unconventional.

"It is a delightfully warm day," he said coaxingly, perhaps sensing that I was weakening.

That was true. The thought of the balmy air on my skin . . . of loving my husband here in the soft grass, under the sky, as if we were back in Eden . . .

I made up my mind. "If I get grass stains on my gown, Henriette will have an apoplexy," I warned him.

"Meaning—?"

I tried to look demure. "Meaning I had best take it off," I said.

With a low laugh of triumph, Atticus picked me up by the waist to lift me over the flimsy barricade before stepping over it himself. He took me by the hand and led me into the lee of the tower, and when he drew to a stop and took me in his arms I saw devotion and desire mingled in his brilliant blue eyes.

CHAPTER TWO

B ecause the day was so unseasonably warm, as Atticus had so persuasively pointed out, I directed Mrs. Threll to have afternoon tea laid for us in the grounds. When Vivi arrived with her husband she looked as bright and flowerlike as the hardy blossoms that still remained in the garden.

Her Titian hair, blue eyes, and high, wide brow proclaimed her a Blackwood, although her precise lineage was not widely advertised, for she was the illegitimate daughter of Richard by way of a village matron, now deceased. She had grown up in France, and many of her habits had a foreign flavor, as when she kissed me on both cheeks in greeting. Her formerly slender figure was noticeably changed now that the baby was well along.

"Aunt Clara," she exclaimed, with a smile that showed her dimples. "How lovely you look in that frock. I hope my uncle has told you so."

"Now, Vivi," replied said uncle with an indulgent smile, "I'm sure you have your hands full managing your own husband without trying to monitor me as well."

"In any case, I have no complaints," I said, slipping my arm through my husband's.

"That must be an attractive feature in a wife," George Bertram said with a grin, winning the pretense of a glare from Vivi. Bertram, a cheerful, honest-faced man in his late twenties, was my husband's agent and an invaluable help in the creation of the Blackwood Homes. He and my niece had courted quickly, for it was clear almost from the day they met that they were suited to each other. Both were enthusiastic and openhearted yet practical. Bertram's advantage in age and experience provided a gentle check on Vivi's enthusiasms when they threatened to carry her away, while she brought delight and excitement into a life that otherwise would have been in danger of being consumed by work.

Indeed, the two men were soon absorbed in a discussion of business, but this suited me for the moment as it made it easy to draw my niece aside. When I whispered my suspicions to her, she clapped a hand over her mouth to stifle a squeal of excitement.

"But Aunt Clara, how perfectly *merveilleuse!*" she exclaimed, but softly enough that our husbands would not overhear. "When shall you tell my uncle?"

"I'm not certain. I hate to distract him when he is so busy."

At that, my niece planted her hands on her hips and gave me a look that took me back to the days of being a chambermaid and being scolded by my mother for some serious breach of my duties. "How can you hesitate? He shall be overjoyed!"

I was nearly certain that she was right, but I craved the comfort of reassurance. "There are risks when a woman as old as I has her first child. I don't want him to fret over me. At least, not until I'm completely certain . . ."

Vivi shook her head decisively, setting her pearl earrings swaying. "From what you have told me, it sounds most certain. And husbands fret in any case. George may look placid now, but you should see how he hovers about me with shawls when the evening draws in and insists that I put up my feet when I sit down for more than one minute by the clock! Do not deny my uncle the pleasure of worrying over you." Then, catching me off guard, she flew at me and hugged me around the waist. "How delighted I am," she whispered, "that my child shall have a cousin! And what perfect parents you and Uncle Atticus will be."

Touched, I returned her embrace. "That is very dear of you to say, Vivi." Over the top of her head I gazed at my husband where he stood deep in conversation with Bertram, and I could not help but smile at the sight of his animated expression, knowing that my news would evoke even more excitement. "Atticus will certainly be a splendid father." The miserable example of his own would tell him exactly what *not* to do as a parent, and I could imagine how overjoyed Atticus would be to give his child all the affection and attention that he had not known himself.

Unless, perhaps, the arrival of a child at this particular time, when he was so busy with his charitable enterprises, proved to be problematic. "Vivi, how did you break the news to George? Was it difficult?"

"Difficult?" She waved that away with an expansive gesture. "He was so eager to hear such news that he practically said the words before I could. You will tell my uncle soon, then?"

"The evening after tomorrow, perhaps," I said. "It's his birthday. He did not want any notice taken of it, but I've planned a rather nice supper for the two of us." We would have complete privacy and freedom from distractions. Delight bubbled up in me at the prospect. What joy would kindle his eyes at the revelation of what lay ahead. At that moment it suddenly seemed an eternity to wait before disclosing the thrilling news.

"Tell me, Aunt Clara," Vivi was saying, and I brought my thoughts back from where they had wandered. "Do you wish for a boy or a girl?"

"I had not even thought that far ahead," I confessed. "I am still so delighted to be able to have a child at all that I cannot imagine being disappointed with either. And you? What is your wish?"

She shrugged in that expressive way that only a French upbringing could endow. "I would be happy with either as well, but I suspect George would like a little girl. Still, with twins running in my family as they do, perhaps we shall have one of each!"

Her peal of laughter caught the attention of her husband, who turned a beaming visage to us. "Come, ladies, join us. We've had enough of our masculine solitude and are in need of feminine company."

We obeyed without hesitation. As my husband put his arm around my waist and smiled down at me, I felt a wave of happiness wash over me, as warm as the sun and as invigorating as iced wine. How perfect was the future that lay before us. A busy, useful life it would be, providing for the needs of women cast off by society and for their children, and raising our own child. When Atticus broke the news about our plan to transform the manor house into a school, though, George sounded a surprising note.

"What about the curse on Gravesend?" he asked. "Aren't you afraid of exposing children to that?"

From the long-ago day that my mother and I had arrived at Gravesend I had known of the curse attached to the place and the family that lived there: the house, so the tale went, would take from its residents whatever they held most dear.

After I had been cast out of the house and had lost Richard, I had blamed the curse. But now, looking back, I knew that my younger self had merely sought in her unhappiness for a scapegoat. Especially now that I was so happy and anticipating such a fulfilling future, the curse seemed nothing more than a superstition. And I saw from a glance at my husband that he was not troubled by the legend either.

"Gravesend has seen its share of sorrow and tragedy," he said. "Perhaps more than other houses; perhaps not. But it has also seen much joy." The way he gazed smilingly into my eyes told me what role I played in that joy. "What do you think, Clara?"

Gravesend deserved a new beginning, I decided, one unhindered by the fears of the past. I said firmly, "The best possible future for the place is for a crowd of children to fill it with their energy and innocence—and chase all the old shadows and superstitions away."

Even now I do not believe that I brought bad luck down upon Atticus and me with those words. A few years before, I might have feared that I was tempting the gods by proclaiming the curse to be a mere superstition, but now that I am older and wiser I know that my scoffing at such a thing did not truly affect what was to come. I do not blame myself—not for that, at least.

Still, if I had known of what short duration my happiness would be, would I have changed anything about that evening? Disclosed my news to Atticus instead of waiting? Drawn out the pleasure of our family gathering, wringing every bright drop of conviviality and contentment to be had?

It is impossible to say. All I know is that this charmed interlude would be the last flowering of our harmonious life before circumstances altered it utterly.

The next day Atticus and I drove into the village after luncheon. He wished to deliver some documents to George Bertram at his office, and I accompanied him so that I might purchase some sewing thread that my maid, Henriette, needed.

If I had known who we would encounter on this errand, I would have done anything within my power to prevent my husband from leaving Gravesend.

As it was, we nearly escaped unscathed. Our visit to Bertram's office was without incident, and the two of us soon proceeded to the dry-goods store. It was only after I had completed my purchase and as we were stepping out the door that the voice hailed us—or rather my husband.

"Why, it's Mr. Blackwood, isn't it? No—Lord Telford now!"

From the street a woman in a tartan dress and a tall, thin man were regarding Atticus with interest.

My husband started ever so slightly. He summoned a smile and doffed his hat as they approached, but a certain stiffness in his bearing betrayed his feelings to someone who knew him as well as I. He was not pleased to see this woman.

He was far too polite to betray the fact, of course. "Miss Norton," he said, briefly clasping the hand she extended in greeting. "This is an unexpected pleasure."

"Indeed, yes. But it's Mrs. Munro now. This is my husband, Cecil Munro." Her eyes darted to me, and Atticus introduced me while Mrs. Munro sized me up, as women of Atticus's lofty circle tended to do. I permitted myself an equally candid scrutiny of her. She was attractive, no older than I, and beneath her fashionable plumed bonnet showed curly hair still brown without a trace of gray. Her tartan walking dress was beautifully tailored, and I was absurdly glad that I was wearing my violet faille polonaise with matching velvet ribbon trim, which was particularly becoming to me.

I could see her bright hazel eyes darting looks at my husband, assessing and approving. Next to Atticus, her own husband could not help but suffer by comparison. In contrast to Atticus with his broad shoulders and air of quiet confidence, Mr. Munro, though tall, was stoop-shouldered and weedy. Perhaps to compensate for his thinning hair, he possessed a moustache so abundant that it obscured his upper lip entirely.

"Cecil darling," she was saying, with a smile that might have been called saucy twenty years ago, "Lord Telford is an old beau of mine."

"Is that so?" Mr. Munro's expression was guarded as he shook hands with Atticus.

"Yes, indeed. Lord Telford owns Gravesend Hall—you remember?"

In the very act of shaking hands, Mr. Munro seemed to pause. In an instant he had recovered, and his manner instantly relaxed. It was as if he had placed Atticus in his memory and realized . . . what? That he posed no threat to his wife's affection?

"Mind you, that was a long time ago." She gave a breathy chuckle, as if her stays were too tight. "My Cecil and I have five children now! But you've not been married very long, have you, Lady Telford?"

"Less than a year," I confirmed.

"Dear me, quite a new bride still! Lord Telford certainly took his time about marrying, although I have to say he was quite attentive to me at one time. There was even talk of us making a match of it." With an air of coquetry, she asked Atticus, "Do you remember?"

"I do remember there was talk," Atticus said, and although his voice was pleasant, something in the words made her smile falter, and she turned back to me.

"My dear, you must tell me all about how you met. And who sews for you? That cashmere paletot is simply cunning. In fact, I should love to ask your opinion on this shawl here in the shop window . . ."

I listened with half my mind and answered absently as she drew me toward the window display. Atticus and Mr. Munro seemed to have found some topic to discuss, for when I looked back I saw that they were now absorbed in discussion of their own.

My uninvited companion must have observed this as well, for her voice suddenly dropped into an entirely different tone: confidential, serious. "You're very brave, my dear," she said.

"Brave?" I repeated, startled.

"To marry the baron, knowing of his—his condition." She glanced over at the two men where they stood talking together and shook her head.

This was why she had drawn me aside—to fish for confidences about our marriage? "My husband is the best of men in all the ways that matter," I said coolly. "I'm proud to be his wife."

She looked at me as if trying to gauge whether I was telling the truth. "Then you don't find it repugnant? His deformed limb?"

In my disgust and anger, I had to fight to keep my voice from rising. "On the contrary, I feel myself the most fortunate of women," I said, biting the words out with icy precision. "Just because you yourself cannot see beyond his affliction does not mean that my husband is in any way deficient."

Her eyes narrowed on my face. "My dear," she said, and her voice was cooler, no longer ingratiating, "it would be foolish of you to pretend that your husband is a normal man."

Was this what most people thought when they looked at him? Dear heaven, what he must have endured. "He is far from normal, as you call it," I snapped. "He is superior to every other man of my acquaintance."

"Your loyalty is most becoming in a wife, of course, but you must give some consideration to what affliction any child of your union might suffer." She actually shuddered, the contemptible woman. "The very thought of wedding a man whose children might be deformed makes my blood run cold. Are you not afraid of what your children might be?"

As if she had the right to speculate about such a thing. Where my voice had been cold before, it was now glacial, and my hands had tightened into fists with the effort to keep control. "I'll thank you to mind your own business, Mrs. Munro," I said in almost a hiss. "I think we have said all we have to say to each other."

Without giving her time to reply, I strode back to the men and slipped my arm through my husband's, and when he broke off what he was saying to smile a welcome to me, I said sweetly, "My love, we mustn't detain the Munros any longer. Lovely to have met you both, but we shouldn't dream of keeping you from your shopping."

Having thus forced him to draw the encounter to a close, after hasty farewells on both sides I led Atticus at a brisk pace to our waiting carriage. I wanted to leave that woman and her odious words far behind and as quickly as possible.

"I gather you didn't take to Mrs. Munro," he said mildly, once we were on our way back home.

"Not one jot. Has she greatly changed from when you knew her?"

"In some ways, I suppose." He was silent for a moment, and then said with gravity, "Her face and form have matured since last we met; I hoped that her mind had followed suit."

"I fear not. She said some things that were outrageous and offensive."

His smile was as weary as if it were a century old. "I think I can guess what they were. She was probably astonished that any woman would take the risk of marrying me."

Sitting across from me in the carriage with his hands folded over his stick, he suddenly seemed remote. I leaned forward and placed a hand over his. "Tell me," I said.

He took a breath and released it in a long sigh. His eyes, always so quick to reflect mirth, were equally prone to be pensive. In a man of his sensitivity, the pain that he had endured in his youth could not help but leave its mark. One hears of eyes being called soulful, and my husband's possessed this quality more than any I had seen. At this moment I was glimpsing the vulnerability that he must have felt as a younger man, which the dreadful Munro woman had awakened in his memory.

"When I found you in Miss Ingram's troupe and proposed to you," he began, "I said that I had wooed women in my own set but had learned that they wanted nothing to do with me."

"I wondered if that story might have been fabricated in an effort to sway me," I admitted.

Again that heartbreakingly exhausted smile. "I confess that I exaggerated the number. Miss Mathilde Norton was the only young lady I courted. It was years after you had left Gravesend, taking my heart with you, and she was the first woman I had met who seemed to me to possess something of your vivacity and spirit . . . the first woman besides you whom I could envision sharing my life with."

I had never heard him speak like this, and I sat silent at this new insight into the man I loved.

He shifted on the cushioned seat as we jounced over ruts in the roadway, and his thoughts seemed to shift as well. "I was lonely, I admit it. Mathilde appeared to be pleased enough with my company, with my attentions. She had a merry disposition and seemed as if she would be an agreeable companion. I had nearly made up my mind to propose to her when I found out, quite by accident, what she truly thought of me."

A pit of sympathetic dread formed in my stomach, but I did not interrupt.

"At a house party at her family's home, I became an unintentional eavesdropper one night. I was in an out-of-the-way alcove in the library when Mathilde and a crowd of her friends burst into the room and settled in for conversation. Before I could make my presence known and excuse myself, I heard my name mentioned . . . and in terms that would have made it too humiliating for all concerned were I to reveal my presence."

He paused for so long that I feared he might not continue. He had dropped his eyes, so I could no longer read them.

"It was my club foot, chiefly, which will not surprise you," he said at length. "To that point I had believed that by dint of the medical treatments and long and arduous practice my affliction was not noticeable in my gait or my dancing, but evidently I had flattered myself. And my condition was hardly a secret. It was rather a shock, however, to learn just how repugnant Mathilde considered it."

My hand tightened over his, and I wished that I had clawed the Munro woman's eyes out when I had the chance. I could only imagine how cutting, how callous, how cruel had been the words Atticus had heard spoken of himself, and which he was refraining now from repeating.

"She and her friends felt that the risk of tainted offspring was one they could not take," he said quietly. "I cannot blame them for that."

Perhaps he could not, but I could—and did.

"The curse also entered into the discussion," he added more briskly. "There was some debate over which was a worse affliction to wed oneself to. But the upshot was that all of the young ladies shuddered at the idea of becoming my wife. I realized then that any thought of marrying was out of the question."

My heart ached with an echo of the pain that those brainless girls had inflicted upon him. For a loving and gregarious person like Atticus, it must have felt like a sentence of exile to believe that he was barred from marrying. "How thankful I am that something happened to upset that idea," I said softly. "What was it?"

"You," he said unhesitatingly, raising his eyes to mine. "I found you. My father's failing health meant that I took on more management of the estate and its resources, and thus more control over my own destiny. Before, my efforts to find you had been constrained by my limited funds and connections, and by the need for secrecy. So when I was able to I relaunched my search for you with the firm intention of making you my wife—by any means short of kidnapping."

That brought a faint, bittersweet smile to my lips. When Atticus had first approached me, I had been so averse to what he proposed that kidnapping might have been the only way for him to have secured me, had circumstances not left me without the means of supporting myself.

"That alias of yours threw me off the scent for a good while," he continued, "as did your travels with Miss Ingram's troupe, but find you I did. So you see"—and he drew me over to sit beside him—"it is actually very fortunate indeed that all of my other possible brides viewed me with such repugnance. Otherwise I would not have been free to marry you."

I threw my arms around him. "That is too frightening a thought to be borne," I exclaimed. "Don't let's ever speak of it again."

"You're happy with me, then?"

I thought there was the ghost of uncertainty in his voice and cursed the woman who had put it there. "More than I can possibly say," I told him. "I wish I could show you just how happy you make me."

"A moving carriage certainly adds a degree of difficulty to such a demonstration," he mused.

I was momentarily taken aback. "Atticus, you don't—I didn't—"

But then the twitching of his lips betrayed him, and I gave his shoulders a little pretend shake. "Wicked rogue," I exclaimed. "Will you never stop teasing me?"

He laughed outright and held me closer to him. "No, I never shall. You are so charmingly indignant when you realize it."

"Well, you shall not always have the advantage of me. Some day I will find a way to astonish you," I told him.

How brilliant were his eyes as he gazed at me. "You already do that every day, my darling," he said softly.

So perfect was this moment, so loving this embrace, that I thought I might tell him my news. "That Mathilde and her friends were fools," I said, placing my hand against his cheek. "Any woman given the chance to bear your children should thank heaven for it."

But his face went grave, and all the merriment of a moment ago fled. "On the contrary," he said quietly. "I understand entirely why she felt as she did. It is natural for a woman to want whole, healthy children."

"But Atticus, surely—"

"The likelihood of having a crippled child is nothing to be taken lightly. Indeed, it is probably better for a man of my condition not to have children at all."

That silenced me. Mistaking the reason for my dismay, he took my hand. "It's just as well that we are of an age when it is unlikely to happen," he said.

That *I* was of an age, he meant—but he was too tactful to say that. "It is still possible," I ventured.

"Have no fear, my love. If it were going to happen, it probably would have by now. As it is"—and he patted my hand—"everything has worked out for the best."

For a time we drove without speaking, the only sounds being the thud of the horses' hooves and the rumbling, clattering carriage. We still sat side by side, but each lost in our own thoughts.

Are you not afraid? the Munro woman had asked. And I had dismissed the question.

But I was afraid now. Not of bearing a child that was less than perfect, and not that Atticus would not love such a child. Afraid, perhaps, that he would blame himself for any physical disadvantage he might pass on. That the remorse and fear would destroy his happiness in being a father.

That he might even, in his most secret heart, blame me for bringing a child into the world who might suffer for carrying Blackwood blood in his veins.

CHAPTER THREE

The next day was Atticus's birthday. If my mood was less than celebratory after our sobering conversation of the day before, it was not improved by the sight of another letter with the Burleigh seal resting by my breakfast plate.

As soon as I was able, I withdrew to my sitting room with the letter so that I could read it in solitude. The writing was unlike that on the previous letter. The hand was shaky, the ink strokes so delicate that the words seemed to try to vanish into the page. Too nervous to sit, I paced while I read.

Dear Clara,

I believe my son has recently invited you to visit what remains of your late mother's family, here at Thurnley Hall. He probably expressed himself very ill, but I beg that you will consider the invitation as coming from me. My health is very poor indeed, and my physicians tell me that I have scant time left

*upon this earth. It is my most urgent wish to meet
my granddaughter before I pass away. Can you
find it in your heart to forgive the wrongs done your
dear mother—or at least to set aside your anger,
just though it is, long enough to meet me? There are
things that you must know, things about the past that
may do untold evil if they remain buried. I beg of you,
come to me once, before the silence of the tomb closes
about me.*

Your devoted grandmother,
Elena Burleigh

What a dreadful dilemma. It would be churlish to deny an
ill old woman her deathbed wish, but I was reluctant to involve
myself in what already seemed to be an eccentric and possibly
deranged branch of my family. And of course, this was assuming
that they were genuinely my relatives and not merely passing themselves off as such. The Telford wealth would be reason
enough for impostors to approach me.

And if this purported grandmother was genuine? It was
a terrible time for me to absent myself from the household.
Although I was not integral to the planning and execution of
the Blackwood Homes and school, I was deeply involved in the
schemes, and Atticus had turned over several areas to me to
advise him upon. It was out of the question for him to set all of
this aside to travel to Yorkshire for an indefinite stay, and I was
reluctant to walk into this unknown situation alone.

Between this thorny problem and my anxiety following
the encounter in the village, I was in a far from festive mood
as the hour for supper approached. Henriette, my maid, was
perplexed that I was so subdued as she helped me change into
my dinner gown. This was a new and splendid ensemble, much
more formal than my usual garb for supping with my husband,
of claret-red figured velvet with festoons of antique lace. I had
directed the seamstress myself on its construction, looking forward to surprising Atticus with my splendor on this occasion.
Frequently in the evenings I simply wore a negligee, relish-
ing the opportunity to escape from my stays, and sometimes I
would wear my hair loose as well, for Atticus said he enjoyed

29

seeing it so. Some evenings after our meal he would brush it for me, plying the brush in long, slow strokes that evoked an almost meditative state.

A bit of that peacefulness would have been welcome that evening. I tried to tamp down my troubled thoughts as Henriette put the finishing touches to my hair and offered me a hand mirror in which to assess the effect of the cluster of ringlets into which she had coaxed my unruly locks.

"It's quite lovely, Henriette, thank you," I said, but the distant tone as much as the vague words made her shake her head at me and say something in French that I did not catch. My knowledge of the language had improved greatly since the first days of our association, when I could do little besides point and gesture to communicate with her, but sometimes I suspected that she took advantage of my comparative ignorance to vent her own feelings without fear of reprisal.

Not that she had anything to fear. Her prickly exterior and sometimes high-handed managing of my wardrobe and hair were little enough to weigh against her kindness, loyalty, and honesty. Of an indeterminate age between forty and sixty, with graying hair and a wiry frame, Henriette might not have been a prepossessing figure, but she had become dear to me, and I apparently to her, for she had stoutly rejected all offers of a change of employment to something less strenuous than attending to me. I reflected that in the much smaller quarters of the lodge she would find it far easier to carry out her duties, and the thought made me glad.

She was looking perplexed now that I was not happier with how grand she had made me look. Impulsively I stood and embraced her. "*Merci*," I said. "You are a marvel, Henriette."

"*Trés bien, madame.*" Mollified, she stood aside as I swept past her to the connecting door to my private sitting room.

Even now the footmen were laying our supper at a small table near the fire. On nights when Atticus and I had no guests to entertain, it was our habit to take the evening meal together here. Our private suppers were a custom that had begun during the days when our marriage was but a show, as a way for us to plan and discuss strategy without being overheard. Now, however, what once had been a strategic necessity had become a cherished custom for both of us—a time to enjoy unhurried, uninterrupted time together, especially precious if the events of the day had separated us. A time when we did not have to be baron and baroness but simply Atticus and Clara.

Despite my trouble of mind, my spirits could not help but revive at the sight of Atticus, splendid in his evening clothes. As always, the stark black and white attire set off the brilliant blue of his eyes—eyes that widened appreciatively when he saw me.

"Clara, you're magnificent," he said, taking my hand and raising it to his lips. "I had wondered why Sterry laid out my white tie."

"Your birthday calls for something festive," I said as he held my chair for me. "Even though our celebration is private, it doesn't have to be plain. I had Birch choose something special from the wine cellar, and Henriette tells me that Cook has outdone herself."

"How thoughtful of you, my love."

It was so easy to be thoughtful where Atticus was concerned, perhaps because he was always thinking of others besides himself. I was learning kindness from him, I sometimes thought. Or trying to restore the balance, to make up for all the years in which he had no one to think of him or try to make him happy. At the same time, I was bringing balance to my own life after all the years in which I had had no one to care for. I had learned that I found great pleasure in thinking of ways to delight him.

It certainly seemed that I had done so this evening. The menu met with his approbation, and when the footmen had departed and I presented his birthday gift to him, he exclaimed over it as though it were the crown jewels.

"It's the finest waistcoat I've ever seen," he pronounced, lifting it out of its wrappings. "Do I detect the skilled hand of my wife in this?"

"Sewing a waistcoat isn't difficult," I said, embarrassed. "But I remembered your saying they never have enough pockets, so I hid an extra one under this lapel—right here."

"The perfect place to tuck a *billet-doux* from you." He held it up to himself. "And I like the color very much."

I smiled. As royal blue was the color of his two favorite waistcoats, it had not been difficult to deduce that he would like a third in that shade. To enliven it I had done the piping and lapels in brocade of the same color as his eyes. He would not encounter another man wearing such a waistcoat.

He leaned across the table to kiss me. "It is splendid, my love. I pity the unhappy men who have to make shift with lesser garments."

"It isn't as fine as all that," I scoffed. "We'd best eat before our meal grows cold, after Cook went to so much effort." But secretly I was delighted by his pleasure. It made me proud that something I made could give him happiness, even something as minor as a waistcoat.

As we supped, Atticus grew even more animated as he told me of the architect he and George Bertram were consulting about the plans for the new Home. Normally I took great interest in details of this sort, but tonight, despite my pleasure at the reception of my gift, my thoughts wandered to dispiriting matters: the conversation with Mathilde Munro and the peculiar letter. Especially the letter.

If only my family had never come to know of my existence, how much simpler things would be. If only I knew for certain whether they *were* my family. If only . . .

A pause in Atticus's words brought me back to myself, and I found him gazing at me with a pensive air.

"I'm so sorry," I said at once. "I must be a little tired. Pray go on."

But he did not take up where he had left off. "I'm being very selfish," he said instead, his husky voice thoughtful. "I'm not giving you the chance to speak at all."

"There's no need. Please, don't let me interrupt."

"But you aren't, my love. I always look forward to these times alone with you, for talking something out with you can help me see it with greater clarity." He put his hand out, and I laid mine in it, finding comfort in the clasp of his long, sensitive fingers. "The other morning," he continued, "when I said that my favorite time of day was the end of it, I was thinking of more than just the delights of the marriage bed. No matter how exhausting or frustrating or frantic the business of the day, I find myself replenished when we have this time together. My joys are magnified when I tell you of them, my difficulties diminished."

"I feel just the same," I said, but my gaze wavered and fell. I was ashamed that I had been giving my husband, my life's companion, so little of my attention tonight. A fine helpmeet I was, thinking only of my own concerns.

His piercing blue eyes seemed to penetrate directly into my heart. "You are my sanctuary, Clara. I want to be that to you. Won't you tell me what is troubling you?"

Abashed, I withdrew my hand from his. "I don't want to spoil your birthday."

"You mean far more to me than any date on the calendar. Please let me help, if I can."

I stared down at the linen napkin in my lap, prey to indecision. In all the years of earning my own living, I had had no confidante or defender, and so I had become accustomed to keeping my troubles to myself. It was all very well for the poet Donne to claim that no man was an island; this woman certainly had been, for all of her adult life. The habits of those years had toughened me, had woven themselves into my very grain, it sometimes felt. As much as my curly hair and brown eyes, a stubborn, guarded independence seemed to have become part of me.

Now that I had the opportunity to unburden myself of my worries, even to reach out my hand for help in banishing them, I found I scarcely knew how. It hardly seemed right, after all, to shunt my burden onto my husband, who had more than enough responsibilities to shoulder already. Yet the matter involved him, even if only to the extent that he might be parted from me for the duration of a visit to these people who claimed kinship with me. And in truth, by remaining silent I might cause him even more disquiet than if I shared the cause of my worry.

The temptation to confide in him was strong. What blessed relief it would be if he were to take on some of the weight of this problem! When I glanced across the table at him I saw that he was still regarding me with grave attentiveness, and a worried crease had formed between his brows. My conscience twinged.

"The last thing I wish to do is add to your burdens," I said. "You have far more important matters to attend to."

"Nothing is more important to me than you, my love." When I did not reply, he added lightly, "Just think what satisfaction it will afford my masculine vanity if I can relieve you of something distressing. Every husband wants to plume himself on having played the gallant knight for his wife, even if he plies his sword and shield against nothing more threatening than a spider in her teacup."

That penetrated my defenses and made me smile. How well Atticus knew me. I might be able to withstand tenderness from him—though only with difficulty—but if he was able to tickle my sense of humor, I could hold out against him no longer. Besides, he deserved to know the reason for my distraction. And he might be able to bring insight to the matter that I could not.

"Very well," I said, rising. "I'll just be a moment."

I had hidden the two letters—feeling furtive as I did so—beneath a stack of handkerchiefs in my bureau. When I returned, I showed them to Atticus in the order in which they had reached me: first the one from Horace Burleigh, then the one signed Elena Burleigh. He read each in silence, his eyes thoughtful, and when he had done awaited my explanation.

"I've not told you much about my family," I said, "for the very good reason that I know so little myself. My mother scarcely spoke of her own people, not at all of my father's. I always had the impression that my father was from a lower social sphere, so perhaps he was ashamed of them and did not associate with them."

"Or perhaps he had no family," Atticus suggested. "He might have been a foreigner, or the last remaining member of a line that had died off."

"That's possible. In any case, my mother never looked to any connections of his for assistance after my father died—not to my knowledge."

"And what of her own people?"

I glanced again at the wax seal with its bold initial B and tried to quell a surge of anger on her behalf. "She gave me to understand that they had cast her off when she married my father. They never spoke again as far as I am aware. I can't say for certain that she never appealed to them for help, but I remember her as fiercely proud. I suspect she would rather have starved than asked them for assistance."

"But she had your welfare to think of."

"That's so." Proud though she was, and often a stern parent, nevertheless she was protective of me, and there had never been a time that she had put her own welfare before mine. Not until I had been dismissed from Gravesend . . . but she had not abandoned me, not exactly. She had found shelter for me and made certain I had a new position. It was not her fault that I had been unable to keep it. Had she left Gravesend with me, there would have been two of us in search of a living, and she would have been unable to send me money to assist with my keep.

I brought my thoughts back to the discussion at hand. "As I say, I am not certain. It is quite possible she appealed to them for help and was rebuffed. There would have been no reason for her to share the fact with me; she might have feared raising my hopes."

"A redoubtable lady she was. It must have taken great strength of character for her to survive with no protector, let alone to rise to so high a position in domestic service."

A new thought made me raise my head from where I had been sunk in contemplation of the flames, and I looked across the table at my husband. "I wonder how she came to your mother's notice. I never thought to inquire about that. Perhaps there is correspondence that would tell us? That might fill in some of my mother's background."

But he shook his head. "It's an excellent thought, but unfortunately my father had all of my mother's letters burnt upon her death. When I began my search for you in good earnest I had the same thought, but it came to naught. And I'm afraid I don't recall hearing anything at the time that might be useful. I would have been no older than ten or eleven when you and she came to live here."

For some reason it had not occurred to me that he would have his own distinct memories of my mother. "Do you think I am like her?" I asked, and I could not have said what I hoped his answer would be.

He rubbed his jaw as he searched his memory. "I don't remember her very well, for as you have observed, in the past I did not always pay a great deal attention to the staff. But it seems to me that you carry yourself very much as she did: your back as straight as a queen's, your head held high. You have a gift for stillness that she did not, however."

"She had little leisure in which to be still," I said ruefully. Little leisure to spend with her daughter, for that matter. I had always longed to have more time with her that was not spent on lessons and chores. When I looked back now, I could not remember her doing a single thing for pure pleasure. Always, always she had been busy about household tasks or teaching me or directing other servants.

"What do you wish to do?" Atticus asked me, drawing me out of my musings. "Would you like to meet the Burleighs? If these letters are to be believed, your grandmother may not have much time left."

"I wish I knew if they were genuine," I said fretfully. "It is so clear that my uncle is interested in us only for the Telford fortune and status. His connection to me may be far more tenuous than he claims. And even if we are as closely related as he says, he sounds like someone I would rather keep at a distance." I stopped. "But my grandmother . . . it worries me that she may be speaking the truth. It would be unforgiveable to deny a dying woman her wish for reconciliation."

"As to the truth of the letters, I can have Bertram make some inquiries about the Burleigh family and this branch in particular. If everything is in order, we could send word for them to expect us within the week."

"Us?" I echoed in surprise, as hope lifted my heart. "You would accompany me?"

"It's a poor husband who would send his wife to face the unknown all alone," he said lightly. "You may find it dispiriting to meet the people who cast you and your mother out, and my place is by your side, lending you whatever strength you may need."

"But you are needed here," I said, touched at his readiness to set aside his own concerns. "I couldn't possibly ask you to leave just now."

His broad shoulders moved in a shrug. "Construction on the new building can be carried out under Bertram's supervision. My presence is not vital here, and if I did stay I would not be easy in my mind until you returned."

"You would do this for the sake of an old woman you have never met," I marveled.

This made him laugh. "Make no mistake, it is not for her that I do it."

Deny it though he might, I knew that his sense of compassion had been roused by the letter. I rose from my chair and moved swiftly around the table to him, so swiftly that in his surprise he had scarcely begun to push his chair back to stand when I reached him. Before he could rise, I seated myself on his lap. Taking his face in my hands, I kissed him long and deep, and I felt his arms slip about my waist.

It was a long time before I raised my head. "How did I become so fortunate?" I wondered aloud, smoothing his chestnut hair back from his high brow. "What am I that I should deserve as fine a husband as you?"

At such close quarters his smile was bewitching. "I am happy that you believe yourself to be the fortunate one," he murmured, "but I know for a certainty that I am." His hands moved from my waist to the buttons on my bodice. "Fortunate also that your gown fastens in the front," he added, with an undertone of mischief in his husky voice.

"That gains you very little," I said, amused, "as there remain more layers of clothing beneath."

For a man of such integrity, my husband could look quite the rogue when he grinned, as he did now. "But I observe that your chemise also buttons in front."

Though delighted as always by his attentions, at the same time I felt a perverse dart of disappointment. I had hoped my new dress would win higher praise than this. "Is that all you have noticed about what I am wearing?" I asked, hearing the plaintive note in my own voice.

"Far from it," he assured me. "I notice that your new gown is a color that brings a glow to your skin and heightens the red of your lips. I see that the sleeves end just below the elbow, so that if I slide this one up just a fraction I shall be able to kiss the tender place in the crook of your arm . . ."

He suited action to the words, drawing a sigh from my lips.

After a moment he continued. "And I observe that the low neckline is designed to draw the eye to your exquisite décolletage." The rakish grin flashed again. "For my benefit, I take it?"

"Nothing of the sort," I protested. "It is the fashion." He cocked an eyebrow at me in skepticism, for I was quite liable to ignore fashion's dictates when it suited me. I cast about for another reason—for I had had one, I was certain. "And I thought it would set off the Telford collar to advantage," I offered. The magnificent necklace of pigeon's-blood rubies was a family heirloom.

He reached up to trace the line of my collarbone. "But you aren't wearing the Telford collar, my love," he said softly.

"Ah." I tried to think this over, but the touch of his hand made thinking difficult. "I seem to have forgotten it," I said finally.

"No matter. Your body is so beautiful it needs no adornment."

"You say the loveliest things. Did you spend all the years that we were apart thinking up compliments for me?" When he did not answer, I felt a sudden, terrible fear that my teasing words had wounded him. "Oh, Atticus, how clumsy of me. I am so sorry—"

"Hush, sweetheart," he whispered, his lips very close to mine. "Not to worry. You aren't far from the truth, at that." He kissed me lingeringly, one hand stroking my throat. "But on the whole, I believe we have talked enough for this evening, don't you think?"

The meaning in his eyes, as much as the ardency of his caresses, made me suddenly breathless.

"Yes," I whispered. And for a long time after, that was all I said. *Yes. Yes . . .*

Chapter Four

In just a few days we were on our way to Thurnley Hall. I had written to my uncle telling him to expect us and in return had received an effusive letter with directions regarding what trains to take and when his carriage would be awaiting us at the station.

I say "my uncle" because, as best as Atticus and George Bertram had been able to ascertain, Horace Burleigh was telling the truth. George had unearthed further history, not all of it reassuring.

"The Burleighs have been settled in West Yorkshire for hundreds of years, and Thurnley Hall dates to the 17th century," he had told me a few days before, when he paid a visit to Gravesend. "They were a prosperous family—mostly from woolen cloth— until about sixty or seventy years ago, when their fortunes took a drastic turn."

"What happened?"

George shook his head. "That depends on who is telling the story, as best I can tell. Tenant farmers complained that the sheep began dying from some mysterious ailment. Other accounts say that a once-rich coal seam played out. Both those conditions could have made it more favorable to townsfolk to leave Coley—that is the name of the parish—for one of the new factory towns, where they could make a more dependable living. In the last ten years, the situation has worsened more quickly, and the area appears to have practically emptied itself. Burleigh probably has scarcely enough tenants now to keep him in milk and cheese."

"And the family? What have you learned of them?"

For the first time George hesitated, and he seemed to search for words. I suspected that, kindhearted as the young man was, he was seeking a way to gently break some unpleasant truth to me. "Until their reverses, they seemed quite respected," he said eventually. "There was a mild uproar when Percival Burleigh, your grandfather, wedded a foreigner. The family was Romanian, I believe. At any rate, she brought her servants with her from her home country, which I gather disrupted the household and set the neighborhood talking."

"Perhaps Burleigh's tenants and neighbors resented the arrival of a foreign influence and began to depart as opportunity offered," Atticus suggested. "If the marriage brought that about, the family might well have considered it unlucky."

I did not have to ask why the mere fact of the bride's being foreign might have put the neighborhood at sixes and sevens. From what I had observed of life outside London, it appeared that anything that set a person apart in the least from what was considered normal . . . anything, for example, like a club foot . . . could give rise to suspicion and hostility.

"That seems quite possible," George affirmed. "Whatever the cause, your uncle may now find himself in a precarious position, Lady Telford."

I was still unaccustomed to being addressed by my title, especially from George, who was part of the family. But he had been rather shocked when I had suggested he address me as "Aunt Clara," as Vivi did, so I had stopped urging him to do so.

"Precarious in what way?" I asked.

"Unless he can hit upon a solution, he may be forced to sell, and I'm certain he has no wish to let the property go out of the family."

"Has he no children?" Atticus asked. "The usual course would seem to be to seek a wealthy alliance for his heirs through marriage."

"He is a bachelor, so he could easily seek to marry money himself were he so moved. But for whatever reason, he seems never to have sought a wife, wealthy or otherwise." George turned a page in his notebook. "Lady Telford, your mother seems to have been his elder sister by some four years. She was disowned when she left Thurnley Hall to marry your father, who had been one of the tenants before their elopement. She must have been no older than nineteen."

Such a young age, it seemed to me now, to have left behind everything she had known for an entirely new life—a life of labor, of struggle. "Have you learned anything of my father?" I asked, even though that fell outside the purview of his inquiries.

Sure enough, he shook his head again. "I'm afraid not. I'll keep inquiring, if you wish."

"Don't go to any trouble. I can probably learn more from Mr. Burleigh once we meet." I knew that Bertram and Atticus had plenty of business to discuss, including the hiring of a new assistant for the duration of our absence, and I rose to let them do so. Vivi had not accompanied her husband that day, and I was grateful that I did not have to tell her that I had not made my announcement to Atticus.

Compared to the chaotic conditions of traveling with Sybil Ingram and her theater troupe, our journey came together with astonishing efficiency. Sooner than seemed possible, Atticus and I were on our way. We broke our journey with an overnight stay in London, where I made a few purchases, and by early the next afternoon we were entering Yorkshire.

Though the views of the dales were verdant and lovely as our train neared Coley, with each mile closer to the family seat of the Burleighs the knots in my stomach tightened. Atticus squeezed my hand in reassurance. "Perhaps we'll be pleasantly surprised," he suggested. "And think how exciting it will be to learn more of your parents."

In this entire expedition that was the only prospect that seemed favorable. I yearned to know how my mother and father had met, courted, and married, and what kind of people they had been . . . unless they had resembled my uncle, in which case blissful ignorance would be preferable.

When the train stopped at the next station, I descended to the platform for some fresh air and a distraction from my thoughts. I was surprised to find Sterry, my husband's valet, hurrying across the platform to me from the direction of the second-class carriage.

"Is anything amiss?" I asked.

"My lady, I beg your pardon, but I fear Mademoiselle Henriette is ill."

"Ill!" I exclaimed. "That is rather sudden. She seemed well this morning."

Sterry avoided my eye. "I fear she felt it coming on before we left, ma'am, but she did not want to inconvenience you. She hoped it would soon pass. But now that fever has set in . . ."

"Take me to her," I said at once. "That does not sound like something that should be ignored."

Indeed, as soon as we joined her in the second-class carriage, I saw that poor Henriette was looking quite wan. After one glimpse, I ordered her to disembark. "Sterry, you must accompany her back to Gravesend," I said.

Instantly Henriette shook her head. "*Mais non, madame!*" she exclaimed, and out poured feverish utterances that she would not desert me thus.

"Be still," I told her gently. "You must not agitate yourself. Sterry will see that you get home so you can recover."

"But his lordship—" the valet ventured.

"He can spare you for a little while. You can come after us as soon as you see Henriette safely home." I dabbed at Henriette's clammy forehead with my handkerchief. "And do make certain to send for the doctor as soon as you can. Tell Mrs. Threll to have her well looked after."

When I returned to Atticus, I found to my dismay that a new passenger had taken a seat in the compartment. He sat nearly invisible behind a copy of the *Yorkshire Post,* so that I could see only striped gray trousers, worn black boots, and the top of a high black hat. The open newspaper was an implicit request for privacy that afforded it to us as well, and I felt free to converse with Atticus almost as if we were alone.

As soon as I had explained what had happened, he gave his unhesitating approval of my decision. "Far more important to see to Henriette's health than to arrive at Thurnley with a full complement of servants," he said.

"I thought you might make do with one of my uncle's servants in the meantime."

"Of course." He leaned closer so that his lips were near my ear and there was no danger of being overheard. "And if in Henriette's absence you need someone to help you dress, I can oblige."

So innocent was his expression that I laughed before I could help myself. A belated glance at our traveling companion's newsprint barrier showed no sign of his having heard us, but I nonetheless took up the newspaper Atticus had brought and raised it before us as an additional shield. "My dear husband," I whispered, "you have proven quite adept at removing my clothes, but as for putting them on me? That isn't something you have much practice with."

"I suspect it would be less pleasurable to dress you than to it is to undress you, but I'm willing to make the experiment."

"Such a generous offer," I teased. "How like you to put my needs before your own."

"That is every husband's duty, isn't it?"

"And what of my wifely duty? Shall I take Sterry's place and be your valet?"

Silent laughter showed in the dear crinkles at the corners of his eyes. "As tempting as that sounds, I foresee a problem with that arrangement," he murmured. "If you were to dress me, I should want you to undress me again straightaway."

So diverting was this conversation that it succeeded in distracting me from my fears about what lay ahead of us. And so, perhaps, was my husband's intent. In any case, by the time we disembarked at the Coley station and looked about us for the carriage that had been sent to meet us, my spirits had revived considerably.

The scenery that met our eyes also did its part in improving my mood. Sun and shadow alternated in a windswept sky over land that stretched out farther than any I had ever seen. Gentle green slopes were stitched together like the squares of a giant quilt with what I later learned to be low stone walls. The wind was brisk enough that I was glad of the warmth of my fur-trimmed mantle, but it was not bitter cold, and I had not even begun to feel impatient when a rumbling noise announced the arrival of our carriage.

The equipage had certainly passed its prime. The dark blue paint was peeling, and the remains of an initial B in crimson had faded and flaked until I might not have known it was there had I not been expecting it. The horses seemed nervous and twitchy but otherwise in sound enough shape, at least to my ignorant eye; they were great beasts with heavy locks growing down over their eyes and hooves.

The coachman, too, was great in size, as I saw when he leapt down from his seat. Clad in rough leather breeches and a home-spun smock that could have done little to keep out the cold, he had hands twice as big as mine and stood taller even than Atticus. Without so much as glancing at us he took my trunk from the porter, raising it to his shoulder with scarcely an effort. He wore a cloth cap over bristling black hair, and his beard and heavy eyebrows obscured his face to the point that it was impossible to read his expression. Beneath the rolled-up sleeves of his smock, great muscles strained as he lifted my trunk to the top of the coach.

"Good day to you," Atticus said to him. "You must be from Thurnley Hall."

For the first time the man looked at him, and, to my aston-ishment, his eyes went wide in what looked like fear. He fell back a pace and whispered something that sounded like "*strigoi!*"

Atticus looked puzzled at this but continued. "Mr. Burleigh is expecting us. There hasn't been any trouble, I hope."

The coachman shook his head rapidly and retreated another pace, throwing his hands up before him as if Atticus were advanc-ing on him. My husband and I exchanged looks of confusion.

"Grigore speaks little English," said a deferential voice. "Understands little either, I'm afraid."

Unheard, a man had joined us, and I realized from his dress that he was the avid reader from our compartment. Now that he was not hidden behind a wall of newsprint, I saw that he was slender, just below Atticus's height, and appeared to be in his middle twenties. Clean-shaven, he had a scholarly pallor that gave his fine features rather the look of an ivory carving. When he tipped his hat I saw that his dark hair was smoothly brushed back from his high forehead, and his brown eyes were of a peculiarly mild and attentive expression. Raising his voice, he addressed the coachman in a language I neither understood nor recognized.

The servant made a terse reply in what must have been the same language. His voice emerged from his massive chest as a deep rumble. But as the other countered in conciliatory tones, his tense posture relaxed somewhat. Although he cast sidelong looks at Atticus, he approached near enough to retrieve the remainder of our trunks and load them onto the carriage. Evidently the strange young man's words had been persuasive.

"Thank you for your assistance," Atticus said. "I'm not certain how I managed to alarm Grigore, but your intervention was most convenient. Allow me to introduce myself."

"There is no need, for I have the advantage of you," the young man said amiably. "It is a pleasure to meet you, Lord and Lady Telford. I am Victor Lynch," he said, reaching now to shake my husband's offered hand. "Mr. Burleigh is my guardian."

There had been no mention in the letters of my uncle's having a ward, and I regarded him with increased curiosity. His caped overcoat betrayed some age, for I saw that the collar had been turned. The coat might even have been made for another person, for the cape gave his shoulders an uneven appearance. When I stretched out my hand, he clasped it lightly in his gloved fingers and bowed deeply but did not kiss it, showing a restraint of which I heartily approved. I disliked it when strange men kissed my hand, but that was something that happened frequently now that I was a baroness.

"When I heard the delightful news that you would be visiting us," he continued, "I hoped I might encounter you along the way."

"Why did you not make yourself known to us on the train?" I asked, surprised.

His smile was gentle. "You and his lordship seemed to be perfectly content with each other's company," he said. "It would have been inconsiderate to impose my presence upon you."

I felt a dart of self-consciousness that this stranger had been observing us so closely, but Atticus merely chuckled and tucked my hand into the crook of his arm. "Your tact is appreciated, Mr. Lynch."

"Were I fortunate enough to be wedded to such a lady as your wife, I know that I should resent intrusions into my time with her." Mr. Lynch's tone was not insinuating, however, merely pleasant and even sympathetic. "I believe Grigore has retrieved all of our belongings; shall we depart?"

We assented, and Atticus handed me into the coach. Inside, the blue velvet upholstery betrayed some fading and baldness near the seams, but it was comfortable enough. I had certainly been accustomed to far more Spartan transportation before I married Atticus. How quickly, I thought in bemusement, I had grown used to luxury. Mr. Lynch gave an incomprehensible command to the coachman, and we were on our way.

"What language is that?" Atticus inquired. "It sounded rather like Italian." I ought to have known that with Atticus's education and inquisitive mind he would know what the Italian language sounded like.

"It is Romanian. Some of the older servants came to us from Romania, where Mr. Burleigh's mother was born. Grigore was born in Yorkshire, but he hews stubbornly to the language and customs of his parents, who came to us from Romania with my guardian's mother. I fear he is also a touch slow, but that is scarcely his fault." Mr. Lynch regarded us with friendly interest from across the carriage. "Is this your first visit to these parts?"

"It is mine," I said. "I admit it is far pleasanter than I had expected. One hears of the bleakness of the moors, but everything is so green and lush."

"We had an abundance of rain this summer. An overabundance, in fact, for the river flooded its banks where it cuts across the Burleigh demesne. We lost two of the few remaining sheep . . . but that is neither here nor there."

"What are the patches of purple?" I asked, peering out the window as the road ascended into hillier territory. The low, bushy growth contrasted charmingly with the many shades of green and with the darker, almost black areas where nothing seemed to be growing at all.

"That's heather. It's fortunate that the bloom hasn't faded, so you see it at its best. If you had come to us just a month or so later in the year, we might not have been able to show you so fine a face."

"You are a resident of Thurnley Hall, then?" Atticus asked.

Despite his proprietary air, he shook his head. "Alas, no, Lord Telford. I should like to be, but the regrettable fact is that I must earn my living. I am always pleased to visit for as long as my guardian will have me, though. I confess that I think of Thurnley Hall as my home, although I have no real right to claim it."

"I'm certain your guardian is happy for you to consider it thus," Atticus said, but a faint frown contracted our new friend's brows.

"My presence is, I fear, not entirely a pleasure for him."

"Whyever not?" I exclaimed.

"Pray don't blame him, Lady Telford. He has a great many worries weighing on his mind, not the least of which is his inability to offer me the lifestyle to which he says I was born." My lips compressed at this: further evidence that my uncle was sorely in need of money and had probably summoned me and Atticus in hopes of our solving this problem. Unaware of the effect of his words, Mr. Lynch continued, "It is to his credit that he found me the place I hold now."

"And what is that?" Atticus asked.

"I am cataloging the library of a gentleman in Coventry. He has an impressive collection of medieval texts on agronomy."

"Ah!" Interest animated my husband's face. "Does he have de' Crescenzi's *Ruralia commoda?* I have been hoping to acquire that ever since reading about it in the Royal Agricultural Society *Journal.*"

Mr. Lynch's smile was no less engaging for being wry. "I must confess my interest in the topic extends only as far as my work is concerned. My own taste in reading tends more toward folklore and works of the fantastic."

As they conversed, I let my attention return to the view. The higher we ascended, the more impressive the scenery became. It astonished me how far I could see across the tranquil slopes and how vast the sky seemed above it all. The banks of white and gray clouds cast great shadows on the verdant scene beneath, and one of these shadows fell over the carriage as it started down a long gravel drive.

After the wild beauty of the surrounding landscape, my first sight of Thurnley Hall was something of a shock. Accustomed as I had become to the classical white facade of Gravesend, I had imagined that Thurnley Hall would be somewhat similar. Now I saw how mistaken that assumption had been.

The first surprise was the sooty dark gray of the stone facade, so dark that one might almost have thought the house had been scorched in a fire. Memories of London flashed into my mind, for so much of that city's brick and stonework bore the marks of the barrage of factory chimneys. Here in what was almost wilderness, I had not expected to see such grime. I knew that it was not an omen, but I cannot deny that it struck a qualm in my heart. Thurnley Hall seemed corrupted somehow, befouled by the blackness that clung to its stone.

Immediately I scolded myself. There was no significance to the sight except to confirm that Mr. Burleigh lacked the funds to hire a team to clean the front of his house—or he felt, most likely with good reason, that resources were better diverted to crucial areas of his estate rather than mere cosmetic appearance. But when I tried to imagine my mother, with her fierce pride and high standards, living in this house, I could not compass the idea.

Another unexpected observation was the house's age. It was clear almost at once that this was an older building than Gravesend, and I wondered if the rose window atop the arched entrance meant that it had once been an abbey. Gables topped with spires rose above the top story, and there were a great many large square windows with diamond-shaped leaded panes. To the left a one-story wing with a peaked roof led to another, higher section with gables like the first . . . but something was awry with them, for as we drew nearer I could see that there was no glass in the high round gable windows, and stones had fallen away from the leftmost one, leaving a ragged gouge. At the sound of our approach, a crow rose flapping and cawing from one of the empty windows, and I could not repress a shiver.

"You'll see that one wing has fallen into disrepair," came the voice of Mr. Lynch, and I started at the suddenness and the way he had seemed to read my thoughts. "You needn't worry, though, Lady Telford—the rest is sound enough."

"It certainly looks it," I said. Indeed, even with the spectacle of time eating away at the place, the main portion of the house was so solid and imposing as to be a bit grim. The dingy, discolored stone certainly added to that impression, as did the leaden pall that had fallen across the lawn as the gray clouds massed and blotted out the blue sky. The grass had been let to grow high, and I remembered what Mr. Lynch had said about the sheep. Perhaps there were too few now even to keep the grass cropped.

The sound of rushing water came to my ears, and then the horses' hooves were drumming on a short wooden bridge spanning the river. This was a narrow channel, but as I peered out of the window I saw that it was indeed running high—and swiftly, to judge by the speed with which a twig was borne out of my sight along the surface of the green water.

As the coach drew up before the arched entranceway, an elderly male servant in faded livery appeared, followed by a slight girl in an apron and a plump woman with a chatelaine of keys at her waist. The manservant handed me down from the coach, and as Atticus and Mr. Lynch descended after me I distinctly heard a gasp.

When I looked at the housekeeper and maid, though, I could not tell which had gasped—or why. The little maid stood with her eyes downcast, and the housekeeper's face was expressionless. Both now made their curtseys, and the older woman said, "Welcome, Lord and Lady Telford. I am Mrs. Furness."

Atticus thanked her while I took her measure. In her forties, I judged, with graying fair hair drawn smoothly back beneath her white mob cap. Her voice was brisk, her eyes alert, and her straight posture gave me the sense that she had both herself and the household well under control. The comparative wildness of the grounds and the exterior was clearly no indicator that Thurnley Hall was managed by a slack hand.

"Mr. Lynch, I am sorry to say that your room is not ready for you," she continued. "We did not receive word that you were arriving."

"It was what you might call an impromptu decision," he said in his mild voice. "I could not pass up the opportunity to meet the baron and baroness."

"I'll inform Mr. Burleigh of your arrival and ask Cook if she has any of your favorite pigeon pie. Lady Telford, are your servants following behind?"

"Not at present. A bit of an emergency detained them. Can any of your staff be spared to attend to my husband and me? We don't take a great deal of attending to, I assure you."

"Naturally. Ann here will see that you're looked after, my lady." As she ushered us through the arched stone entrance and into the great hall, I looked about us with curiosity. The two-story hall was centuries older than Gravesend, looking almost medieval in comparison. The floor was of flagstone, and the walls, too, were of stone, but of a creamy buff color. An enormous fireplace was the most notable feature, along with the stairway that ran along the near wall. The stair rail of dark wood put me in mind of a cathedral, as did the elaborately carved armchairs near the hearth. A great wheel-like chandelier, unlit at this hour, hung from the high half-timbered ceiling. I was so absorbed in examining my surroundings that I was caught off guard when Mrs. Furness said, "I've put you in the Cradle Room, my lady."

"The *what* room?" I exclaimed before I could stop myself. Always at the edge of my mind hovered thoughts of the coming baby, and for a startled moment it was as though the housekeeper had seen into my mind and glimpsed my anxieties.

My interruption did not perturb her, fortunately. "It isn't a nursery, my lady, but the oldest of the bedchambers, and it was named for a sixteenth-century bed and cradle that are original to the house. Mr. Burleigh always puts his most distinguished guests there. I assure you, if you are concerned about its being spacious enough for you both, it will be quite adequate."

"I don't doubt it." Hastily I sought a reason to request a change. "I had rather hoped that we could be put in the room that was my mother's," I said.

"Unfortunately, all of the furnishings were moved out of that room years ago."

"Oh." I glanced at Atticus, but his face was untroubled; evidently I was the only one who felt that the cradle would be a painful presence. "The Cradle Room will be fine," I said.

"Excellent. As soon as you have had a chance to refresh yourselves, Mr. Burleigh will be pleased to welcome you."

I'm sure he shall, I thought. After all this time, I was finally to meet my mother's family . . . but I was far from certain that any of us would enjoy the experience.

CHAPTER FIVE

The Cradle Room proved to be a gloomy chamber made dark by the oak paneling and the great four-poster bed, whose headboard and canopy were carved in intricate designs. The central panel on the headboard depicted what seemed to be Adam and Eve being expelled from Eden by the angel with the flaming sword . . . not, I would have thought, a scene conducive to peaceful sleep. The namesake cradle at the foot of the bed was carved in more innocuous designs of wheat sheaves and flowers.

I averted my eyes from it as Ann, the little maid, helped me change my dress and tidy my hair. Great thought had gone into my choice of dresses when Henriette and I packed my trunks for the journey—far more than such a minor matter warranted. I had found myself wanting to impress upon my mother's relatives how successfully I had made my way in the world despite their having abandoned her, to prove that they had not harmed or humbled us. I wanted to show that despite their neglect I was doing quite well for myself. At the same time, I resented my own wish to impress them. They had failed my mother, had shown she did not matter to them. Why should I care what they thought of me now? Yet I did care. I felt I had to prove myself somehow. For my mother's sake more than my own, perhaps, but I could not let them think that they had won.

"Won what?" was Atticus's perfectly reasonable question when I had described my dilemma to him the day before.

"I mean that I don't want them to think that they broke my mother's spirit or succeeded in destroying her life, if that was their intent."

"I know your pride is smarting," he said gently. "Mine would be as well, in your situation. But consider that they may wish to make amends. Perhaps they regretted the breach and had no way of healing it until now."

It seemed ignoble of me to say what I felt—that they deserved to suffer for their treatment of my mother, as she had suffered. "Maybe I can forgive them," I said finally. "If they show me they understand what they did to her and recognize that they did wrong. Without that, I cannot imagine wanting to have anything to do with them."

Concern drew his auburn brows together. "I understand, of course. But you must realize that some people are just not capable of that kind of insight. Not everyone can comprehend the consequences of their actions."

I had to hope that my mother's family did. They were her blood, after all; surely they would regret having caused her pain. If not already, then perhaps after learning from me just how the years of my childhood had been spent. Perhaps they lacked imagination and needed me to fill in the missing years for them.

By the time Atticus emerged from behind the folding screen that set off his dressing area I was dressed in a new gown of taffeta finely striped in black and gold. Black velvet trim accented the underskirt, bodice, and cuffs, and an ivory faille inset at the bodice made it suitable for day. For dinner that evening, I would remove this dickey. I had no idea whether I would be overdressed or underdressed for what lay ahead, but this

ensemble gave me courage and steadied my nerves. I knew that
it looked distinguished—elegant without being fussy or running
to any extreme of fashion—and, to judge from my husband's
expression when he saw me, it suited me very well.

"Will that be all, my lady?" Ann asked. She must have been
no more than fifteen, with wide brown eyes and a great deal of
wispy hair that refused to stay tidily in its bun. She said little,
perhaps from shyness.

"Thank you, Ann, yes. You've made me quite splendid."

"I heartily attest to that," said Atticus, taking my hand. "If
you would just show us where to find Mr. Burleigh?"

"Of course, your lordship!" She scurried to open the door
and point down the passage. "He'll be in the hall, awaitin' you
there. Do you need me to take you?"

Atticus assured her that we could find our way, and she
curtseyed a farewell. We made our way down the hallway, the
only sound being the creaking of the floorboards beneath our
steps. When we approached the stair, I held Atticus back on the
landing before we would emerge into view from the hall below.
He looked questioningly at me when I drew him close, but he
responded to my kiss with a ready enthusiasm.

"For courage," I whispered as I released him.

His smile momentarily drove all anxiety from my mind.
"You never need a reason, my love."

Then, with my hand tucked in the crook of his arm, we
descended into the great hall.

It was empty save for the figure of a stocky man who stood
before the fireplace with his hands clasped behind his back.
His feet were planted wide on the hearth as if he were estab-
lishing his ownership of the flagstones on which he stood,
and the thought occurred to me that this might be a pose as
theatrical as any of those struck by an actor in Sybil Ingram's
troupe.

He had a round head, nearly bald but for a short brush
of gray hair. With his short neck and barrel-shaped body, he
presented the impression of brute strength unrelieved by any
civilizing influence. His bottle-green coat and checked waistcoat
were a silent reproof to Atticus and me for dressing formally. As
we drew into view he looked up and smiled broadly.

That smile was as long as it took for me to take a violent dislike to my uncle. Probably he meant it as a friendly expression of welcome. But somehow it struck me as gloating and avid, not at all suited to one family member's greeting to another.

"Welcome!" he proclaimed as we neared. His eyes were small, even beady, and I did not like how they regarded me. "Welcome at last to the home of your ancestors, my dear Clara. I trust you don't mind if I call you Clara? After all, we are such near relations."

Somehow the sound of my name on his lips grated on my nerves like an iron file. "If it's all the same to you," I said, "I'd rather you didn't."

He drew in his chin, nonplussed. Then he gave a booming laugh. "Like to hear the sound of your title, do you, niece? Well, I can hardly blame you. Marrying a peer is quite an achievement."

"It would have been less of one had my mother and I not been reduced to the level of servants," I said tartly.

To my astonishment, instead of looking shamefaced or embarrassed, he let that great laugh loose again. Echoes bounced from the stone walls and rolled around the room like boisterous puppies. "You waste no time in pourparlers, do you, niece? Good, good. I prefer to speak plainly myself. Most women like to beat about the bush and mince words. I'm happy to find that you have a head on your shoulders. Lord Telford, sir, allow me to welcome you into the family. You've won yourself quite a prize in Cl—in your lovely bride."

Atticus shook his hand. "I agree completely, sir. Thank you for inviting us into your home."

"Not at all, not at all. Delighted to have such a distinguished nephew. I look forward to our further acquaintance. But just now"—and he grimaced—"you are expected most urgently by my mother."

"She wishes to see us already?" I asked.

This time his laughter was more like a wry bark. "She has been impossible to live with ever since you accepted our invitation. Once she learned you'd arrived she has refused to take any rest or nourishment until she speaks with you. I won't keep you from her any longer, but I wanted to greet you first. And I wished also to warn you . . . that is, to prepare you." He appeared to hesitate. "The fact is that she's likely to say some strange things. Pay them no mind."

"Has she been wandering in her wits?" I asked in surprise. Her letter had seemed rational enough.

He wavered, his small, close-set eyes avoiding mine. "I would not say that exactly," he finally answered, "but she has strange fancies. She sometimes takes it into her head that—well, she may confuse stories with actuality."

By that I supposed he meant that she was likely to say unflattering things about him. "We shall bear it in mind," I said. "Does she wish to see us both?"

That toothy smile split his face again. "Oh, assuredly. She's quite eager to assess the baron and determine whether he is worthy of inclusion into the family."

"That suits me, for I am quite eager to set about charming her," said Atticus amiably. "If you care to lead the way, sir?"

As my uncle conducted us to his mother's room, he pointed out features of the house . . . or, more precisely, the lack of them. "This is where a desk once stood that was owned by Oliver Cromwell, it is said. Thurnley Hall is rumored to have a priest's hole dating to those turbulent days." And once, indicating a pale rectangle on the wall where a picture had evidently hung, "We used to have a rather nice Sir Joshua Reynolds there until the roof needed repairing. It leaves a sad gap in the collection."

Old Mrs. Burleigh's room was in the main building of the house, like the Cradle Room but on the opposite end. At the sound of our knock, a thin, imperious voice called, "Come in, and be quick about it!"

A glance told me that the room was even larger and grander than the one Atticus and I had been given. Here none of the riches had been despoiled: a tapestry hung on one wall, fine paintings on another, and the giant four-poster bed could have been the double of ours. But instead of a cradle at the foot there was an antique armchair, and in this chair was my grandmother. And she made the rest of the room dwindle in importance.

The first thing that seized the attention was her eyes: dark and undimmed by age, they almost glittered with the force of her scrutiny. They darted over me, assessing, noting, and I found myself suddenly uncertain, wondering if my hair was in disorder or my dress too gaudy. I felt somehow that nothing, no defects of appearance or character, would escape that shrewd gaze.

Then she released me from that intense examination and turned her attention to Atticus. I was glad to notice that he was not intimidated by her: he stood at his ease, smiling slightly in apparent pleasure at this meeting, and not for the first time I felt a rush of pride that I could call this man my husband. Then, when his hand closed over mine, I remembered that I, too, had every reason to stand tall and proud. There was no reason for me to quail before this old woman.

"At last," she said, in that sharp, vigorous voice. She did not speak loudly, but there was no hesitation or sign of weakness in her words. Nor was there a marked accent, as I had expected. "Horace has taken his time in bringing you to me."

"The baron and baroness needed to rest and refresh themselves after their journey," my uncle protested. "They've not been here more than half an hour."

A thin, fine-boned hand waved him to silence. My grandmother looked as delicate as a porcelain shepherdess, but everything about her manner belied that impression of fragility. Her slight frame was clad in a gown of rust-colored velvet whose spreading skirts must once have been supported by a crinoline. She wore antique lace at her throat and wrists, and pinned to her collar was a large cameo depicting a weeping woman in classical drapery. Her white hair gleamed in the light of the fire that burned on the hearth. But her features were most interesting of all, for in them I thought I saw some resemblance to my own.

"Come closer, child," she ordered. "Let your grandmother have a look at you. Yes, you are Miriam's daughter and no doubt, despite your towering height. That must be from your father's side; your mother was nearly as petite as I. Kneel down so that I may see you better."

I did so, examining her as frankly as she did me. This close to the old woman, I could hear a catch in her chest when she breathed, and I could also see fine wrinkles on her brow and around her eyes. They were especially pronounced around her mouth, and even on such short acquaintance I could imagine that they indicated that she spent a great deal of time with her lips pursed in disapproval. Her skin was thin and delicate with age, and a complexion that must once have been olive like mine had gone sallow with illness. Her cheeks, however, were pink, and I realized that she used rouge. As a belle during the Regency, she had probably grown accustomed to such cosmetic aids. She had a straight, small nose and wide-set eyes with long lashes, nearly white now. There was also something familiar about the determination in the line of her jaw.

"Yes, yes," she muttered. "The hairline, the obstinate chin . . . thank heaven you inherited my ears: small, neat, close to the head. Your mother was not so fortunate. She was always trying to hide hers beneath her hair."

"She was?" I exclaimed. It was details like this that I was eager to learn. I wanted to be able to picture her as a girl and young woman and imagine her life in this house. "What else did she do?"

"All in good time. You may rise now. Introduce me to your husband, child."

"Allow me to present Atticus Blackwood, Lord Telford," I said. So commanding was her manner that I had unthinkingly fallen in with her orders rather than exerting a will of my own. I gave myself a little mental shake. "And how shall I address you, ma'am?"

The dark eyes, so striking against her sallow skin and white hair, raked me again. "Why, as Grandmama, of course."

I had the strong feeling that if she had been displeased with me, her answer would have been different. Evidently I had passed the first hurdle.

Again I silently scolded myself. I was not here to meet with her approval; rather the opposite. But I wanted the old lady to think well of me all the same, to recognize that my mother, her daughter, would have had no reason to be ashamed of me.

Atticus was bowing over her hand. "A pleasure, ma'am," he said, and even just those few words in his warm, genial voice seemed to soften the sharpness of her gaze.

"You are surprisingly well set up, given all that I'd heard. Aren't you a cripple?"

My breath caught in horror, but Atticus merely smiled. "I have a bad limb, but fortunately it does not impede me to any great extent. My stick here is all the assistance I need."

"Hmm. Well, I am glad to hear that. You're charming, to be sure, but that is not necessarily a mark of good character. Still—a baron. That is something." She drummed her fingers on the arm of her chair. "Tell me about your finances. How many acres have you? Any entails on the property?"

The barrage of questions pricked my temper. How dare this old woman question my husband as if he were a schoolboy? I opened my mouth to give vent to my indignation, but Atticus said simply, "I shall be more than happy to assure you of my ability to provide for your granddaughter, ma'am—but at another time. I know my wife is longing to speak with you about family matters, and I could not forgive myself if I postponed that conversation any longer."

The old lady regarded him closely. "It appears you know how to handle yourself," she said, in a milder voice. "Be off with you then, Lord Telford—and you go with him, Horace. I want to speak to my granddaughter alone."

My uncle clasped his hands behind his back and did not budge from where he stood. "You may overtire yourself if I am not here to see that you don't."

My grandmother's eyes locked with his. "Did I ask you to be my nursemaid, pray? You've more talent for getting underfoot than any man I've ever met."

Under that sarcastic tone his face reddened. "Very well, I'll go," he muttered. "I'll return shortly, though."

Atticus caught my eye and gave me a quick, encouraging smile as he left. He was slowly followed by my uncle, under whose heavy tread the floorboards creaked protestingly.

When the door closed behind them, the old lady sighed and relaxed slightly. Her back was still ramrod straight, and I wondered if she had been strictly schooled in posture as a girl, for only now did she permit it to touch the back of the chair. "Thank heaven he consented to go. My wishes do not always carry the weight they should with my son."

"I'm sorry to hear that," I said, but it occurred to me that my uncle might only now be in a position to argue with his mother. I could imagine that growing up under her strong will might have grated on him . . . as it might have done me, had I been reared in this household.

"Draw up that chair and sit with me. He is not all that I would have hoped for," she said as I did so. "As soon as I saw his letter to you I knew it would do more to keep you away than to bring you here. That is why I had to send for you."

"You spoke of secrets," I said. "Secrets that could do terrible damage if you did not disclose them."

"Did I? Perhaps I did. I may have resorted to melodrama in my urgency to meet you. What I said about my health was true enough; I've been given only a few more months to live."

But this evasiveness did not fool me. She knew perfectly well what she had been about, I was certain, and I said firmly, "I am very sorry to hear that, but I deserve to know what you meant."

"And you shall, Clara. Just have a little patience. We have so much to catch up on, and I must make certain of a few things first." Clearly she did not like to be pushed. She would disclose things in her own time, and my pressing her would do no good.

"You seem to have married well," she continued, returning to the earlier topic. "The baron is no weakling who will allow you to order him about, but I see no cruelty in him. Is he intelligent, child?"

The question caught me by surprise. "Very much so," I said.

"That is what I heard. I made inquiries, you may be sure, before writing to you. I learned that he is known for unconventional views, so I feared he might be an inbred idiot who wanted to plant the streets of London with breadfruit trees or some such claptrap."

"I assure you, that is not the case. He is a fine man and I love him dearly, as he does me."

That did not seem to impress her. "Sentimental attachment is unnecessary in a marriage, Clara. You seem like a sensible girl; I would have thought you would know that."

"It may not be strictly necessary," I said with a straight face, "but it makes things much, much nicer."

"Hmm." She regarded me thoughtfully, and her fingers absently touched the cameo at her throat. "The two of you seem well suited, at least. Any children?"

I hesitated. "Not yet," I said, hoping she would not press for details—or guess my secret. I had known women of her age with an uncanny knack for identifying expectant mothers.

To my relief she responded, "In other words, no. And at your age, very unlikely. Thank heaven for that."

"Why do you say that?" I exclaimed, ready on the instant to defend Atticus. "If you are thinking of my husband's club foot—" With a flutter of lace she waved her hand to silence me. "Not at all, child. Be still. But there are reasons . . . tell me, have you any sisters or brothers?"

"No."

"None living? Or none at all?" The questions shot out with a force that startled me. "As far as I know, there were no other children. I was born about a year after my parents married, and my father died soon after, so my mother said."

"Ah!" A curious look of regret softened the old lady's face, and she gazed into the distance. "How I wish I had known. How different everything might have been."

"How do you mean?" I asked.

For a long moment I thought she had not heard me. Then she said, in a gentler voice than I had yet heard from her, "I could have persuaded my husband to let you and Miriam come live here, if we had known you had no brothers."

I stared at her in uncomprehending shock. "You mean you would have forgiven Mother?"

Her eyes closed briefly, and she sank back into the chair. When she next opened her eyes, I was astonished to see tears gathered in them. "It was my husband who forced her out of the house. Oh, I did nothing to stop him, mind you, but if we had known the threat was past—"

"*Threat?* What on earth do you mean?" When she did not reply at once, it was all I could do to keep from seizing her by the shoulders and shaking answers out of her. "Why was my mother cast off?" I demanded. "Was it not because she married beneath her?"

"No," she said softly. "It was because—she married."

In the silence that followed that baffling statement there came the tread of heavy footsteps, and with the most perfunctory of knocks Mr. Burleigh entered.

"Now, now, that's enough of your gossiping for one afternoon," he said with a geniality that irritated me all the more for

61

seeming forced. "I know you womenfolk will talk endlessly if left to yourselves, but it's time for you to rest, Mother. See, Mrs. Furness has brought your draught for you."

"I don't need a draught." Fretfully, the old lady reached for my hand. "Clara, come back tomorrow morning so we may talk more. There are things I must tell you—things you must know about the past—"

"You can tell Clara tomorrow, Mother." He stooped to draw her arms around his shoulders and slip one arm beneath her knees. He lifted her from her chair and carried her to the bed as if she had been no bigger than a doll. "Now it's time for us to dress for dinner. Ann will bring yours on a tray, never you fear."

The prospect of dinner seemed to distract her from her wish to disclose more to me. "What is it to be tonight?" she asked.

Mrs. Furness, who stood by with a medicine bottle and a wine glass, answered her. "Pigeon pie," she said soothingly. "And a glass of Madeira to celebrate Lord and Lady Telford's visit."

"Mind you don't let my pie get cold. My room is not so far from the kitchen as that." The old lady seemed to have forgotten my presence. "Mrs. Furness, I believe I'll take my medicine after all."

"Very good, ma'am."

Mr. Burleigh took my arm, much to my displeasure, and led me to the door. "Good night, Mother," he said, again in that tone of false heartiness, and I called out, "Good night," just as he shut the door firmly behind us.

"As you can see," he said, "she isn't as strong as she thinks she is. Some sleep will set her to rights." His voice was crisp now without the false cheer.

"I wish I did not have to wait until tomorrow to speak to her again," I said, unsettled by how quickly she had seemed to grow confused. "Do you know what confidences she means to tell me?"

He would not meet my eye but kept a firm hold on my arm, leading me down the hall. "Like as not it's nothing important. No doubt she's looking forward to telling you about your mother."

"I gathered it was something urgent, or else she would not have said so in her letter. Why do you—"

He cut me off with a forced laugh. "Now then, there's time enough to discuss such things tomorrow. If she meant to confide in you the secret location of the missing family fortune, I'm certain she would have done so by now! Best not keep your husband waiting, now. The dinner gong will be going any minute."

And to my indignation, the man actually walked me all the way to my door and waited until I had stepped into my room before he would leave me.

CHAPTER SIX

W hen Mrs. Furness rang the small gong in the great
hall, the only person absent was my uncle. Atticus and
I had been the first to descend, followed shortly by
Mr. Lynch.

Like Atticus, my uncle's ward had changed into an evening
coat, and he looked more slight and youthful than he had in
his bulky caped greatcoat. This coat, too, gave his shoulders the
appearance of being uneven, so much so that I wondered if it
was not the coat after all. His dark hair had a tendency to curl
at the ends, an oddly endearing trait, and together with his pale
complexion it gave him something of the look of the late poet
Shelley.

"Lady Telford, how elegant you look," he said, bowing once
more over my hand. "You have enhanced the decor of Thurnley
Hall with your presence—a much-needed improvement. I trust
that my guardian has told you and the baron all about its former
greatness and the fine *objets* it once boasted?"

I tried to hide a smile. "Atticus and I did hear something about a Sir Joshua Reynolds or two," I said.

"And a desk belonging to Oliver Cromwell, or was it Napoleon?"

Atticus cleared his throat warningly, for our host was now descending the stairs, and we fell silent.

"Victor, I see you have met our distinguished guests." Mr. Burleigh's expression was sour. He looked strangled in his high old-fashioned collar, below which was tied a fresh white stock. That and a change of coat seemed to be all that distinguished his ensemble from his day wear. "Mrs. Furness told me of your arrival. I would have expected some word from you before you planted yourself on my doorstep."

"I apologize for having given no warning." Mr. Lynch held out his hand to shake, and after a moment's deliberation, the older man clasped it briefly. "You have always given me to think that Thurnley Hall is as much my home as yours, so I hoped it was unnecessary."

I caught no reproach in his voice, but his guardian's face reddened as if he had taken offense. "I'll not be dictated to by you, sir," he rumbled. "Don't think that the presence of our guests means you can tweak my nose without any consequences."

Mr. Lynch made a slight bow. "Sir, your nose is entirely safe from me."

The older man's lips thinned, but he did not pursue the issue. Instead, he pointedly turned his back on his ward and offered me his arm. "Lady Telford, if you'll allow me?"

I placed my hand on his arm and let him lead me in to dinner. The dining room was much smaller than the great hall, almost cozy in comparison. The dark wood paneling was lightened by an elaborate plasterwork ceiling, and a fire lent the room a more cheerful appearance. Mrs. Furness and Ann moved about the table, filling our glasses and serving the soup. I was surprised at first that no footmen waited on us until the reason dawned on me: naturally footmen were a superfluous expense, one that a struggling estate would find dispensable.

Perhaps I should not have laughed at my uncle, I reflected. I could not blame him for dwelling on the possessions he and my grandmother had been forced to part with, after all. If only his intentions were not so blatantly selfish, I might have been able to feel sympathy with him. And his oafish behavior toward his mother and ward did not endear him to me, certainly. I might have been more forgiving if he were not my kin and thus a reflection on me—and my mother. Would she have ended up like him had she stayed at home instead of marrying? I could not believe it.

In the past few weeks, my stomach had developed a capricious temperament, and the fragrance of the soup did not awaken my appetite. Of greater interest was what I might be able to learn from my host.

"Mr. Burleigh," I said, for I was not yet ready to address him more familiarly, "can you tell me what memories you have of my mother? My grandmother didn't tell me a great deal, and I am so eager to learn what she was like as a girl and young woman."

He shifted in his chair. "There is very little I can tell you, Cl—my lady. I was still in school when the whole scandal took place, and I returned that summer to find her gone and all of her belongings disposed of."

"But before that," I pressed him. "As children you must have spent time together. You were only four years apart in age, weren't you? You must have been playfellows when you were young."

He puffed out an impatient sigh. "I really can tell you very little. Like most boys I preferred to spend my time with other boys getting into mischief, and Miriam, as a young lady, was expected to pursue more decorous activities. I seem to remember that she enjoyed watercolor painting, but I doubt she had much time to spend on it. Mother was training her up in the management of the house so that she would one day be equipped to run it herself."

How strange, yet how fitting, that she would one day earn her living from the training her mother had given her. "Did she enjoy it?" I asked.

His booming laugh smote my ears. "Enjoy it! Not one whit, my girl—that is, my dear Lady Telford. She told me once that she would never be lady of the house. 'It is a prison,' she said. I can hear her now. 'Thurnley Hall is a prison, and to be its lady is to never know freedom. I shall not be trapped here.'"

Overcome with sadness, I set my spoon down and stared at the tablecloth. How cruel that, running from one form of servitude, she had ended up doing much the same work but in another woman's house and with even less freedom.

Atticus, probably guessing the direction of my thoughts, reached across to place his hand over mine. "She may have been grateful after all for her mother's teachings," he said gently. "They meant that she was able to keep you with her."

I thanked him with a look. It was true—in many other occupations she would have had to leave me with strangers. At least we were both spared that. "Perhaps after all she preferred keeping another family's house," I reflected. "She could always walk away from it if she needed to."

"What is that you say?" Mr. Burleigh interrupted. "Do you mean my sister worked for a living?"

"She did," I said coolly. "After the death of my father, since she had no support from her own family, she had no choice."

"Good God, I had no idea. When you said you'd been reduced to the level of servants, I though you were exaggerating, as women do." At first I thought his shock was regret at having been unable to assist us, but his next words gave the lie to that idea. "No wonder our parents never spoke of her again. How humiliated they must have been."

Honest work was nothing to be ashamed of, especially when there was no alternative, and I was about to inform him of this in blistering tones when Atticus squeezed my hand comfortingly. The gesture made me pause to take control of my tongue, and while I was composing myself Mr. Lynch turned the conversation into a new channel.

"This is why I do not understand your persistent desire for me to earn my living, sir," the young man said to his guardian. "I've told you over and over that I would be happier here at Thurnley Hall, helping you manage the estate."

His guardian grunted and gestured for Ann to refill his glass. "And as *I* have told *you* over and over, that is out of the question. How are you finding the work? Do you think cataloging manuscripts will hold your interest?"

Mr. Lynch shrugged. The motion looked so peculiar that again I wondered if there was something amiss with his shoulders other than the fit of his evening coat. "As much as any of the other positions you have procured for me, I suppose," he said idly.

"That is to say, very briefly indeed. After I go to all the trouble to secure work for you, why do you insist on behaving as if it is all some great lark, which you may throw over the moment it ceases to entertain you?"

Atticus and I exchanged a glance. This was a startlingly personal topic of conversation, and I wondered if I should change the subject. But before I could, young Mr. Lynch was speaking again.

"Sir, you went to the trouble and expense to have me educated like a gentleman. To expect me now to earn my own keep strikes me as inconsistent, to say the least." His voice remained mild, even a touch lazy, and the effect was to make my uncle's face darken even further.

"I'll not have you question me, you insolent puppy!"

Atticus looked as taken aback as I felt. Fortunately the housekeeper entered then with the dish of pigeon pie, and he said to her heartily, "Mrs. Furness, this soup is excellent. Please let Cook know how much we are enjoying it."

"I'll tell her, my lord," the housekeeper said. "She'll be ever so pleased."

"Perhaps, if the recipe is not a family secret, she might consent to copy it out for our cook at Gravesend."

"I shall ask her, sir." In a lower voice she said to the maid, "The firewood is running low, girl. Tell Thomas to bring in more at once."

"Thomas?" repeated my uncle, who evidently had sharp ears. "What is Grigore about that he cannot bring it in? It will take him only one trip, whereas Thomas will take three. As long as I have the expense of feeding the giant, let him at least earn his keep."

Mrs. Furness smoothed down her apron nervously. "Grigore begs pardon, sir, but he would rather—that is, he is feeling—"

"For heaven's sake, woman, speak up."

"He's afraid of Lord Telford, sir," she said in a rush.

My uncle's mouth dropped open. "Afraid! What the devil? Does he think the baron's bad leg is contagious?"

Did the man possess no sensitivity at all? Seeing my indignation, Mr. Lynch stepped in to smooth things over.

"I think I can shed some light on that," he said calmly. "When Grigore brought the coach to collect us from the station, he called the baron *strigoi*. He believes that his lordship is a revenant." When none of us responded, he clarified with a mischievous smile. "A vampire."

Atticus burst out laughing, but I was more perplexed than amused. "Why on earth would he think that of Atticus?"

"Grigore's parents are Romanian, as I mentioned. There is a great deal of vampire folklore in that region—extending all the way through Austria-Hungary, Serbia, Styria, even Greece. Romanian legend has it that people with red hair and blue eyes are likely to be vampires. I beg your pardon, my lord, but that is what the lore relates."

My husband shook his head, amused. In his elegant evening clothes, with his hair brushed smoothly back and the lamplight illuminating his aristocratic features, he could not have looked less like the ravening monster of myth. "Of all the things I have been called, *vampire* is a first."

"My only knowledge of such things comes from the penny dreadfuls I read as a girl," I said, "but I remember the vampires in those tales as being more saturnine than my husband."

"Each country has its own superstitions, of course," Mr. Lynch said. "English yarns are much more likely to take their cues from Polidori and Coleridge than from Middle Europe. Lord Telford, I suggest you bear these regional peculiarities in mind if you and your lady wife plan to travel in that area."

"Aren't spooks of that sort generally held to come out at night?" I asked. "Since Grigore met Atticus in daylight, why would he think him a vampire?"

"A great many vampires of both literature and folklore walk by day," our expert informed me. "In some Romanian tales *strigoi* move about freely during the day. So you see, Grigore had logic on his side, after a fashion."

Atticus chuckled. "I confess it is a novelty to be considered frightening. Of course, there has always been the curse dogging my footsteps, but that's rather different."

"Curse?"

I think all of us had forgotten my uncle, so diverting was the conversation, but his hoarse exclamation made us turn to look at him. He was staring at my husband in apprehension bordering on panic, and with both hands he clutched the table as if for support. As we watched, his eyes darted from Atticus to me in consternation. "How did you learn of it?" he demanded in a harsh whisper. "Did my mother say something? I knew I shouldn't have left you alone with her. She'll ruin everything . . ." As we regarded him in startled silence, he seemed to realize that he had taken fright prematurely. He moistened his lips with his tongue, and his small, unpleasant eyes fixed on me again. "What did she tell you of the curse?" he asked, less urgently but with tension still evident in his voice.

"I think you must have misunderstood," I said carefully. Until I knew him better, I found this new side of Mr. Burleigh to be alarmingly unpredictable. "My husband referred to what people call the Gravesend curse."

"It is part of the Blackwood family history," Atticus confirmed. He, too, regarded our host warily, but he spoke in a relaxed tone meant to ease the tension. "A bit of bad luck bestowed upon us by a family forebear, that's all. I don't think it can be the same thing you mean."

"No." My uncle cleared his throat. "No, of course not. I—I misspoke. Where is that deuced Thomas with the firewood?"

If anything, though, he seemed to find the room too warm; he ran a finger around the inside of his high collar as if his stock was too tight. Mr. Lynch took advantage of the momentary silence to ask, "Is the Gravesend curse connected to the mystery of your brother's supposed return from the dead, Lord Telford? One hears the most intriguing accounts, but of course there is much fiction to season the facts."

His tone was merely interested, but the subject was still delicate for Atticus . . . and for me. "I'm sure you'll understand if I wish to refrain from going into the whole story," my husband said. "Personal family matters can be . . . trying."

"The important thing," I said lightly, "is that no member of the Blackwood line is, or has ever been, a vampire. Won't you tell us more of your studies on the subject, Mr. Lynch?"

I suspected that he was disappointed to learn nothing from us, but he had the good manners to try to hide it. "Most willingly, Lady Telford," he said with a charming smile. "But you see, there is such a wealth of lore that I could keep us here all night discussing the subject."

"Pray do not," his guardian rumbled warningly.

"I wouldn't dream of it. I merely meant that, even when one narrows the focus to, say, the distinguishing characteristics of the vampire, they can still be astonishingly numerous and varied. Of course, there are certain constants that recur across many different regions. For example, any physical feature that is noticeably out of the ordinary can suggest a demonic or vampiric quality—even quite innocuous imperfections like the irregularity of my back and shoulders, which I believe you were observing just now, Lady Telford."

"I do beg your pardon," I exclaimed, startled. "I didn't mean to stare."

"Don't worry, my lady." His tone was as gentle as ever, so I could not tell if he was offended. "I have been accustomed to stares from the time that I was a small boy. My deformity seemed to fascinate and repel my schoolfellows."

Understanding touched my husband's eyes, and he nodded. "I know myself how cruel boys can be to those of us who appear at all different. You have my sympathy."

"Please believe I had no such thought in my mind," I said, alarmed that I might have caused the young man pain, however unintentionally. "It is simply that I used to be a seamstress, so I observe clothing. I thought there was asymmetry in the cut of your coat, and I was trying to determine the reason."

"That is observant of you, Lady Telford. That tailoring reduces the visibility of my hunch." His smile reassured me that he had not taken offense.

"A seamstress, eh?" my uncle mused. "That must save some money. Otherwise a gown like that would probably cost six months' rent from one of my tenants."

Embarrassed, I was struggling to form a response when Mr. Lynch said reprovingly, "Sir, what the baroness spends on her gowns is between her and her husband. With all the good works that she does, surely she can be permitted the harmless extravagance of dressing as befits her station."

But my uncle seized on another uncomfortable point. "What happened to your being the widow of some wealthy American, eh? This is the first I've heard of your having been a seamstress."

I hesitated. Atticus and I had ceased to maintain the fictitious background we had invented for me when I came to

Gravesend as his bride. The gossip that spread after his father's murder and the even greater scandals that had followed had damaged our respectability so much that it seemed pointless to whitewash my past. But I resented my uncle's attitude. If it had been Mr. Lynch alone who was asking, I would not have minded telling him my whole story. As long as I could keep it from my snobbish uncle, however, I would do so.

"The past matters little now," I said. "The important thing is my present occupation as wife to Lord Telford—and his advisor and assistant in his charitable work."

My uncle brightened. "So you're interested in charitable efforts, Lord Telford? I daresay you won't find many charities more needy than the maintenance of this estate! I tell you, times are rough and no question. The lead mine is played out, my livestock are dying or being washed away by the river, and a full third of the estate's income is tied up in my mother's dower. My tenants are scattering to the factories—factories! Faugh! As if it weren't bad enough that they steal all my workers and leave my fields to rot, they pump out this vile smoke that has spoiled all the beauty of my house! I tell you, I wish I could burn the lot to the ground."

To this tirade Atticus said mildly, "I'm afraid that would probably increase the amount of soot in the air rather than reducing it."

There was a moment of uncomprehending silence before my uncle laughed heartily. "You have me there, Telford. But I hope it's relief for the landowners who are suffering in this agricultural depression that you are about in this charity work of yours."

"No, it isn't. I agree that it is important for us to pay close attention to the difficulties faced by our tenants, and I am on the point of hiring another agent to make certain that my farmers always have someone close at hand to bring their problems to." He touched his napkin to his mouth and placed it next to his plate. "My chief projects are the Blackwood Homes."

Unexpectedly, Mr. Lynch chimed in. "I've read about your endeavors in the *Times*. The Blackwood Homes offer shelter and vocational training to unattached women in distress, do they not?"

"Exactly. Soon there will also be a school, which will house and teach their children."

My uncle gave one of his barking, incredulous laughs. "Homes for whores and their brats? You are having a jest, Telford."

"I assure you I am not." Atticus's voice had cooled, but our host did not know him well enough to recognize that as a warning.

"How can you possibly be in earnest? These creatures bring their fate on themselves, you know. Let them pay the price for their sin—let them be shunned by decent folk as they deserve to be. As for training them up in a vocation—" He gave a derisive snort. "No daughter of Eve ever needed to be taught to spread her legs, my lord."

I gave a wordless exclamation of disgust, not merely at his crudeness but also at his revolting attitude toward his fellow creatures. I noticed that Mrs. Furness stood listening by the sideboard. Still as a stone she was, but her lips were pressed together so firmly that they had gone white, and her nostrils were pinched. Mr. Burleigh's words had angered her as well.

"There are ladies present, sir." My husband's voice was quietly ominous.

"What have I said to shock any decent female?" my uncle expostulated. "Women know their own. They are as quick as anyone to cast stones when one of them transgresses. It is how they prove their own virtue." He sat back in his chair, puffing out his chest as if he were handing down a verdict of great insight and sagacity. "Tolerance of sin is a weakness," he declared, punctuating the point with an aggressive forefinger. "An abominable weakness! And this so-called charity of yours will do nothing but make the plague of loose women worse."

I had heard quite enough from him about my sex, and Mr. Lynch must have felt the same, for he coughed in a pointed manner. "Sir, we are scarcely making our guests feel at ease," he said mildly. "This is probably not the reception the baroness expected in the home of her ancestors."

Mr. Burleigh's face darkened at this correction, and for a moment I think he was on the point of roaring his ward to silence. Then a glance at my face seemed to give him pause. He said more quietly, "I beg pardon, I'm sure. But on the subject of ancestry, why, may I ask, is it a better use of charity to pay for the keeping of strangers and not your own family?"

I said shortly, "These unfortunates have nothing—which is, I believe, little worse than my mother's position when your parents chose to shut their doors to her. Why should my husband and I contribute to the welfare of the very people who abandoned her?"

"But we are blood!" he practically shouted, bringing his fist down on the table with a force that made the plates jump. "That must count for something. Indeed, it should count for everything."

After the noisy outburst, my husband's quiet words sounded distinct in the silence. "Blood bonds are no guarantee of bona fides," he said, and I knew he was thinking of Richard, who had killed their father and tried to do the same to Atticus.

My uncle, probably unaware of this dark history, would not be deterred. "Look at where you are now, though. The two of you might never have known each other had my parents not cast Miriam off, as you put it, niece. You might have grown up here at Thurnley Hall, learning to scrimp and save and being forced into the sordid contemplation of money in a way most unsuited to your birth. Instead, you have made a fine marriage and gained a secure place in society. You are more than comfortably housed, dressed, and fed, and you have the freedom not to concern yourself with making ends meet. You are far better off for having been barred from your mother's home."

Astonishment at his gall stupefied me. I stared at his red face with its jowls trembling with outrage and wondered how this man could possibly be my kin. "Are you saying," I demanded, "that I owe a debt to you?"

His mouth opened and then closed again. Faced with the bald meaning of his own words, he could not own up to them.

Swiftly I pushed my chair back from the table, and the men stood automatically as I rose. "I'll bid you good evening," I said shortly, speaking more to Mr. Lynch than to my uncle, the sight of whom I felt I could no longer tolerate. "I find myself indisposed for further conversation."

"Now, now, don't get in a pet," my uncle exclaimed. "If I spoke out of turn, I can only apologize. I assure you, I had no intention of offending you." He turned to Atticus in appeal. "Lord Telford, please stop your wife. I meant no harm by what I said."

Atticus regarded him without warmth. "My wife goes where and when she wishes," he said. "Clara's decisions are her own."

"Blast it! I'm too impulsive, I admit it. That's one of the Burleigh failings." He laughed as if he had made a joke, but no one seemed amused, so he tried another tack. "Very well, I promise to curb my tongue," he said grudgingly. "Now won't you stay?"

Looking at Atticus gave me no suggestion as to the action I should take: he was waiting to take his cue from me, no doubt because this was my family rather than his. As I hesitated, Mr. Lynch's low voice fell soothingly on my frayed nerves.

"Please, Lady Telford, stay for dessert at least. Cook is so proud of her plum dumplings, and she's making them especially to welcome you. Her feelings would be terribly hurt if you did not at least try them." His lips quirked in a conspiratorial smile. "And Cook is rather temperamental, it must be said. When her feelings are wounded she is likely to visit any number of inedible horrors upon us for days on end."

I wanted to fling my napkin down like a gauntlet and stalk away. But instead, after an inner struggle, I resumed my seat. "Very well," I said shortly. I did not want to spoil the cook's kind gesture . . . even though it meant enduring more of my uncle's odious comments.

But he seemed to have learned his lesson, for he turned the conversation to more anodyne topics for the rest of the evening. Mr. Lynch did his part to keep things light and pleasant, for which I was grateful.

Nevertheless, I retired as early as I reasonably could. The reason I gave was the rigors of the day, but the truth was that I was feeling a most unfamilial urge to kick my uncle in the shins, and I was not certain how much longer I could suppress it.

CHAPTER SEVEN

A tticus lingered with the other men for brandy and cigars, but he did not tarry long before joining me in our room. Almost as soon as the door shut behind him, I burst out, "What a dreadful man my uncle is!"

"He is certainly far from the ideal dining companion." Atticus slipped off his coat and replaced it with his maroon dressing gown as he spoke. "As infuriating as his views are, though, they are not unusual for men of his standing and background. You know how widespread that unenlightened perspective on women is."

"That's true, but he revolts me." I was too restless to settle, and Atticus watched me from the divan as I paced back and forth.

"And me as well," he said, "but consider that he probably hurts himself more than he hurts anyone else."

"Perhaps," I allowed. "With no wife or daughter to feel the brunt of his prejudices, at least the damage he can do is limited."

As often happened, talking a matter out with Atticus helped me find a measure of calm. I ceased pacing and sat down beside him on the divan, and was rewarded when he put his arm around my waist and drew me close. "You are so much kinder and more forgiving than I am," I said.

That made him smile, although there was resignation in the lift of his eyebrows. "Not at all. I want to horsewhip him from one end of Yorkshire to the other. I merely know from experience that it's difficult, if not impossible, to change the minds of men whose opinions are as deeply entrenched as his."

My anger revived as another memory surfaced. "And he is so grasping. It outrages me that after what his parents did to my mother he thinks I shall meekly turn the other cheek and give him money, to boot!"

He gave a low chuckle and pressed his lips to my temple. "My love, I don't think that anyone who has spent more than five minutes with you would make the mistake of considering you meek. But it's true that these are difficult times for your uncle and others like him."

Thinking of the litany of troubles my uncle had listed made me sigh. They were no less valid for coming from that source. Now, looking down at the black and gold taffeta of my gown, I felt shamefaced. His speculation about its cost had touched home—the money might have gone far toward replacing his lost livestock, or for a new greatcoat for his ward. But giving him money outright would feel like rewarding him for being what he was.

I finally said, "I think what upsets me most is that I am disappointed. And I fear you are disappointed as well."

He tipped my chin up so that he could look into my eyes, and the tender concern in his face eased my anxiety. "My love, it is you I am married to, not—I rejoice to say it—Mr. Burleigh."

That mental picture won a smile from me. "I'm very glad of that myself."

"I'm sorry you are finding this reunion less than you hoped it might be, though. We can leave any time you desire."

Just having the freedom to leave made it feel less urgent to do so. "I must spend more time with my grandmother," I said. "She has not yet told me what this great secret is that is weighing on her. And I want to learn more from her about my parents."

"Yes, you mustn't let yourself be diverted from that. This visit may yet prove to be precious to you."

No one could help me through turmoil of mind better than Atticus. His embrace enfolded me in comfort and security, and gratitude flooded my heart at having such a husband. "Thank you for coming here with me," I said.

"I know you're strong enough to face anything alone, but I'm happy if I'm able to make it easier," he said softly.

"You do. Everything is easier when I face it with you." Calmer now, I rested my head against his shoulder. "Do you think me very terrible for not wanting to help my uncle?"

"Not terrible at all." His warm, husky voice soothed me as much as his words. "You have a strong sense of the injustice done your mother, as any proper daughter would. And I happily admit that the idea of letting your uncle live off us, considering his selfishness and backward thinking, goes against the grain for me as well." He tucked a stray tendril of my hair behind my ear. "However," he said softly, "he made a good point in saying that the actions of his father, however cruel, did set in motion the events that led you to Gravesend . . . and to me. I am selfish enough to be grateful for that. The thought that we might never have met is unbearable to me."

"To me as well," I whispered. The knowledge that he and I might not be together now but for a tenuous web of circumstance made me shiver.

"Perhaps you should sleep on the matter," he suggested. "Your happiness means a great deal to me, and I would hate for you to make a decision in haste that you might regret later. Morning is soon enough to take up your trouble of mind again."

"How did you become such a sage?" I teased.

His smile was peaceful. "I merely want what is best for you, my love."

"As I do for you," I said, touched, "even though you might not think it from my having brought you to this place."

He shook his head gently. "Clara, no one is keeping score. Did I not tell you that you are my sanctuary? You and I help each other all the days of our life together."

At that, I drew his face down toward mine to kiss him. As wonderful as it was that he took such pleasure in being my staunch support and comforter, it made me even happier that he could lean on me as well in his turn when occasion arose. For the years before my marriage, my primary concern had been simply keeping myself fed and sheltered. But as Atticus's wife, I had a higher purpose: giving back to him all the love and strength and encouragement that he lavished on me.

Soon, indeed, I would have a purpose higher still . . . but whether Atticus would find it a joy or a burden was a question I could not yet answer.

The thought unsettled me enough that I freed myself from his arms and went to the dressing table, ostensibly to remove my jewelry. In truth, I feared that with his keen insight into my moods he would intuit my thoughts and raise the one topic I was still unprepared to confront.

"I noticed your leg seemed to be giving you trouble earlier," I said to change the subject. "If you like, I can rub it with liniment."

"It's just a bit stiff, that's all. Probably we'll have rain soon." He stretched his leg experimentally and added, "If it doesn't improve, I may go for a walk."

I replaced my amber earrings in their case and unfastened the catch of the matching necklace. It was not nearly as impressive as the Telford collar, but I had judged that pigeon's-blood rubies would be too ostentatious for this visit. The impulse had definitely been the right one: I could imagine how it would have infuriated my uncle had I declined to give him money while wearing a small fortune around my throat. Were I in his place I would have had much the same reaction, I had to admit.

As I drew the necklace away from my throat, I was perplexed to see a small red mark on my skin. "I shall have to see about getting this repaired," I said. "I think it has scratched me. One of the prongs must have bent."

He came over to see and touched the scratch with a gentle fingertip. "As toothsome as you are, I'm not surprised if even your jewelry wishes to take a bite out of you."

"Ridiculous man." But he had made me laugh for the first time during this wearing evening.

"It isn't ridiculous to say that you are delicious, for you are." He lifted my hair off my neck and stooped to put his lips to my skin. Then the light touch of his teeth made me start. "You are reason enough for any man to turn vampire," he said into my throat. Even though his voice was muffled, I could hear the note of amusement.

I reached up to caress his hair, but the laughing reply that was on my lips died when I heard a choking cry. In the mirror I saw the horrified face of Ann, who had just opened the door and now stood frozen on the threshold. It was clear from her expression what she thought she was seeing.

"Ann, don't be alarmed—" I began.

But the door banged shut behind her, and the sound of running footsteps receded down the corridor.

I ought to be ashamed to say that Atticus and I promptly burst into laughter. Even if we had had any inkling of how serious the matter really was, we would not have believed it. After all, how could moldy superstitions of impossible creatures like vampires harm us?

When we had composed ourselves I rang for the housekeeper and explained what had happened. To judge by the length of time it took Ann to return to my room, Mrs. Furness must have had to do a great deal of persuading, but the maid finally returned to help me undress. She kept casting nervous glances at the screen behind which Atticus had retreated, and more than once I had to prompt her to unfasten something. Finally, though, I was ready to climb into the antique bed, beneath the coverlet of which she had placed a hot brick to warm the sheets.

"You do understand, don't you," I said gently, "that there are no such things as monsters who crawl out of graves to drink our blood?"

She nodded, but she would not look at me, and I feared that she was merely humoring me. I stifled a sigh. "Very good. What time does Mrs. Burleigh rise in the morning?"

"At seven, my lady. Shall I wake you then as well?"

"If you please. That will be all for tonight, Ann, thank you."

She withdrew as quickly as she could without being rude, and Atticus emerged to draw the heavy brocade curtains of the bed. "This is quite cozy," he remarked as he pulled the covers over us and drew me close. "In fact, what a perfect solution to our difficulty at Gravesend. If we had a curtained bed, we would have all the privacy we needed."

"It is like our own little room within the room," I agreed. The heavy draperies shut out the draft, and between the hot brick to warm my feet and my husband to warm the rest of me, I felt quite snug. Perhaps Thurnley Hall had its good points after all.

Then, as my husband's lips found mine, I revised that theory. It was not that the destination had improved upon acquaintance, but that my traveling companion rendered any location better. In my husband's arms I let go of all troubling thoughts of the day before. Indeed, in the sweetness of his embrace I let go of thought altogether.

~⟲~

Next morning I set out for my grandmother's room as soon as I thought she might be finished breaking her fast, reasoning that at this early hour she would be at her most alert—and Mr. Burleigh less likely to be present. But as soon as the thin voice bade me enter and I opened the door, I found that I had been mistaken: my uncle stood by the windows, arms folded across his barrel chest, as if he were a guard assigned to protect his mother from hostile intrusions.

Behind him, rivulets of rain streamed down the glass. Atticus's prophecy had come true.

My grandmother was in bed today rather than in the chair, and I wondered with some anxiety whether that meant she was feeling weaker. She wore a bed jacket clasped at the throat with her cameo, and she was propped up on pillows so that she was nearly sitting upright. "There you are, child," she said. "I had expected you earlier than this."

"I'm sorry to have kept you waiting," I said politely, while I wondered how I was supposed to have intuited her wishes. "I hope you're well today?"

"She is very weak this morning," my uncle informed me. "I mean to make certain she does not overtire herself during your visit."

"Horace, you interfering clod, I've told you a dozen times to go." The old lady's voice was peevish, and I could not blame her. "There is no harm at all in leaving me and my granddaughter to converse in privacy."

He shook his round head vigorously. "On no account, Mother. I'll not leave myself open to accusations later that I neglected my duty by you."

The old lady sighed. "You see how it is, Clara. He is afraid I'll tell you something that will drive you away and make you reluctant to own us as your family."

"He has made a capital start at that himself," I said dryly, and took a mean pleasure in the red flush that spread over my uncle's face. He started to defend himself, but my grandmother cut him off with a laugh.

"Yes, that is just like Horace. No more tact than a wild boar. There is no real harm in him, though."

"I'm sure," I said, but only to be polite. "His ward has been doing his best to act as peacemaker, however."

The old lady's eyes sharpened. "What's that?" she exclaimed. "Is Victor here, Horace? You neglected to tell me that."

My uncle's jaw tightened briefly, but his voice betrayed no anger when he said, "I must have forgotten in my pleasure at meeting my niece and her husband. Yes, he is stopping here briefly to meet the baron and baroness. I'm certain that at any moment he'll return to his duties at Coventry."

"He must not do so without coming to see me first. Do you hear, Horace? I insist upon it."

Her voice carried so much force that he nodded, though with clear reluctance.

The old lady gave a sigh as if the effort of exerting her authority had taxed her. "Come, child, sit by the bed that I need not raise my voice," she said to me in a milder tone. "But before you do, fetch that daguerreotype from my bureau."

The bureau surface was covered with treasures that must have been accumulated over her long life: delicate blown-glass perfume flacons, a large jewel case ornamented with enameled flowers, silver-backed brushes, ivory combs, and framed miniatures, both paintings and photographs. But there was no question what daguerreotype she meant: I recognized my mother's face at once.

She must have been only sixteen or seventeen, for she still wore her hair down. It fell past her shoulders, far more tidily than mine had ever behaved. Her dress was in a floral pattern with a lace collar, more festive apparel than I had ever seen her wear. Rather to my surprise, her expression was serious. Or perhaps *determined* was a better word. Despite my uncle's account I had hoped that I would find her carefree and smiling during the years before she had lost first her home and then my father, but now I was forced to wonder: had her girlhood been fraught with conflict with her parents? Or consumed by some inner life that they knew nothing of? Looking at the dark eyes that gazed out at me with such intensity from the photograph, I had to conclude that my mother was still very much a mystery to me.

"What was she like?" I asked, and I was unable to entirely quell a wistful note in my voice.

My grandmother's laugh turned quickly into a cough, and I had to wait for the spell to pass. She took a sip of water from the glass I held out to her, then sighed and rested her head against the pillow. "Willful," she said. "She took after me in that respect. We rarely agreed, and she hated more than anything to give in. It's that stubbornness that led her to elope, I'm certain of it."

"What do you mean?"

"As soon as she learned that she would never be permitted to marry—she and Horace both—she would not give me a moment's peace on the subject. She pestered the life out of me for a solid fortnight." She paused to catch her breath, and I could hear a slight rasp in her throat. "She would have pestered her father, too, except that the first time she questioned him on the subject he boxed her ears. I would never raise a hand to her, but I could not answer her questions either. Perhaps that is why it happened."

My fists clenched at the thought of my mother being struck by her father, but I forced myself to ask, "How did it happen?"

Her hands made a fitful gesture against the counterpane. "It is so long ago, I don't recall exactly."

"I think you do," I said evenly.

Her eyes met mine, and in a moment she gave a sad little smile. "How like her you are," she said, almost to herself.

"It is just as well that I am, for she never let anything get the better of her." *Nothing except death,* I silently added.

She moved restlessly against the pillows, and I rearranged them to better support her head. "Thank you, child," she said when I was done. "I believe Horace has told you how impatient your mother was with the life she was born into, of being mistress of an estate."

"He said she felt trapped."

"Trapped. Yes. And in those circumstances it was not surprising that she sought a means to escape. At the same time, she sought a way to prove to her father and me that we did not have the final say in her future. Marrying Robert Crofton must have seemed the perfect means to bring about both those ends."

"Are you saying that she didn't marry for love?" When she pulled a sour face at the word, I remembered her term for it. "I mean, do you suggest there was no sentimental attachment between them? That she cared nothing for my father but as a way to free herself from her life here?"

The apprehension in my words seemed to puzzle her. "Why should she have felt any attachment to the man? She scarcely knew him. A tenant, a mere farmer. They can have spoken hardly two dozen words together until she persuaded him to elope." She gave a dry laugh. "Not that I imagine he took much persuading. He probably believed he was gaining access to a higher social sphere than he ever could have attained as a farmer."

I tried to hide my dismay. I knew she would think it foolish of me, but I had imagined that my parents had been devoted to each other. Mother had scarcely ever spoken of my father to me. I took that to mean that losing him was so painful that she could not bear to be reminded of him. But perhaps it meant only that he rarely crossed her mind after he died. Why was the idea so painful to me?

Because it was a gulf between us, I decided. I had loved with my whole heart, not once but twice, and the idea of a life in which that emotion never played a role was abhorrent. If my mother had been incapable of that kind of attachment, it made her seem more of a stranger to me than ever. I didn't want that to be the case—I wanted to feel that she and I were connected by temperament as well as by blood.

"Do you know anything about my father besides that?" I asked.

She shook her head, mussing the arrangement of her white locks on the pillow, and waved one of her thin hands dismissively. "No, and I do not need to. He was unimportant."

Anger flared in me at hearing my father dismissed this way, but she continued, unaware. "Your mother would have married a tinker to spite her father and me. But I understand why she felt that way. She was my daughter, after all, and I married partly for spite. Had they not forbidden me to marry a foreigner? Yet I did, despite my father making the most terrible threats and . . . and reproaching me for my ingratitude."

That had not been what she had started out to say, I felt sure. Then a half-smothered yawn came from my uncle, and I realized his presence might be making her circumspect. I had grown so absorbed in our conversation, and my uncle had been so uncharacteristically quiet, that I had forgotten he was still in the room. "You do not sound Romanian," I said to my grandmother.

The old lady frowned at me. "I was educated in Switzerland and France, like any well-bred girl of my status. My family always spoke English, French, and German; Romanian was for the servants." Then she sighed. "It was wrong of me to defy my parents," she said in a low voice. "Wrong of me to choose to obey my husband instead of heeding my father. When misfortune struck, I was instrumental in bringing it upon us. That is what I wanted to tell you . . ."

"Mother," my uncle said warningly, "you mustn't get worked up. It isn't good for your health."

"My health is immaterial," she retorted. "We all know I have few enough days left on this earth, and before I go I must tell Clara the source of all the family's ill luck. She must—"

But as my uncle moved toward her with, I was certain, the intent of silencing her, her words died away into coughs. Her son picked up the glass on her bedside table, poured a few drops into it, and held it to her lips as soon as the paroxysm had passed. She took a few sips before letting her head fall wearily back on the pillow.

"I weaken daily," she said. "You cannot conceive of how frustrating it is when one's soul is as vital as ever but bound to a decaying machine. Fortunate girl, you still have so many years before you."

"Please," I said, "is there anything else you can tell me? I feel I still know so little of her. Is it true that all of her possessions were removed after she married?"

"Her father wanted all traces of her removed from our lives. But she left behind a trunk that I think she meant to take with her. It contained a few of her favorite books, her best dress, a few other oddments. It was found in the great hall, as if she had carried it to the front door only to leave it at the last minute. Perhaps she found it too heavy."

"If she disappeared, how did you know she had married?"

"She left a letter full of defiance, or so my husband said. He threw it in the fire." Her voice had developed a wheeze, and at her gesture I picked up the glass and held it to her lips so that she could drink.

"I suppose he also destroyed the trunk?" I said, bracing myself for disappointment. But to my astonished delight, she shook her head.

"There, by the bureau—I had Horace fetch it for you. All those years ago I hid it in the eaves where my husband would not find it, and now it is yours."

Without intending to I found that I had risen to my feet. "May I—?"

"Of course, child. It belongs to you now."

The words had scarcely left her lips before I was kneeling by the trunk—quite a small one—and raising the flat lid. The contents were sparse enough, but their meaning sent my heart knocking against my ribs in excitement. My mother had handled these things, had valued them enough to wish to take them with her into her new life.

They were few in number, to be sure. A half dozen books, mainly translations of classical verse; a dress of robin's-egg blue satin with enormous puffed sleeves; a matching pair of satin slippers; and a box containing some modest pieces of jewelry as well as a fan, handkerchiefs, and the like. I did not want to examine them all under the gaze of my uncle, who was openly staring, so I closed the lid and made to pick the trunk up.

"Steady there!" my uncle boomed. "I'll have one of the servants take the box to your room. Why do we have them if not to carry things for us?"

"I don't mind," I said, reluctant to let the precious thing out of my grasp. "Truly."

My grandmother closed her eyes as if I wearied her. "A woman in your position should not lift a hand on her own account."

"For years I had no servant and had to do my own carrying," I said stubbornly.

But my grandmother was determined. "It's well past the time when you should have left that behind you. To think that I would need to school a baroness on her stature!"

Another coughing fit seized her, and my uncle announced, "That's a long enough visit for today. You can speak to Mother again tomorrow morning, if she is feeling well enough for visitors."

She raised her head from the pillow again. "Come," she croaked, "give your grandmother a kiss before you leave, child."

Though surprised at this sentimentality, I returned to the bedside and bent over to touch my lips to her cheek. Her hand clutched my arm, and so strong and unexpected was her grip that I nearly yelped.

Hissing the words into my ear, she whispered, "Come back at five o'clock, without that oaf of a son of mine. Then we may speak freely."

"Yes, Grandmama," I said, and then added for my uncle's ears, "I'll return tomorrow morning."

She did not reply, as another fit of coughing seized her. My uncle actually took my elbow to hurry me toward the door, so eager was he to be rid of me.

"You needn't push me about," I snapped.

The look he gave me was neither friendly nor avuncular, and his grip did not ease. "You have worn her out with your questions. I should have seen you out long before this."

"You won't be able to stop her from talking to me," I told him. "Whatever it is that you don't want me to learn, I assure you I will find it out."

For answer he merely propelled me out the door and into the hallway, releasing his grip on me at last and shutting the door smartly behind me. The sound of my grandmother's coughing penetrated through it.

I rubbed the place on my arm where his grip had pinched me and reluctantly withdrew. I had a strong suspicion that before the trunk made its way to me its contents would be subjected to close scrutiny. And with my grandmother weakening so quickly, I hated to waste another minute before talking of whatever it was that was weighing on her so. Just what was it that my uncle was so determined I should not learn?

CHAPTER EIGHT

As always when I was troubled in mind, I felt that discussing the matter with Atticus would bring me some measure of comfort. When I went in search of him, Mrs. Furness told me that he was in the library, a room I had not yet seen.

Its leaded glass windows offered a fine view of the meadowland at the front of the house where it stretched down to the river and beyond. The rain had stopped, but the sky was still gray, and the trees bent and swayed under a high wind, which shrilled around the edges of the windows. Even from here I could see the river foaming around the rocks in its path, and I remembered what Mr. Lynch had said about its having overflowed this summer. It still looked as if it were running high and fast enough to pose a danger to the unwary.

Closer at hand, the view was considerably more attractive, for Atticus sat at a table with a book open before him. Whatever it was, it had made him smile.

"What are you reading?" I asked, coming to peer over his shoulder at the page.

"Finished already? It's an eighteenth-century guide to supernatural creatures. I'm reading about vampires." He turned a page and read in portentous tones:

> These vampires were corpses, who went out of their graves at night to suck the blood of the living, either at their throats or stomachs, after which they returned to their cemeteries. The persons so sucked waned, grew pale, and fell into consumption; while the sucking corpses grew fat, got rosy, and enjoyed an excellent appetite. It was in Poland, Hungary, Silesia, Moravia, Austria, and Lorraine, that the dead made this good cheer.

I shook my head. "It's remarkable that men of learning took such legends seriously enough to devote themselves to their study."

"I don't know," Atticus mused. "It seems to me that an important part of scientific inquiry is finding the grounds to separate assumption from fact. Sometimes that may mean assembling definite observations instead of dismissing ideas out of hand, even when the ideas seem ludicrous on the surface."

"Well put, Lord Telford," came a quiet voice, and I found that Mr. Lynch had joined us unheard. "It is not necessarily a sign of superstition but of an open mind to study lore such as this. For all we know, there could be astonishing revelations about the world we live in hiding in stories that are dismissed as sensational fiction." He gestured toward the shelves beside which we were standing. "This is my collection," he said. "Or as much of it as I can bear to leave behind during my time away from Thurnley."

The titles ranged from popular fiction, like Mrs. Shelley's *Frankenstein* and the fantastical stories of Théophile Gautier, to obscure treatises, like Foxe's *Book of Martyrs* and the volume Atticus held, *The History and Philosophy of Spirits, Apparitions, & c.* by one Augustine Calmet. I hoped that Mr. Lynch had not thought we were mocking his taste in reading, but I could not keep from observing, "It is an unusual collection. How did your taste for such subjects begin?"

His shrug drew my eye to the unevenness of his shoulders, plainer now in the light of day that streamed through the windows. "Certain events in my youth planted a seed, shall we say, that grew into a devouring curiosity. It fascinates me to learn what the men of different lands and different centuries labeled with the word 'monstrous.'"

"One can learn a great deal about people by studying what they choose to demonize," Atticus agreed. "Have your studies disclosed anything surprising?"

For the first time Mr. Lynch's smile betrayed a hint of steel. "Disappointing, yes," he said. "Surprising? Given what I have observed firsthand over the years, no."

"There you are!" The booming voice belonged, of course, to my uncle, who stood on the threshold regarding us. "I've been looking for you, niece. I thought I might take you and your husband round to the cow barn and the other outbuildings. When you see them you'll understand how vital it is to carry out extensive repairs."

Atticus, no doubt gauging that this scheme would drive me completely out of patience, performed the hero's part and stepped in front of the bullet. "I don't believe Clara has finished her exploration of the library, but I should be delighted to accompany you," he said. "I hope you'll tell me about all the work that needs to be carried out on the estate."

"That would take more than one afternoon," Mr. Lynch said gently, and his guardian shot him a look that was positively hostile before shepherding Atticus out of the room and away from us.

"Your husband is an interesting person," said my companion. "He does not seem to feel the need to bluster and stamp about as my guardian does to make his presence felt, yet he makes a powerful impression all the same."

I smiled my agreement. "Atticus is a remarkable man, especially given his upbringing."

"Oh?"

"He was not raised to hold himself in any regard," I said. "His physical imperfection, though minor, was enough to cause

91

the ignorant to draw away from him. Even his parents disdained him for it." I suspected that Mr. Lynch had experienced something similar, and I was curious enough to want to draw him out.

"I am not surprised to hear it." His dark eyes were thoughtful as he gazed into space . . . or into his past. "You will probably not be astonished to learn that my schoolfellows were merciless about my slight curvature of the back. They called me . . . well, no matter. The fact that children can be cruel will not surprise you, I am certain. I still hope to find some knowledge from studying accounts both historical and fictional that would explain why we are so hostile to those who are different, especially in our youth. Still, one hopes for better from adults, who ought to have the wisdom of age and experience to give them insight."

"Adults like my uncle?"

He rubbed his chin, avoiding my eyes. With his high forehead and slender hands he reminded me a trifle of Atticus, and I wondered if that was part of the reason that I felt suddenly protective of him. "I never knew my parents," he said presently, "and my guardian insists that it's better for me to remain ignorant of them. That makes me fear they surrendered me willingly to his care—that they did not want a deformed child and rejoiced to find that they need not keep me."

"Do you know this for certain?" I exclaimed, shocked. Even Atticus's parents, neglectful though they had been, had not abandoned him outright.

A gentle smile. "No, it's mere supposition. But the fact that even my guardian prefers to keep me at a distance—by sending me away to school, then to work—tells me how the world must view me. He has never bothered to conceal that he does not want me nearby. As the world goes, it is not so great a burden, but it is still unpleasant to feel that one is an inconvenience to those who should have one's welfare at heart."

Abruptly I remembered feeling something very similar in my girlhood. "My mother sent me away," I said without having intended to.

The warm brown eyes were attentive. "When?"

"I was seventeen. I was a maid at Gravesend Hall then, and she the housekeeper. I was dismissed for being too familiar with a member of the family. I don't like to make any of this generally known," I added, "for I should hate for Atticus to be looked down on for having a wife of such humble origins."

"I'll not breathe a word to Mr. Burleigh," he assured me.

"Thank you. It isn't exactly a secret anymore, but it makes it more embarrassing that the young man I was caught trysting with was Atticus's brother, Richard."

"Ah! He who returned from the dead."

I cast a reproving look at him but otherwise ignored this quip. "Lady Telford dismissed me, and my mother carried out her orders. Mind you, Mother made certain I had the means of finding lodgings and employment, and it would have been disastrous for us both had she thrown over her position in protest, but . . . at the time I almost wished she had. I felt rather as you did, that she found me a problem to be packed off to London, out of sight and where I could do no further damage." I came back to the present to find my young companion's eyes fixed on me with such concern that I laughed in embarrassment. "Please don't feel sorry for me, Mr. Lynch—I felt quite sorry enough for myself. As you can imagine, a seventeen-year-old girl could generate enough self-pity for a lifetime. And you see, everything worked out in the end, for Atticus sought me out and made me his wife."

"Did everything work out for your mother?" he inquired. "Did she retain her position?"

"Until her death. Which followed all too quickly after my departure." I wondered now whether, if she had walked out of Gravesend with me, she would have succumbed to some other illness. Or would she have lived many years more?

Letting my thoughts wander in that direction would only be tormenting myself, and indeed, there were already tears in my eyes. I had found that I wept more readily now that I was expecting a child, and it was embarrassing for it to happen before a new acquaintance.

I reached for my handkerchief, but Mr. Lynch had already produced one. With a murmured "If you'll permit me . . . ," he touched it gently to the corners of my eyes. Under his intent gaze I felt foolish.

"Please forgive my display," I said. "Talking with my grand-mother seems to have stirred up my emotions. After all these years, finally to learn something of my mother's past has been a bit unsettling."

"I shall forgive it and with pleasure, if you will answer a question for me."

Though his tone was deferential, I felt a little spark of resent-ment. I disliked having conditions foisted upon me.

"Well?" I said, more coolly.

His expression was so gentle that I almost felt guilty for having taken that tone with him. "How did your husband's brother contrive to come back to life?" he asked.

Uncertain whether he was entirely in earnest, I said, "He didn't. He had led everyone to believe he was dead, but all the time he was alive, either in disguise or in hiding. He was not one of the revenants from the folklore you study, Mr. Lynch."

His response was so strange that, long after the rest of that conversation had dimmed in my mind, it remained clear in my memory . . . along with the curiously penetrating expression that accompanied the words.

"How do you know for certain?" he asked.

Perhaps it was foolish of me to be so disconcerted by his question. I said something inconsequential and then remem-bered that I had promised my grandmother that I would send him to her, and told him so. He made a polite farewell—his manners were always irreproachable except with his guardian, I had noticed—leaving me alone in the library.

I welcomed this opportunity to peruse it uninterrupted. My mother must have had an unusually impressive education for a woman to have schooled me as she had, and if any of her books remained here still they might give me another window into her personality. True, my grandmother had said that everything of hers except for what was in the trunk had been disposed of, but I suspected that schoolbooks might have been kept so that her brother, a few years younger, might use them in his turn. Like-wise, literary classics might well remain here, and I hoped that I might find marginalia left by my mother.

But another look around the room revealed many empty shelves. There was room for perhaps five times as many books as were present. I wondered if my grandmother and uncle had sold off many of the books as their financial straits worsened. My uncle struck me as the kind of man who would rather spend his time shooting than reading, and as for my grandmother, reading was probably difficult now for her . . . and all too soon she would have no need of any earthly possessions.

The books that remained seemed to bear out my theory, for there were few that looked valuable, either for their plates or for their age; almanacs there were, and bound issues of *Cornhill Magazine* and *Odds and Ends,* and of course Mr. Lynch's collection of fantastic reading. I found a primer much written in with pencil, but the childish, straggling letters might have belonged to any youngster. The range of books seemed to reveal differing tastes among members of the household: a volume of Trollope rested cheek by jowl with the essays of Dr. Johnson, which in turn rubbed shoulders with a guide to diseases of sheep and cattle. I riffled the pages of any that were old enough to have been present during my mother's tenancy, but found little besides an occasional underlined passage. Either my mother's books truly had been removed, or she had had too much respect for their sanctity to mark up their pages with her own thoughts. It occurred to me that had she been less conscientious I might have more clues to her inner life.

When Atticus returned I was turning the pages of a volume of Donne's poetry. "I asked your uncle if we could postpone the remainder of the tour," he announced. "I thought you and I could take a turn and enjoy some fresh air together while the rain has stopped. Your countenance and conversation are exactly what I need after two hours with our host."

I assented at once, and as soon as we had donned outerwear that would fend off the wind and drizzle, we left the house.

The fresh, cold air was bracing, and I inhaled it gladly even though its force whipped my cloak about me. The fine precipitation was almost more mist than rain, and it was refreshing against my face as we rounded the corner of the main wing and came upon the cobbled courtyard held in the bend where the two main wings met. As we neared the tumbledown portion

I saw to my consternation that a tree was actually growing out of an embrasure that had once held a window. "This part of the house must not have been habitable for many years," I exclaimed. There was even a gable that held the outline of what must once have been another rose window; now it was bare and open to the wind.

The sound of a thin voice raised in a hymn, coupled with the sound of stone scraping against stone, drew us onward. Last night's storm seemed to have loosened some of the masonry in the ruined wing, for great blocks of stone were strewn on the gravel. The stooped figure with the straggling white beard who had met our coach the first day must be Thomas. He was shoveling smaller rocks and crumbled bits of masonry into the cart. He was dwarfed by a massive figure with his back to us, who could only be Grigore. He was picking up the large blocks of stone and setting them into the cart as if they had been no more substantial than cubes of sugar. As we approached, Thomas broke off his singing and touched his cap to us, and Grigore turned to see who he was greeting.

His eyes widened at the sight of us, and he crossed himself swiftly. Muttering to himself in what I supposed to be Romanian, he fumbled at the neck of his smock and drew out a crucifix that hung from a thong around his neck. He held it out as if it would fend us off. There was something eerie as well as absurd about this giant of a man cringing before my husband, who had never done a cruel deed in his life.

"Good morning," said Atticus cheerfully, evidently hoping to convince the man that he meant no harm, but Grigore continued to mutter to himself. A prayer to ward off evil? I wondered.

"Good mornin', my lord," said Thomas in his thin treble, and raised his cap to me. "My lady." But even as I returned the greeting, his eyes slid to the other man, full of apprehension. What did he expect the man to do?

His anxiety had not escaped Atticus, who sighed. "We had best take another route for our walk, Clara," he said in an undertone. "I think our presence will agitate Grigore too greatly."

"As if you were not the kindest man anyone could encounter!" I said in an indignant whisper, but I did not argue as we turned our steps away from the house and to a rough path that led gently uphill.

The rain from the night before made the route slippery. Atticus relied much on his stick, and mud squelched beneath our feet with every step. But the view as we ascended was worth a bit of messiness. The green dales divided by lines of stone spread out beneath us, and the hillsides were tufted with purple heather and wildly misshapen trees, evidently tortured into these strange contortions from decades of the persistent wind. Outcroppings of rock showed their jagged shapes against the sky. The slate-gray clouds overhead seemed to stretch out endlessly, a foreboding but bleakly beautiful sight, and beneath them the sooty gray walls of Thurnley Hall seemed like an earthbound thundercloud.

"What a remarkable view," I said, drawing Atticus to a stop. "It is as if there is more sky here than anywhere else in the world."

"It is remarkable, as you say. But some day I want to take you to Europe with me. You will be enraptured by the Black Forest—there is nothing that inspires such awe as the Alps. And how you shall love Florence!" Catching himself up short, he laughed at his own enthusiasm. "How patient you've been, Clara, not pressing me to take you on a wedding tour. It is high time we planned one."

"I never expected such a thing," I said, startled, but he had seized my imagination. My thoughts were suddenly filled with scenes I only knew from paintings and engravings. The chance to see them in the company of my husband, to learn about them through the lens of his education and experience, tempted me greatly. "With the school and the new Home, can we think of going away for any length of time?"

"Perhaps next summer. By then they will require less attention and can be safely left in Bertram's hands for a few months. Would you like that?"

"Like it!" I exclaimed, even though I wondered how the coming child would complicate this scheme. Mentally I counted ahead. Even if our child was old enough by then to travel, we would need a nursemaid. Indeed, we would need one in any case, which meant that soon I ought to begin seeking one. There were so many preparations not yet begun, and still I did not know how to broach the subject.

I realized that we had been standing in silence for some minutes, and I came to myself to find Atticus regarding me with concern in the set of his brows. "Is there something about the idea that troubles you?" he asked.

"Not at all!" I said hastily. "I was just thinking about all the arrangements that will need to be made. It's a wonderful idea, Atticus. You are so generous to me."

My words chased the faint crease from his brow. "It is my pleasure to spoil you, my love."

I linked my arm through his as the wind rose again, buffeting me with a force that might have pushed me off balance were it not for him to anchor me. *Two against the wind,* I thought, and smiled. Yet another way in which the going was easier for two rather than one alone.

How quickly, I realized, I had come to rely on his presence. For nearly two decades before our marriage, I had made my way in the world alone. I had friends, but they were neither numerous nor intimate; in all important ways, I had been solitary. Self-sufficiency had held a degree of satisfaction, but it had been a cold life. I had become wary and distrustful, certain that I could rely on no one, and believing that I was destined to live the rest of my life without love since the man I had thought I adored above all else had been taken from me. A joyless existence it had been—yet I had been so slow to leave it behind, to let myself trust in Atticus and at last to love him.

Now I knew how wondrous it was to have a companion in the great adventure of life. Just as I had someone with whom to share my joys, I no longer had to bear my troubles alone. How exhausting it had been to bear the sole responsibility for my existence. No one in those days would make certain that I was fed or clothed or tended when sick—not until Sybil Ingram had taken me under her wing, although she had been so flighty that even her patronage had carried no guarantee of security. Now, however, I could lean on Atticus, resting in the certainty that I was more than a few coins away from poverty . . . and, what was far more important, that no matter what adversity might strike us, we would face it together, stronger for being united. Poverty with Atticus would never be as terrifying a prospect as that of poverty faced alone.

The unexpected thought occurred to me that my uncle's life must be more difficult for not having a helpmeet to confront his difficulties with him. Had his prejudices prevented any woman from accepting him as a suitor? If so, I applauded the good judgment of the local belles. Or had my grandmother been in earnest when she said he and my mother had been forbidden to marry? The prohibition made no sense, and I resolved to pursue the reason for it. At the same time, I felt a flicker of compassion for my uncle at the idea that he had been forbidden that experience. Why, perhaps his odious views on women might even have been corrected had he married and learned firsthand what worthy creatures we could be.

Perhaps I should be generous to him after all. I could afford to be, for I had all that any mortal woman could wish for.

"I wonder if there is a way for us to help my uncle without supporting him outright," I mused. "If we knew more about the particulars of the property, we might see a way out of the worst of his difficulties. If there is unfarmed land that could be sold without loss of income, or another lead seam that might be worked if we advanced him the necessary capital . . . you know better than I the kind of thing to look for."

"There may also be investments that could be retrenched, or something of that sort. And there may be a part of the property that would be attractive for expansion of one of the railway lines. Just because he has not found a good solution doesn't mean none exists." Atticus leaned over to kiss my cheek. "An excellent idea, my love. I'll see if he's willing to enter into a discussion that does not begin with the premise of our funding his partridge and port for the rest of his days."

I knew it would not be a pleasant or easy task that lay before him, and gratitude flooded my heart that he would take it upon himself for my sake. "Are you certain you don't mind? It is a great deal to ask you to do for someone who isn't even your blood relation."

"Remember that I have your welfare at heart, and I think this is the best way to bring you peace of mind." Perhaps I looked taken aback, for he added reassuringly, "I don't mean that you owe him anything, for you don't. But your conscience is a persistent one, and it might trouble you in years to come if you had the chance to do a good turn for the man and chose not to. I would prefer to save you from the risk of living with that."

His blue eyes were so earnest that I could hardly keep from teasing him, even though I knew he believed every word he said. "You have such a talent," I said, "for making it sound like I am doing you a favor by letting you solve my problems."

He smiled. "It isn't that I solve your problems, sweetheart, merely that I help you in confronting them. And that—like being your husband—is my honor and privilege."

"Thank you, dearest," I said, but the words were inadequate. I drew him to me and tried to convey my feelings in a kiss.

"I very much like the way you say thank you," he said presently. With a smile both tender and mischievous, he drew me closer. "Indeed, I could happily let you express your gratitude for hours on end."

But the weather made such open-air trysting uncomfortable, and shortly we descended from our windswept aerie and returned to our room to shed our muddy boots and change our clothes for dry things. It was a relief to warm ourselves by the fire, and I was glad I had brought my scarlet wool melton dress, one of my warmest garments.

The wind had torn my hair from its chignon and turned it into a wild tangle that gave me the look of a maenad, and I had just finished combing it out and repinning it when a diffident knock at the door sounded. When I called out a welcome, it opened to reveal Mr. Lynch.

"I hope I'm not disturbing you," he said, "but I wondered if you knew whether Mrs. Burleigh is resting. I went to visit her earlier, but there was no answer."

The mantel clock showed the time to be nearly noon. "I imagine that Ann will be taking her something to eat soon, so we may as well go round to her room and see," I said. Even though she had told me to return at five o'clock, it was just possible that my uncle had overheard her say so, I reasoned, so it might be wise to make my visit earlier.

The massive grandfather clock that stood on the landing opposite my grandmother's door was just beginning to strike the hour when we reached it, and perhaps for that reason there was no immediate response to Mr. Lynch's soft tap at the door. I knocked more firmly, and this time the door opened. My uncle stood on the threshold—but how changed he was. His usually ruddy face was curiously pale, and his eyes were fixed and glassy. He looked at us as if he did not recognize us.

"Sir?" his ward said, and from the puzzled tone of his voice I knew that the strangeness of the older man's appearance had not escaped him. "Is something the matter?"

Mr. Burleigh's lips moved inaudibly, and he put a hand to the doorframe as if to steady himself. Then he repeated, "The matter . . ."

Dread was gathering in my stomach. "Is my grandmother unwell?" I asked, even though I was not certain I wanted to know the answer.

My uncle's eyes alighted on mine, and in them shock had erased all other expression. In a hoarse voice he said, "She is dead."

In the silence that formed around these words the clock finished striking. It was noon.

CHAPTER NINE

"I am truly sorry to hear such grievous news," said Mr. Lynch as the last echoes of the chime died away. His voice was so sympathetic that it was difficult to believe he had spoken to his guardian with such discourtesy the night before. "What a terrible loss for you, sir. I suppose it was another paroxysm?"

My uncle's hand went to his forehead, and then he lowered it and stared as if not understanding what it was for. His fingers were trembling. "Paroxysm?" he said as if uncomprehending.

"I gathered from Lady Telford that she was suffering from her cough a great deal this morning."

My uncle's gaze now fixed itself upon him. "Yes," he said, as if struck by a new idea. "Yes, she was."

"But she said the doctors had given her months yet to live," I protested, as though that could make a difference. It did not seem possible for her to be gone so suddenly, with so little warning.

Mr. Lynch gave me a sad smile. "Doctors have been known to make mistakes, my lady."

I had had so much yet to learn from her, though. And when I thought of the ferocity with which she had clung to life even as her body began to fail her, I felt a spark of surprising regret. Even though she had not been a warm or lovable person, she had given me precious knowledge about my heritage and my mother, and she had been a fascinating person in her own right. It seemed bitterly unfair for her to have departed before she was ready . . . and before *I* was ready, although I was ashamed of so selfish a thought. Now she would never get to meet her great-grandchild, either.

"May I see her?" I said suddenly, startling the two men—and myself as well. Since they were staring at me, I sought a way to explain this impulse. "Just to—to pay my final respects. I had so very little time in which to get to know her, and . . . this is terribly sudden." I felt as though her death would not be truly real to me unless I could confirm it with my own eyes.

"I'm afraid that won't be possible," said my uncle. The color was creeping back into his face, although his gaze still seemed remote and stricken. "The body is—I mean, she is in considerable disarray."

I tried not to let myself form any mental images of what that might mean. "Nonetheless. I should like to say goodbye."

He frowned. "I cannot allow it. Your sensibilities would not be sufficient to the shock. Her illness was not kind, and the strain of the final fit has left her . . . well, it is not a pretty sight." He was beginning to sound more like his usual obstreperous self. His hand came down heavily on my shoulder in what I supposed to have been meant as a gesture of sympathy but which felt more like an attempt to fend me off. "I would hate for you to remember her that way," he said decisively. "Now I must notify Mrs. Furness and tell Thomas to summon the priest and send a wire to our solicitor. Excuse me, niece. There are many things to be done."

He withdrew his hand from my shoulder, for which I was grateful, and shut the door firmly behind him. His peculiar state of shock had passed.

103

"Is there any way in which I can help?" I asked.

"No, there's no need to trouble yourself."

"What can I do, sir?" his ward asked. "I shall be happy to go into town and summon the doctor. I am entirely at your disposal."

This seemed to catch my uncle off guard, and he simply stared for a moment. Then, thoughtfully, he said, "Yes, that would be helpful. I'll write a few lines for you to take to him. Come to my study."

Then, to my astonishment, he produced a key and locked the door of my grandmother's room. He was determined that we should not catch a glimpse inside.

No doubt it was for the best, and he might have been sincere in wishing to protect me from the ugly reality of death caused by sickness. But when this combined with his peculiar behavior, it awoke the gravest misgivings in me. Like everyone else, my uncle had known that his mother's death was approaching. Why should it have shaken him so much unless something about it had been unnatural? And if that was what he was attempting to hide, that meant he knew—or at least suspected—the true cause of her death.

⌇⌇⌇

When I told Atticus the news, he folded me in his arms and held me close. "I am so sorry, my love," he whispered. Feeling the comforting strength of his body supporting me, the protective embrace of his arms, I closed my eyes and let the tears come. Without his having to say it, I knew that he comprehended all that this loss meant to me. Not only the loss of my grandmother herself, one of my all too few relatives, but of all that she could have taught and told me. Part of my past was gone, never to be fully known or understood.

"Can we stay for the funeral?" I asked at length, plucking the handkerchief from his breast pocket and applying it to my eyes. "It may prolong our visit past what we had intended."

"Of course we'll stay. I'll go into town and wire Bertram."

"I'll go with you. I believe Thomas will be taking Mr. Lynch, so we can ride together." I tried to think about practicalities—something with which to occupy myself so that my thoughts would not endlessly dwell on the cause of my distress. Atticus and I had stopped wearing mourning for his father some months before, so we had no appropriate clothing with us. "We shall need some black dye. I can probably find some in town if Mrs. Furness has none. And plenty of crape . . . I shall ask her to make a list."

The housekeeper seemed glad enough for me to make the purchases for her, but when I offered to speak to someone about preparing my grandmother's remains, she said it would not be necessary. She would be washing and dressing the body.

This surprised me somewhat. For a family of the Burleighs' status, I would have expected more ceremony. "Do you not need assistance?" I asked. "Is there not a woman in town who does for families in these cases?"

She shook her head decidedly. "No, my lady. It's only right that I attend to the lady this last time. I've been with the family so long."

"How long is that?" I asked.

"Twenty-five years, my lady."

That was indeed a long time—so long that her loyalty to Mr. Burleigh might keep her silent about any peculiarities my grandmother's body might betray. It would not surprise me if my uncle was somehow forcing her to be complicit in this manner. "I am her family," I said. "It would be entirely fitting for me to help you."

But she was unyielding. "Thank you," she said, "but it will not be necessary." Her gray eyes did not waver under my gaze, and they betrayed no weakness of will. Even though her face and figure were comfortably plump and she was too short to be imposing, she managed to create the impression of being unassailable—unmovable, even.

I could not say that I was entirely sorry to be rebuffed, for preparing my grandmother's body for burial was not a task that I would be likely to carry out with equanimity. With my shopping list, I withdrew.

When Atticus and I set out for the village in the company of Mr. Lynch, I was reminded of when the three of us arrived at Thurnley such a short time before, although this time it was old Thomas and not Grigore who drove us. Mr. Lynch accepted my husband's condolences gracefully. "She and I were never close," he explained. "I gathered that she disapproved of her son's taking me as his ward. But if that was what she summoned me to discuss, I shall never know."

That was something I had not considered: what had my grandmother wanted to discuss with him so shortly before her death? It occurred to me to wonder if Mr. Lynch was my uncle's natural son. I knew that the title of ward was sometimes a euphemism for a gentleman's child born out of wedlock. If my uncle had indeed been forbidden to marry, it was not altogether surprising that he might have sought feminine company, which could all too easily have led to a child.

If that was the case, though, would there not be some resemblance between them? Yet two more dissimilar men it would be difficult to imagine. There was also the question of whether Mr. Lynch's origins would have been kept secret if he were really my uncle's son. My time in the elevated world of my husband, though brief, had already taught me that most connections of this type were an open secret, with no one troubling to maintain secrecy as long as a respectable appearance could be upheld. Still, there were bound to be exceptions. Whatever mysterious reason lay behind the Burleighs' prohibition against marriage might be a vital part of the mystery, and I wished that I had sought the answer from my grandmother. I doubted that my uncle would be forthcoming about it, as he had sought to prevent her from confiding anything to me.

Our first stop was the railway station. There was no longer a proper post office in Coley, for as the town had dwindled to a village, many businesses had shuttered. This meant that Atticus and Mr. Lynch had to send their telegrams from the station. By chance, one was waiting for us, letting us know that Sterry, too, had taken ill and could not join us at Thurnley yet. Mrs. Threll offered to send another servant, but Atticus felt that he could do without a valet for the duration and said as much in his answering message.

After this was accomplished, Thomas took us to the general store, where Atticus and I alighted. Mr. Lynch was leaning out of the carriage window to discuss particulars of where and when he would fetch us after his errand to the doctor when I noticed that two elderly pedestrians had halted in the street to stare at us. Their faces wore an expression so surprising that I could not be certain I was interpreting it correctly. The expression was fear.

I had no time to hail them and inquire, though, for as soon as they realized they had been observed they turned and almost fled in the direction from which they had come. From their simple clothing and cloth caps I deduced that they were laborers, but the reason for their consternation baffled me.

Then Mr. Lynch bade us farewell and the carriage moved on, and Atticus linked arms with me. "We should have a good half hour, perhaps three quarters, before Thomas and Lynch return with the doctor. That should be more than enough time for you to make your purchases, shouldn't it?"

"Of course," I said absently. A pale sunshine had broken through the clouds during our stop at the station, and in the light my husband's hair looked very red indeed. Was that what had frightened the men? Did they, too, believe in stories of vampires? Perhaps some of the townspeople had come over from Romania with my grandmother's retinue.

With the help of the shop girl it did not take me long to assemble the items Mrs. Furness had requested. Fortunately the store was thoroughly stocked with all the necessities of mourning, including armbands and hatbands, black-bordered stationery and handkerchiefs, crape veils, and white ribbon. I added a few other items that I thought might be welcome, such as a pound of Assam tea, wax tapers, and paraffin oil. I had plenty of spending money with me, and it gave me a warm sense of satisfaction to be able to provide some necessaries for the household.

There was even a small selection of ready-made clothes, which made me pause a moment in thought. Remembering Mr. Lynch's shabby greatcoat, I wondered if he would accept a new coat as a present from Atticus and me. Clothing was a somewhat intimate gift between those who were not related, but we were close to family, after all, and these were special circumstances.

Then an even better idea occurred to me, and I had the girl measure off generous lengths of black bombazine and crape. I would offer to make mourning clothes for those in the household who wished for them, I decided. It would give me a healthy way of occupying the time before the funeral, and it might prove that Mr. Lynch would accept new clothes offered thus. It would also provide an excellent excuse for me to make a new dress for myself, and I was in need of one. My waistline had begun to expand, so I would need to either let out the dresses I had brought with me—an alteration that might be conspicuous—or fashion something new to fit my increasing size.

"Do you need a lad to carry them, my lady?" the young woman asked me after I had paid for my purchases.

"No, thank you. Mr. Burleigh's carriage will be coming for my husband and me at any moment."

I thought I saw a change of expression flit over the girl's face, but at the sound of the approaching carriage outside I made abbreviated goodbyes and left the shop with Atticus and my parcels.

To my surprise, only Mr. Lynch was present in the carriage. "Will the doctor be following later?" Atticus asked.

Mr. Lynch shook his head serenely. "He felt it unnecessary to perform an examination. Based on what my guardian told me, he felt quite confident in making out the death certificate and sending it back to Mr. Burleigh with me."

Startled, I glanced at Atticus to see what he made of this. But his face had taken on the appearance of a polite mask, and there was no way for me to know what his thoughts were until I had the opportunity to ask him in private. Was this normal when a family held such power and a protracted, fatal illness was involved? Our doctor had certainly made the journey to Gravesend upon the death of Atticus's father, and it was a good thing he had, for it was he who saw the signs that the old baron had not died naturally. It would have eased my mind had Dr. Brandt been present now. Acerbic and impolite he might be, but he was trustworthy.

But perhaps this man had certain instructions from my uncle. For a brief instant I wondered if Mr. Lynch might have carried a bribe with him, but then I dismissed the thought. He and his guardian were not on such close and sympathetic terms that my uncle would have entrusted such a task to him, even if his ward would have accepted something so dishonest.

When we arrived back at Thurnley Hall, Thomas took my parcels to Mrs. Furness, and I followed, paying no heed to his astonishment that I should enter the servants' quarters. Mrs. Furness was giving instructions to Cook as the latter, a stout elderly woman with gray hair mostly concealed under her cap, worked dough vigorously at the kitchen table. When I entered, she made a startled curtsey and stared at me with intent dark eyes.

"Mrs. Furness, may I have a word with you?" I asked after the housekeeper had made the introductions and I had shaken hands with Mrs. Antonescu, as Cook was more properly known.

"Of course, my lady. If you'll come to my sitting room?"

The housekeeper's sitting room was small and furnished with what were clearly unwanted pieces of furniture from the main part of the house, but the chair she showed me to was comfortable despite its threadbare cushion, and though the hearth was a small one, the fire that burned there was welcome after the carriage journey. I explained to her my scheme to make mourning clothes for any who wished for them, and she approved it heartily. "Mr. Lynch in particular could use a new suit," she said. "Of course, you are aware of his condition. That will present a challenge."

"I am certain I can produce something suitable, as long as you think he will accept it. I suppose I have come to feel an almost maternal interest in him," I admitted, "so I tend to forget that we are not actually related." *Not that we know for certain,* I added silently.

Mrs. Furness's expression had softened. "I understand entirely, my lady," she said. "He has a way about him that makes one rather protective of him. I'm certain he'll take your interest very kindly."

Now that she was in such an amiable frame of mind, this might be my best opportunity. "It troubles me that I did not get to say a real goodbye to my grandmother," I said. "I'm certain you are feeling her loss very keenly yourself, so you must understand how I long for one last glimpse of her."

But her eyes had gone wary. "I regret to say, my lady, that Mr. Burleigh insists that there be no viewing. He knows how distressing it would be for her family to see Mrs. Burleigh in such a sad state."

"It must have been distressing for you," I ventured, "seeing the ravages of her illness."

This gained me nothing, however, as she merely bowed her head momentarily. I dared not question her more minutely; it would be gruesome and even cruel were I to ask for particulars about my late grandmother's appearance. If only I could learn whether the housekeeper had any suspicions herself. Her guarded expression revealed nothing. Had her employer forced her to keep silent in this fashion?

"Mrs. Furness," I said, lowering my voice, "if my uncle has asked anything of you that makes you at all uneasy, please feel free to confide in me."

That did produce results, but not what I had expected. There was a flicker of something in her eyes, and she asked quietly, "And what would you be able to do about it if he had, my lady?"

Startled, I could not at once find an answer. It was true that I had no authority here, an unsettling fact that I had managed to forget. "You could come work for my husband and me," I offered.

She shook her head. "I cannot leave Thurnley Hall," she said. She made the statement sound like a prison sentence rather than a testament of her loyalty, and I wondered what web of events and emotions made her feel that she had no alternative to this dreary estate, which might not even be able to afford to keep her on.

Perhaps after a quarter century she did not feel she could adjust to a new household and new faces. I could well imagine that being the case with any servant who had been with one family for so long—and, of course, in some cases their tenure was even longer. That brought to mind an avenue of inquiry about my family history that I had not fully explored.

"Mrs. Furness, are there others still with the estate who might have known my parents?" I asked.

"Thomas is the only member of the staff who was here that long ago. I regret to say that age has affected his mind, though. I doubt you'll learn much from him."

That was dismaying. "And outside the house? How about any of the tenants?"

"I'll be happy to make inquiries, my lady," the housekeeper said. "I believe, though, that all who were on the estate in your mother's day are gone."

"All?" I repeated.

Mrs. Furness gave me a look that mixed patience with pity. "Your parents left the area around thirty-five years ago, did they not? In that time, things have changed a great deal, my lady. Even at that time, so I understood from Mrs. Burleigh, many had already given up farming to go to the factories. As you can imagine, that has only grown more common in all the years since."

"I hope my uncle appreciates your devotion," I said, feeling that it was a feeble response.

At that, she rose to go to the small cherry-wood sewing cabinet—evidently banished from upstairs for the gash on one leg—and opened the top drawer. From it she retrieved something that she held out to me. "That reminds me," she said, and her voice was brisk now. "Mr. Burleigh told me that your grandmother wished for you to have this."

"This" was the cameo that the old lady had worn both times I had seen her. The carved weeping lady stood out in sharp relief against the background. It was a large piece, and even to my ignorant eye a beautifully carved one.

"Mrs. Burleigh wore it every day that I knew her," she said. "I never saw her without it. Your uncle said that he hopes it will help you feel as though your grandmother were still close to you."

A pretty thought, to be sure. But my thoughts at that moment were concerned less with the brooch's sentimental value and more with the question of whether my uncle intended it to distract me from my interest in knowing more about my grandmother's death.

"Perhaps it's a mourning brooch," Atticus suggested, turning it so that the firelight illuminated the relief. "I wonder whose memory it honored. The figure of Niobe would suggest a child."

"Niobe?" I repeated. "As in *Hamlet*—'all tears'?"

He nodded, and the firelight cast a ruddy gleam on his hair. We had taken our evening meal on a tray in our room, as had the other members of the household. Tonight, my uncle had decided, we would all prefer privacy and solitude rather than a formal dinner together. Although I suspected that the decision was for his own convenience, so that I would not have an opportunity to plague him with questions, I found it very pleasant to sup privately with Atticus, rather as if we were at home at Gravesend. It was also a relief not to have to hide my tormenting thoughts in the presence of my uncle.

I tried to dismiss the thought and focus on the present. My years associated with the theater had increased my familiarity with figures of mythology and history, but there were still gaps in my knowledge. This woman's story was new to me. "Tell me about her," I said.

"Niobe was a queen in ancient Greece," he began, and I settled back in the divan, enjoying the rich sound of his voice. It was almost tactile, like the soft pile of a Persian rug beneath one's bare feet. "She boasted of her twelve children until her pride angered the gods, and to punish her Artemis and Apollo slew them all. She fled to Mount Sipylos and grieved so pitifully that Zeus took pity on her and turned her to stone, and they say she weeps even still. She is the most famous bereaved mother of legend."

"How horrible," I said, and took the cameo from him to examine it again. The weeping figure in her classical garb and diadem was hunched in utter despair beside what I now saw to be a faintly sketched plot of earth. "Only one grave," I observed. "But perhaps the artist felt it would have been impractical to try to crowd the other eleven into so small a space. So this brooch might have been created to commemorate a child that died."

"Quite possibly. But whose?"

I turned the brooch over, and on the back of the gold frame was engraved the date *20 December 1815*. "It is a puzzle," I agreed. "The date is well after Grandmama's marriage, but no one ever mentioned that she had any children but my mother and my uncle. Perhaps the subject carries no special significance and she simply thought it was beautiful." And now she was dead and it was in my keeping . . . thanks to my uncle. My uncle, who might have killed her. What was my responsibility in such a situation? Should I have insisted upon going back for the doctor—or a constable?

I did not realize how long I had been silent, staring into the flames, until my husband's voice brought me out of my reverie. He said gently, "You have had a grueling day. Shall I brush your hair for you?"

"That would be lovely, Atticus. Thank you."

He seated himself behind me on the divan, and soon I could feel his fingers working gently in my hair, finding and removing the pins that held it in its coil. As he drew each one from my hair, I felt a sense of relief, a release of tension. But only tension of the body. My troubled mind and heart were not yet willing to be calmed.

As he began to draw the brush through my hair, I realized that sitting thus, when he could not see my face, I had the courage to broach the grotesque suspicion that haunted me. I knew that he would never be deliberately unkind to me, but still I feared the unintended minute flash of horror that I could entertain so dreadful a suspicion. Yet I had to tell him. He would know whether I was right to be afraid or whether there might be some benign explanation that would ease my anguish.

"Atticus?"

"Yes, my love?"

I took a deep breath. "I'm very much afraid that Mr. Burleigh may have killed my grandmother."

There was only the briefest pause before the hairbrush resumed its slow, soothing rhythm. "What makes you think that?"

He spoke so reasonably, without any trace of censure, that my courage grew. Anything that troubled me would receive his most serious attention, as I knew by now.

"He acted so strangely when Mr. Lynch and I came upon him," I said. "I wish you had been there to see him. He seemed horrified, shaken—nearly undone."

"I can well imagine guilt showing itself that way." He fell silent for a moment, and the only sound was the sibilance of bristles moving over my hair. Each stroke of the hairbrush seemed to draw tension out of my body, releasing minute aches and pangs that I had not even been conscious of. "But might it not have been the reaction of an innocent person who stumbles upon the sight of his parent's lifeless body?"

"It might," I admitted. "What would I not give to know for certain! I wish the doctor had come to examine her. Why do you suppose he refused?"

"That struck me as odd as well. I suppose he was so familiar with your grandmother's condition that he felt entirely confident declaring the cause of death from Lynch's letter—"

"—which was written by my uncle."

"Indeed. I should like very much to know what the letter said."

I felt the same. It was appalling to think of my uncle not only committing murder but deliberately covering his tracks by writing a false account to the doctor. Again I had to gather the courage to speak my worst fear. "If I had not been so reluctant to offer him financial help," I said haltingly, "perhaps he would not have been driven to such a measure. He himself told us that her dower diverted a third of the estate's income away from him."

My husband's voice was soothing against the faint susurration that the hairbrush made. "You have no reason to reproach yourself, Clara. You didn't force him to take any action. And motive and appearances alone are a long way from the fact of murder. Remember that not very long ago, appearances made it look as though I killed my father."

That brought a tiny spark of hope, but it died all too soon. "No one who knows you would imagine for a moment that you could do something so vile. Whereas my uncle . . ." I pictured him at dinner that first evening, red-faced, jowls trembling, pounding the table as he spewed vitriol. He was someone whom I could envision committing murder.

And what was even more frightening was that this man was my near relation. Did that mean I had inherited that capacity as well? Even if I was not quite capable of that worst of acts, moreover, I might have inherited qualities that were nearly that disturbing. "My grandmother was not exactly loveable," I said. "She could be spiteful and selfish and a bit of a bully, just like him."

"Age and illness may have played a part in that," Atticus observed. "We were not seeing her at her best."

True enough. From what she told me, however, I had the impression that even my mother had not been all that I wished her to have been. A rebellious child who eloped to spite her parents—this was not the heritage I wanted. "Do you think I'm like them?" I asked, even as I feared the answer.

But with Atticus I never needed to fear. He said at once, "You are like yourself, my love."

I turned to beam at him, and he kissed my lips before gently turning my head back so that he could resume brushing my hair. "Mind you, I understand how you feel," he said in a new voice, an almost somber one. "It still sickens me that my own brother had the capacity and the will to commit murder." The motion of the hairbrush stilled for a moment. "He was my twin, practically my other self. It raises doubts in my mind about the kind of man I am."

"There is no doubt whatever in *my* mind," I said fiercely, turning to face him once more so that he could see my conviction. "It doesn't matter what your parents or your brother were. You are entirely different."

A faint smile touched his mouth, and he set the hairbrush aside. "That is what I am saying about you," he told me, taking my hand. "You are gloriously, completely yourself, not some derivative of those who happen to share your bloodline."

"I hope you're right," I said. But my gaze slid away from his face and over his shoulder to the shadowed part of the room. The antique cradle crouched there at the foot of the bed, the foreboding reminder that no matter what pretty fantasies Atticus and I spun about my character and my heritage, neither of us could truly know what I might pass on to our child—or what kind of mother I would prove to be.

CHAPTER TEN

The next day brought the arrival of a solicitor who was to go over the disposal of property with my uncle. For next few days, they were closeted together for long periods, joined by Atticus, who was lending his wisdom and experience to my uncle. As grateful to him as I was for this sacrifice, it left me alone for much of the time, and I would have fallen prey to loneliness without two pursuits: sewing and seeking more information about my mother.

There was little enough of the latter, unfortunately. I continued to prowl through the books in the library, and I made a thorough investigation of the empty room that Mrs. Furness said had belonged to her. I thought some signs of her tenancy might remain, even if it was no more than her initials scratched into the windowsill. But it was as if my mother had never set foot in the house—exactly the impression that her father had evidently wished to create.

Sewing gave my mind and hands something constructive to do, but it was still a solitary occupation. The drawing room seemed to be one of the least-used rooms in the house, and it more than any other I had seen spoke of the diminishing of the Burleigh family's stature and fortunes. The room had been redecorated in the last century, so that instead of the heavy, antique carved oak pieces from Cavalier days it boasted spindly, delicate rococo confections with a great deal of gilt, painted porcelain, and tufted satin. Sadly, these pieces had not endured the passage of time as hardily as the older furnishings. The satin cushions and hangings were faded and torn, the gilt patchy with mildew. The ornately framed mirror that hung over the mantel was blotched and misty, yielding a reflection that made me flinch away and resolve not to look again. No doubt death was too much on my mind, but the vision of my face in that mirror made me think of decay and corruption.

Sewing improved my spirits somewhat, for it always gave me satisfaction to see something tangible take form under my hands. First I ran up a new black waistcoat for Atticus to be worn with the black suit coat that Sterry had providentially packed for him. Then I began work on the truly challenging garment: the new frock coat for Mr. Lynch. I had just finished the long side seams of the toile when the sound of my name spoken directly behind me made me practically leap from my chair.

"Mr. Lynch!" I pressed my hand against my bodice as if I could force my heart to slow to its normal pace. "You startled me," I said inadequately.

He put his hand to his heart in an unintentional echo of my gesture. "I am so sorry, my lady," he said gently, his dark eyes dwelling with mild concern on my face. "I hadn't realized that the noise of the machine covered my footsteps."

"It does make a racket," I said. I was still flustered at having been so badly startled. "Did you wish to speak with me?"

"Mrs. Furness said that you needed me for a fitting. If this is an inconvenient time—"

"No, this is perfect." I raised the presser foot, drew the fabric away from the machine, and snipped the threads. I had fashioned the toile from black broadcloth so that it could double as the coat lining. "Here you are. As soon as I've made certain the shoulders are right, I can add the sleeves and check them for length."

He took the toile from me and drew one slender hand across the fabric, feeling the texture. "I really cannot thank you enough," he said. When he spoke softly like this, his voice was almost musical. I wondered with an inward smile if he had many young women pining over him back in Coventry. His poetic quality had probably stirred many a feminine heart. "Your kindness overwhelms me."

"Oh, heavens," I said, embarrassed. "It makes me feel useful."

"Still. I thank you a thousand times, Lady Telford." He made a neat bow. "I shall return at once and tell you how it fits."

"Wait!" I exclaimed with a laugh. "That will not do. I need to see the thing on you to fit it properly. Do you mind trying it on here?"

He hesitated for a moment, and in a rush of understanding I realized that he must be reluctant to let me see his shoulders' asymmetry without the disguise of his coat. Or perhaps he was equally concerned that anyone who passed by the door would see him thus. Almost at once I decided there would be no harm in closing the door. It could not be scandalous since we were practically family.

"I'll just shut the door and give us some privacy," I said, turning away from him. I moved unhurriedly, even stopping to pretend to examine a knickknack, to give him time enough to don the toile so that he would have at least that much covering over his shirt and waistcoat.

When at last I closed the door and turned around, he had removed his coat and put on the toile, which looked like some kind of strange clerical garb against the snowy white of his shirt. He stood staring directly ahead, very straight and stiff, like a soldier at attention . . . or like someone bracing himself for a blow. "I am sorry that you have to see this, my lady," he said in a low voice.

This was the clearest view I had yet had of what he called his hunch, and I did not think it such a great abnormality. The unevenness of his shoulders was not at all severe. Clever use of padding would make it almost invisible except for the roundness of his upper back.

"Why, there's nothing to apologize for," I said, but the tension in his face did not abate until I stepped close to him and began tugging the toile into place, smoothing it over his shoulders, and examining the effect.

The fact that I touched him unhesitatingly must have been significant to him, for when he next spoke his voice was almost inaudible with amazement. "You don't find me repulsive?" he almost whispered.

"Good heavens, no! What a thing to say."

But he was gazing at me with wonder in his eyes. Was it truly so astonishing that I did not shrink from him in horror? I wondered what terrible reactions he had endured in the past to make him so skittish now. I said firmly, "A bit of padding will do the trick, I should think. Really, it is scarcely noticeable at all."

"Perhaps you are accustomed to deformity," he said, and now his voice was pensive. "Because of the baron's."

"I don't think of my husband as having a deformity." I tucked some cotton wadding under the toile on the side of the lower shoulder and stood back to gauge the effect.

"Truly? You are a remarkable woman, Clara."

I laughed. "Hardly."

"No, it's true. Most people . . ." He did not finish the thought, and I could only guess what unpleasant memories must be gathering in his mind.

"Never mind most people," I said briskly. "Those who are governed by ignorance and prejudice are not worth a snap of your fingers." The recollection of Mathilde Munro and the scars she had inflicted on Atticus lent my words conviction, if not outright asperity.

He continued to stand perfectly still while I pinned and adjusted and repinned. I had never had so patient and obedient a mannequin. "Sewing must be a lonely occupation," he said presently, and it pleased me to hear his voice sounding relaxed and normal again. "Scarcely anyone ever ventures into this part of the house. Has no one offered to read to you while you sew? Some Trollope might be a congenial companion."

It took me a startled moment before I realized he was naming the author rather than referring to the unlucky type of woman whom we welcomed at the Blackwood Homes. I hid a smile at my misinterpretation but said only, "That's very kind of you. I'm afraid the noise of the machine would be a constant interruption, though."

I smoothed the fabric down over his chest to make it lie properly and realized abruptly that our respective positions were rather intimate. It was a foolishly conventional thought, but once in my mind it would not be dislodged. I was standing so close to Mr. Lynch that if he but bent his head a little he could whisper directly into my ear.

He would never take advantage of this closeness, I was certain, but I nevertheless stepped back and directed him, "Turn around, please, so that I can see how it lies in back."

Obediently he did so. Suddenly I realized that this might be the perfect opportunity to inquire whether he shared my suspicions of his guardian. It would be a delicate subject to broach, but I would be so much easier in my mind if I knew whether my terrible theory had any grounds. When I had asked Atticus his advice, he had recommended that I not act on my suspicions until I acquired evidence pointing one way or the other. But this was difficult to come by. Mr. Lynch might prove to be a valuable source of information.

"Mr. Burleigh has certainly been much occupied with estate matters," I began. "When I do catch a glimpse of him, he seems greatly troubled in mind."

There was a moment's silence before Mr. Lynch said, "Naturally he would be feeling the loss of his mother."

The words were not rebuking as much as guarded. I would tread a bit further and see whether he would be more forthcoming. "He was certainly in terrible distress when we encountered him that morning," I said. "It was almost as if there were something besides my grandmother's death that had unsettled him."

Another pause. "What do you suppose it might have been?" he asked, again in that tone that gave no clue as to his feelings.

I decided to take the gamble of being open with him. "It was no secret that he needed money badly, and that his mother's dower was part of the cause. In such a situation, when she was so ill already, with but a few months to live . . ." I took a breath. My heart was hammering in my throat with apprehension at my own daring. "One can understand why he would have been greatly tempted to—to hasten nature in its course."

He went perfectly still. For the space of four heartbeats he gave no sign that he had even heard except for his unnatural stillness, as if he had turned to stone. Then, slowly, he turned to face me.

He seemed paler, and his dark eyes were almost shocking in contrast. I had feared that he would wear a face like thunder and would hail condemnation down upon me for speaking as I had, but it was perplexity, not anger, that contracted his brow. "Are you certain?" he whispered in a bewildered voice. "Would he really have done such a thing—to his own mother?"

"I don't know," I hastened to say. "Indeed, I have no certainty whatever." My voice had fallen to a whisper as well. "But his manner seemed so guilty that the suspicion has lodged in my heart, and I cannot move it." When he didn't speak, I bit my lip in remorse. "I should not have spoken of it," I said. "Please forgive me for saying such things. It was a mad idea."

But now his eyes were turning pensive, and I could almost see the thoughts passing behind his eyes. "He has decided against a viewing," he mused. "Did you know? And he was adamant that he would not let you say a last goodbye to her."

"Yes! As if he were afraid that someone would see a sign that her death was not natural." I darted a look at the door to make certain it was still closed, and continued breathlessly. "Mrs. Furness herself prepared the body, when usually a woman in the village is brought in for that purpose."

His eyebrows rose. "Do you think Mrs. Furness is in his confidence?"

"In his power, more likely," I said grimly. "She would not quite admit to it, but I can well imagine how vulnerable a position she is in unless she doesn't care about losing her place here. And she was most emphatic that she has to stay. I cannot blame her, for finding a similar position at her age would probably be very difficult without connections."

Mr. Lynch drew his hand over his chin and shook his head slowly. "It is horrifying to contemplate such a thing," he said. "All the more horrifying that one cannot dismiss it out of hand. It is all too plausible." He took a deep breath and released it in a sigh, then met my eyes. "What do you plan to do?"

I spread my hands helplessly. "I have no plan. I can do nothing when all I have is suspicion, not proof. Believe me, I would be overjoyed to find that my fears are groundless."

"As would I," he said swiftly. "Perhaps I can help in that regard."

"Help?"

"To seek evidence clearing my guardian. I feel now that I won't be easy in my mind until I know he is innocent." Then his face clouded again. "Although it seems all too unlikely, now that you have opened my eyes to the signs. I should have seen them myself, except . . ."

"Except that he is your guardian. I know." I laid my hand on his arm in sympathy. "It must be terribly painful for you to contemplate such a side to the man who has been like a father to you."

He nodded slowly. But there was resolve in his voice when he said, "The truth is more important than anything else. I realize that now." Placing his hand firmly over mine, he gazed into my eyes and said in words as solemn as a vow, "I'll not fail you, Clara—in this, or in anything."

It was as if he were pledging himself to me like a knight . . . or a husband. Taken aback, I was still trying to form a response when the door opened. In that instant, Mr. Lynch quickly withdrew his hand from mine, and that rendered furtive what could have been meant as simply a companionable gesture.

To my pleasure, and also somewhat to my relief, it was Atticus who entered. "Clara, there you are," he said. "I beg your pardon, Mr. Lynch. I didn't mean to interrupt a fitting."

"We were just finishing," I said, stepping away from the young man.

"Excellent. I hoped you might join me for a walk, unless it's inconvenient."

"That would be lovely. Mr. Lynch, do you need assistance extricating yourself from the toile?"

He smiled and shook his head. The disquieting intensity had vanished, and he was merely friendly once more. "Don't let me delay your walk," he said.

Atticus and I collected our wraps before departing. Outdoors the world was cloaked in a heavy mist, through which isolated objects reared up unexpectedly: a pillar, a gnarled tree, a heap of rock where a wall had collapsed. The mist muffled everything, dampening even the sound of our voices. Our footsteps were almost inaudible, as if we were drifting like ghosts.

"Mrs. Furness told me that there are dangerous places around," I recalled, "like ravines from old lead works, even tunnels. I wouldn't want to tumble into one of them."

"You'd best hold very tightly to me so that you don't," Atticus said with a smile. "Is Lynch's coat coming along satisfactorily?"

"Yes, quite well." I wasn't certain that he would approve of what I had broached with my uncle's ward, but I felt it was important to be entirely open with him . . . about this particular topic, at least. "When you came in I had just finished telling him of my fears about my grandmother's death."

"How did he respond?" His voice indicated neither approval nor disapproval.

"He was shocked, of course, to consider that my uncle might have been complicit, but he didn't dismiss the idea entirely. He is determined now to seek out the truth."

"Determined to impress you, at least. I think you have gained an admirer."

"Oh, fiddlesticks," I said, embarrassed. "He was simply quite pleased about the coat. It was really very touching."

"I don't think it was just the coat, my love. The way he looked at you was rather proprietary."

The undercurrent of concern in his voice echoed my own uneasiness. "I do hope that's not true," I said. "Perhaps we misunderstood the nature of his attention. After all, I must be at least ten years older than he."

At that, he drew to a stop and reached out to twine a lock of my hair around his finger. "You are too lovely for a mere ten years' difference to prevent a man from losing his heart to you," he declared. "You don't know the extent of your power to attract, my love."

"You say that because you are my husband, Atticus."

His lips quirked in a smile. "Oh, is it a contractual obligation? I'd no idea."

I gave him a reproving look. "You know what I meant. Just because you see me that way doesn't mean other men do. Mind you, I suppose he must be lonely, as he seems to have no friends hereabouts, and goodness knows his relationship with his guardian is rather fraught."

"Exactly," he said, and the laughter had left his voice. "In such circumstances, it would be all too easy for him to become fixated upon you."

I wanted to deny it, but that oddly solemn speech Mr. Lynch had made to me just before Atticus had come upon us still echoed in my mind. Moreover, he had called me *Clara,* and without my having invited him to do so. Remembering this, and his obvious emotion when I had not shrunk from the sight of him in his shirtsleeves, I felt my unease growing. "Do you think I oughtn't to have done the fitting alone?" I asked. "Next time perhaps I should ring for Ann and find some reason for her to attend us."

"Mrs. Furness would be even better," he said. "Not that I believe you are in any danger from the fellow, but it might prevent him from getting it into his head to make the conversation more personal than you would like."

The pleasure of my good deed had dwindled considerably. "I hope you're mistaken about him," I said, "but I'll avoid being alone with him from now on if you think it best."

"For your sake, that would make me easier in my mind." He kissed me as if to seal my pledge, then kissed me again with greater thoroughness. "How I miss you when I'm closeted with Durrington and your uncle for so much of the day!" he exclaimed. "That reminds me, I asked after the trunk you were promised, but Durrington says he must look through it first and compare the contents to his inventory to make certain that it contains nothing disposed otherwise by the will. The man seems sound, but he is taking a great deal of time making certain that everything is carried out properly."

"Thank you for asking after it, at least." I stifled a sigh. My desire to learn more of my mother seemed to be thwarted at every turn.

Even with Mr. Lynch's coat to finish, I still had time over the next few days to make a simple new dress for myself. And not a moment too soon, for my other dresses were straining at the seams.

It was not long before Ann noticed my increasing waist. On the evening before the funeral when dressing me for dinner she tugged in perplexity at my corset laces. I caught her eye in the dressing-table mirror just as she was opening her lips to comment, I was certain, on the impossibility of lacing me as tightly as before. My quick, urgent shake of the head made her blink and shut her mouth with a puzzled look. I tipped my head slightly toward the screen, behind which Atticus could be heard whistling as he changed his clothes, and put a finger to my lips.

Ann's eyes grew wide, but she gave a solemn nod to indicate that she understood and would keep my secret.

I was fortunate that she did not ask why I wanted to keep my husband from knowing of my condition, for I might not have been able to justify it. Every day my fear struggled with the conviction that I must not continue to keep him in the dark. This was especially true since Atticus continued to speak of our traveling to Europe come summer, and the presence of an infant would doubtless affect those plans.

Despite this knowledge, my fear had not lessened; if anything, it grew stronger with the passing of the days as it became clear that it would not be possible to keep my condition secret for much longer. Although to this point I had at least been spared the nausea Vivi had warned me of, I was surprised that Atticus had not noticed my changed waistline during any of the times that he embraced me when I was not wearing my stays. Perhaps he had noticed and had ascribed it to Cook's rich fare. Or perhaps he was distracted by the matters we had left behind in Cornwall.

"How are George and Vivi faring during our absence?" I called, hoping to distract myself from my internal struggle. "Is construction going well?"

"Do you know, that's an odd thing," Atticus said. "Aside from a short telegram saying how busy they are, I've not received a single letter from Bertram during our stay here."

"Perhaps he meant that he is too busy to write," I suggested, but that was unlikely: George was too conscientious not to keep

Atticus informed. "I've not heard from Vivi, for that matter," I added as realization came to me. And that was not like her. I ought to have been receiving long effervescent letters full of plans for the babies—both hers and mine. "Nor has Mrs. Threll sent word of whether Henriette and Sterry are recovering. Do you suppose the mails are so much worse out here where we are so remote?"

"Quite possibly, but they shouldn't be delayed this severely," Atticus said, emerging from behind the screen to look in the mirror beside me as he fumbled with his tie. Ann was still uneasy in my husband's presence, liable to stare and drop things, so I dismissed her with a nod. She bobbed the briefest of curtseys before making a hasty exit. "I shall speak to Burleigh about it," he said, unaware of this small domestic drama.

"How does he seem to you?" I asked.

"By which you mean, is he acting like a guilty man? That's hard to say." He gave up on his tie and dropped his hands, turning toward me with a self-conscious smile, and I took up the ends so that I could finish the task. "Something is certainly troubling him," he said, "and if I were forced to guess I would say it seems to be more than his mother's death. I doubt it's money, for Durrington seems to think his standing is more secure than before."

"A not unexpected development," I pointed out, "and a mighty strong motive."

"Now, my love, I know you are wondering whether I think he is guilty, but I have discovered nothing we did not already know that would support such a theory. Which is not to say that it's impossible, only that I am no closer to certain than before."

I sighed and stepped back to gauge the effect of his tie. "I just wish we *could* know for certain. It is wretched knowing that my suspicions may be altogether unfounded and I could be wronging him terribly."

"I wouldn't say they were entirely unfounded," said Atticus. "His behavior has been decidedly odd. But it is unfortunate that it isn't odd in a more explicit way."

That made me laugh, something I had not done much lately, and I stepped closer to him and slipped my arms around his waist. "Thank you for not scoffing at my suspicions," I said. "It means a great deal to me that you take me seriously." He stroked one knuckle across my cheek. "I would never scoff at you, my love. But I confess it makes me sad to see you so agitated. I want to see you happy again." His husky voice was soothing to my frayed nerves, so that I already felt less on edge than before. "I would love nothing more than for us to leave here within the hour," I said wistfully. "We could be back at Gravesend in a trice, taking tea with George and Vivi. But I feel as though we have a responsibility to determine whether something is amiss here."

"I entirely agree, my love." He touched his lips to my forehead. "I promise to help you in any way I can. My conscience would not permit us to leave Thurnley Hall now even if yours could."

My husband's conscience, as I well knew, was a stern one. Still, I wondered if he was exaggerating slightly out of his desire to support me in all my undertakings. It was a question that I was content to brush aside at that moment, but later it would come back to haunt me. My own determination to stay at Thurnley Hall, not his, might have been what held Atticus there . . . and my conscience would later have terrible cause to reproach me on that point.

CHAPTER ELEVEN

The evening meal, like all of those at Thurnley Hall, was short on cheerful conviviality. The lawyer Durrington was not a merry addition to our company, although in his defense it must be said that we had been forced upon him as much as he on us.

He was a thin gentleman of indeterminate age, with a domed bare pate encircled by a scanty fringe of dark hair. Throughout the meal I noticed his pale eyes taking note of the room's accoutrements: the handsome sideboard with its elaborate carvings, the silver we ate with, even the two hunting scenes in oil that brightened the dark paneling. Perhaps he was merely noting the presence of items whose existence he had read about in my grandmother's will, but it was unsettling, and I half expected to find his emotionless gaze resting on me with the same calculation, as if itemizing me for a catalog. *One baroness of recent vintage but imperfect provenance, together with an inconveniently vivid imagination and a large degree of stubborn conviction.*

A glance at my uncle drove such fancies out of my mind, however. To put it mildly, he did not look well. His jaw was stubbled with several days' growth of beard, and his linen was dingy at the neck and wrists, as if he had not changed it in days. As he reached for his wine glass his hand trembled, and he gulped the beverage quickly and then jerked his head at Mrs. Furness to pour him more. His eyes were furtive, rarely meeting those of any of us at the table. He looked like a man with a wretched conscience, but whether he was guilty of more than thought was impossible to say. It was entirely plausible that he had wished his ailing mother dead and then been stricken with guilt when her death had seemed to fulfill that wish. That did not explain his having refused to let anyone see her body, however.

Sadly, staring at my uncle across the dinner table would not bring me answers. I let my gaze wander to the rest of the company and found Mr. Lynch watching his guardian with an expression of detached interest. I wondered what conclusions he was drawing, if any, from what he saw.

Now my uncle had begun to describe the proceedings of the funeral the next day. After the church service, the family would accompany the casket to the mausoleum on the Thurnley Hall grounds. The small family burial ground was located on a slight rise, well back from the house and outbuildings but clearly visible from the oldest part of the house. Atticus and I had visited it on one of our daily walks, but we had given it only a glance before continuing on our way.

My mind was called back from my musings when I heard my uncle say, "Of course you may say a few words on your wife's behalf, Lord Telford."

"I can speak on my own behalf," I said, bristling at his high-handed manner.

Startled at the interruption, he gave me an ill-tempered glower. "Naturally you won't attend the service. You know that ladies have no place at a respectable funeral."

"I most certainly will attend. This is my grandmother, after all."

He put down his wine glass with an emphasis that made liquid slop over the rim. "It won't do at all to have a female there making a scene and becoming hysterical," he snapped.

"I assure you," I told him icily, "I am quite capable of maintaining all the composure you could desire. The only reason I would make a scene, as you put it, would be if I were forbidden to witness my grandmother's final journey."

He flung his hands up in exasperation. "I don't see why you're so set on it, when you didn't know she was in the world even one month ago."

I did not say so, but I felt as if I had failed my grandmother somehow, that I had not helped her unburden herself as she had seemed to wish. Aloud I said, "This is the last time it will be in my power to do something for her, and I don't see that it's a great deal to ask."

My uncle looked at Atticus as if seeking help in dissuading me, but if that was the case he found no help from that quarter. My husband met his mute appeal with a bland expression.

"Very well," he said at last, grudgingly. "But you can't blame me, Lord Telford, if any of the hired mourners make an indecent advance on your wife. Her presence there may well provoke them regardless of her degree of dignity and reserve."

Atticus said calmly, "The responsibility for their behavior does not lie with Clara. If the mourners you have hired are too drunk or unmannerly to maintain their own decorum, they should be dismissed."

My uncle's expression darkened again. "It wouldn't be proper for my own mother to go to her grave with only a few paltry mourners in the procession."

Atticus gave him a friendly smile. "In that case, I hope you won't take it amiss if I correct their behavior as I see fit."

"As you wish." My uncle's expression was skeptical. "I'm not certain a lecture will have great effect."

It gave me great satisfaction to tell him, "My husband is skilled in bare-knuckle fighting, Mr. Burleigh. His methods of correction will be quite effective."

Up to this point the lawyer had seemed contented to stay out of the wrangling—and for that I could not blame him—but that seemed to pique his interest. "Is that true, Lord Telford?" he inquired. "How interesting. I would have thought fighting would be difficult for you with your, ah, disadvantage."

"My club foot forced me to seek ways to improve my balance, and pugilism addressed that," Atticus explained. "Working to overcome my difficulty in staying on my feet has served me in good stead."

Mr. Lynch had been silent for so long that the sound of his voice, though gentle as always, made me start. "How fortunate are you and I both, my lord," he said, "that our parents did not practice the ancient Greek custom of exposing infants who were not perfect physical specimens."

An explosive sound drew my eyes back to my uncle, who seemed to be choking on his wine. Although his eyes streamed with tears and his face turned nearly purple, he waved the lawyer violently away when he made to rise to go to his aid. "Why would you say that?" he demanded in a croaking voice when the coughing fit had subsided. "What in God's name are you about?"

His ward frowned slightly as if perplexed at so vehement a response. "I was merely making a historical allusion," he said. "I meant no harm by it, I'm sure."

His guardian's eyes narrowed. "You're a liar. You said it because you . . ."

But he fell silent without finishing the thought. It was just as well, for I had caught Mr. Lynch's tensing at the word *liar*. The conversation might all too quickly become fisticuffs, it seemed to me.

Mr. Durrington must have felt the same, for he cleared his throat and said in a soothing tone, "Now, Mr. Burleigh, I'm sure your ward wouldn't lie to you. I think perhaps the strain of your dear mother's passing may be inclining you toward, shall we say, a heightened state of emotion."

This was enhanced, no doubt, by the quantity of wine he had consumed. The lawyer was too tactful to mention that, however, even when my uncle pushed back his chair and stood so abruptly that he had to clutch at the table to keep his balance.

"I don't have to listen to any more of this," he announced, squinting at us each in turn as if he suspected us all of collusion. "I won't sit here and be insulted at my own table. I just hope you all have more civil tongues in your heads at the funeral tomorrow. If you won't respect me, the least you can do is show respect for the sorrowful occasion—and for my mother, may God rest her soul."

Grabbing the claret decanter from Mrs. Furness, who had stood silently by, he strode unsteadily from the room. His ward observed his exit with an expression that made me wonder whether he felt, as I did, that this behavior might well be significant. Was my uncle merely concerned with presenting a respectable appearance to his neighbors when he tried so hard to dissuade me from attending the obsequies? Or was there a more urgent reason that he wished me elsewhere? His behavior seemed so unstable that I wondered if we should expect some kind of outburst from him.

The funeral service the next day proceeded smoothly, however. My uncle looked nearly respectable in clean white linen and a suit of sober black, and I surmised that Grigore or Thomas had shaved him and made him presentable. He made no objections to my presence beyond a hostile glare, but even this lessened in intensity over the course of the proceedings. The eulogy struck me as being impersonal and vague, as if the priest either had not known my grandmother well or was deliberately glossing over the incidents of her life in order to cast her in a better light. I realized that I would not have been able to supply him with anything more favorable to say about her, and that, too, depressed me.

There were few enough people in attendance at the church, and I wondered if that was another reflection of the general movement away from the vicinity toward the towns and cities, or whether the decline in the Burleigh family's social importance meant that they numbered few acquaintances now who would travel to Coley for a funeral. I could understand why he had hired mourners . . . who, I was pleased to find, behaved with a reasonable degree of decorum and did not require any correction from Atticus. He remained by my side to give my hand a comforting squeeze at intervals, and I was grateful for his reassuring presence.

The mausoleum on the Thurnley Hall grounds was a dignified affair of once-white granite, which had sadly been discolored, like the house. Inside there was room for only the priest, my uncle, Mr. Lynch, Atticus, and me. Two candles in wall brackets cast a sickly light, and I let my eyes roam over the inscriptions marking where my progenitors lay while the priest spoke his last words. When he bade us all bow our heads and join him in prayer, our every word echoed from the domed roof, creating a gloomy clamor.

After all was done and we filed outdoors, the overcast day seemed almost bright compared to the gloom inside the house of the dead. I turned to look back after all of us had exited and found my uncle closing the iron gates that served as doors. The noise was so great it might have been a giant discordant bell.

Then, to my surprise, he drew a length of chain through the bars and snapped a padlock on it to secure the gates. When he noticed me observing him, he gave an unconvincing smile.

"So many vandals hereabouts," he said. "I dare not leave the mausoleum open. If anyone desecrated my mother's resting place I would never forgive myself."

This was the first I had heard of any vandals in the area, and my skepticism must have conveyed itself to my uncle, for he turned and led the way back to the house. I dawdled at the end of the procession, looking back at the locked mausoleum. The chain and padlock seemed to me like my uncle's final attempt to prevent anyone from examining my grandmother's body for signs of foul play.

⌭

In the darkness I reached out for something to guide me. My outstretched hands met only stone. The walls on either side of me were rough against my fingertips, and with every step my stocking feet met with the same unforgiving rock. When I reached up, the roof of the passage was just inches above my head. I had no light, no companion, nothing to help me on my way, yet I hurried as fast as I could because somewhere at the end of this passage was Atticus, and he needed me.

Pebbles skittered under my footsteps, and I winced as the rough surface abraded the soles of my feet through the flimsy protection of my stockings. My fingertips smarted from being drawn across the walls, but I relied on them to tell me which way to walk.

But now the passage was narrowing. Whereas before my arms could stretch almost to their full length on either side, now I had to draw them in more and more. Soon I was holding them almost straight in front of me.

With a bump the crown of my head grazed the roof. I bowed my head as my heart began to make quick, anxious thumps in my breast. I forced myself to take one more step, then another. Somehow I must reach Atticus. Richard had a pistol. If I did not reach them in time—

The rock pressed down, and I crouched like an old woman. Still the passage grew lower, and soon I had to get down on my hands and knees and crawl. My skirt hindered my progress, tangling around my legs until I could have wept in frustration. Then my shoulders snagged against the rock on either side. I struggled to move forward, but the passage was too narrow; I was stuck like a cork in the mouth of a bottle.

If I could make my way back the way I had come, I thought feverishly, there might be another route, a different way of reaching Atticus. But when I fumbled backward, my heels bumped against stone. There was no way of going back. Frantically I felt ahead of me with my hands in a desperate hope that the passage would widen again, but my fingers encountered nothing but cold stone. I was sealed in.

Fighting the scream that rose in my throat, I hammered my fists against the unyielding rock until the warm blood trickled over my broken skin. Closer and closer the walls pressed, until I could no longer draw breath, and my lungs burned with the need for air. With a Herculean effort I strained against the encroaching stone, exerting all of my strength . . .

. . . and awoke in bed, gasping for breath.

My heart was galloping as if it would burst out of my ribcage. Still gulping great mouthfuls of the blessed air, I reached out in the darkness and felt a renewed dart of panic until my hand fell upon the reassuring form of my husband. With a gasp of relief I moved over until I lay beside him, feeling the comforting warmth of his body against mine. When I laid my head on his chest, the tickle of hairs against my cheek made me smile. The soothing, regular rise and fall of his chest and the beating of his heart brought me back to the here and now. I was safe. I was with Atticus.

Though in the enveloping darkness with the bed curtains closed I might not be able to see him, my body knew the shape of his. The breadth of his shoulders, the round swell of muscle in his arms told me this could be no one but Atticus. This was still novel enough to be faintly miraculous. How astonishing that in so short a time I had become so intimately acquainted with this man that his body felt almost as familiar to me as my own. I could lie with him naked yet completely without shame or nervousness, as if we truly were two halves of one beautiful, inevitable whole.

Yet less than a year ago I had been a spinster, with no idea that I would ever share my bed with a man—let alone that I should like it so well. The Clara of a year ago had slept alone in her narrow bed, and if she woke in the night with a frightening dream she had no one to make her feel safe and protected. Of course, not just any man would have made me feel this way. Only Atticus could have transformed my life—transformed *me*—like this.

As if sensing my thoughts, he stirred and gave a sigh. His arms closed around me, and I could feel the words rumble in his chest when he said sleepily, "Clara? Are you all right?"

"Yes," I whispered. "Go back to sleep."

His lips brushed the crown of my head. "I was dreaming I was a knight in the age of chivalry," he said. His fingertips touched my shoulder, stroked lightly down my arm and back up again. "I was in single combat with another knight. Every now and then I would catch a blow from his sword on my shield, and it would make the most terrific noise."

"That doesn't sound restful."

"It wasn't. Wait—there it is now. It wasn't in my dream after all."

This time I had heard it too: a harsh, metallic sound like a violent blow of metal on metal. It did not sound near, but it was nevertheless distinct. I sat up just as Atticus swung his feet to the floor and parted the curtains. "What do you think it can be?" I asked, as he walked to the window.

"There's a light. Not from any of the outbuildings, as far as I can tell." Then he turned to look at me. "I think it's coming from the burial ground," he said.

That was the last thing I would have expected. "But who would be there at this hour?"

He reached for his dressing gown and put it on. "I'm going outside to take a look," he said as he knotted the sash.

"Wait a moment," I said, pushing back the bedclothes. "I'll come with you."

Soon the two of us were making our way to the burial ground with outdoor wraps thrown over our quilted dressing gowns to protect us from the chill that was so different from the mild climate of Cornwall. Atticus had his walking stick, which might be useful as a weapon depending on what we found, and I carried a lantern but had not yet needed to light it, since the moon was particularly brilliant. This made it all the more curious that someone would need a light to see by. But then, all depended upon what kind of work was being done . . . and by whom.

As we neared the fenced area, we could see a figure at the mausoleum. For an instant I thought it must be my uncle, embarking upon some new and sinister business. Was he attempting to hide something? Quickly, however, it became apparent that the figure was Grigore. No one else of that height and bulk was known to us. The lamp that rested close by him cast a distorted shadow on the granite face of the tomb, imbuing the spectacle with an eerie quality, as if he were an evil troll in some old folk tale.

Even though the reality was reassuring, the question remained: what possible business could he have at the mausoleum? It baffled me. Had he come to pay his respects in some rite unknown outside Romania?

As we neared, he grabbed the chain that held the gates fast and yanked it fiercely, as if he were trying to snap it with his bare hands. Then, as we watched, he released it. Stepping back, he picked up an axe and swung it down in a swift arc. The jarring clanging noise rang out, making me start, and I realized he must be trying to break the padlock and get the gates open.

"Good evening," Atticus said pleasantly.

The effect was astonishing. Grigore whirled around at the sound of his voice and gave a short, hoarse cry as he recognized Atticus. He was dressed in his usual garb of smock and trousers, but with a coat of fur skins and a strange garland of white objects around his neck. It was peculiar to see a man of his size and evident strength shrinking before us. He dropped his axe and plunged his hand into a pocket, then made a gesture as if he had retrieved something and thrown it toward us.

Atticus and I both flinched automatically, and in that instant the manservant took to his heels and ran. Soon he was out of sight.

At first I could not tell what he had thrown at us, for I had seen and felt nothing. Only a faint patter on the granite stoop of the mausoleum confirmed the presence of something falling to the ground. Bracing himself with one hand on his cane, Atticus stooped and felt around on the stoop.

"Peppercorns," he said, and the confusion in his voice mirrored what I felt. "Or some kind of seed. I need better light to be certain." Rising, he extended his hand to me, and in his palm I could see what looked like beads or tiny pebbles.

"Is the man mad?" I exclaimed. "Why would he throw such a thing at us?"

"Lady Telford?" said a new voice some distance away. "Lord Telford? What brings you here at this hour?"

Victor Lynch was approaching us. Despite the advanced hour, it seemed that he had not yet retired, for he was wearing his caped topcoat over what appeared to be his daytime garb. In the moonlight, which leached all color from the scene, his skin was as pale as marble. He might have been a sculpture that had wandered here from some other graveyard monument.

As he neared he tipped his hat to us, an incongruous note of formality in the circumstances. "Good evening to you both," he said, and the pleasant, mild voice was a welcome dose of normality. "Or perhaps I should say good morning." When he bowed to me I felt a flush of self-consciousness, realizing how I must look with my hair falling loose down my back and wearing my dressing gown beneath my mantle. But he was too polite to take notice of that. Instead he asked, "Was that Grigore who went haring off just now? What was he doing out here?"

"My wife and I wondered the same thing," Atticus said. "It was a noise that first caught our attention. He was evidently trying to break the lock or chain with that axe, and the sound woke us."

Mr. Lynch bent to retrieve it, but it looked like any ordinary axe as far as I could tell. "I suppose he was trying to get inside the mausoleum," he said. "Otherwise he would not have needed a lantern, for outdoors the moonlight is quite bright enough to see by."

"What could he possibly have intended to do inside?" I wondered. I took up the lantern, which the manservant had left behind in his hurry, and held it out to cast its light around us in search of other clues. I saw nothing at first, but then the glint of the light off metal captured my eye, and I pointed.

Atticus picked the thing up, but cautiously, for the light gleamed on a sharp, curved edge. "A scythe blade," he mused. "I don't see a handle anywhere about. What could he have planned to do with that?"

"And this," I said, bending to pick up a half brick that was rough with age but untouched by moss. "I don't think it can have been here before; we would have seen it when we were all here earlier. And it can't have fallen from the mausoleum, for it isn't granite."

"Between that and the seeds, it's a motley enough assortment." Atticus shook his head in perplexity. "Lynch, you mentioned before that this fellow was a bit . . . touched, did you say? Is some mania of his at work? I confess I find myself baffled. And he fled from us—well, from me—as if I were death itself."

"Seeds?" the other man echoed. "Did I hear you aright?"

"Yes," I said. "At least, we believe that's what they are. He threw them at us just before he took to his heels." I offered Mr. Lynch the lantern, and he squatted down to observe the tiny objects that were scattered on the stoop. In a moment he straightened, and I was startled to observe that he was smiling. "Do they have some significance to you?" I asked.

"They do," he said, and I was surprised at the amusement in his voice. "You recall, sir, how Grigore shrank from you before, calling you a *strigoi*. I'm afraid that all this is a sign that his fear is stronger than ever. He is convinced that you are a vampire, Lord Telford."

"But that's preposterous!" I cried, my voice rising with indignation. "How can he not see that my husband is the furthest thing on earth from some vicious, bloodsucking demon?"

"My love, your loyalty is very touching," Atticus said more quietly, putting his arm around my shoulders, "but perhaps we should avoid waking any more of the household. Lynch, why do you say that?"

The younger man gestured to the blade of the scythe. "It looks very much to me as though Grigore believes that Mrs. Burleigh was attacked by a vampire and might rise from her coffin. According to the primitive beliefs of men like him, a stone or brick placed in the mouth of the deceased may temper their taste for blood. But if she was still inclined to rise"—he raised the scythe blade, which shone eerily in the moonlight—"this was to be placed across her neck to trap her in her casket."

Anger flared in me at the thought of Grigore breaking open my grandmother's coffin to defile it with these objects of primitive superstition. "My uncle must be told of this," I said, this time remembering to moderate my tone.

"Why did he throw the seeds when we drew near?" Atticus asked. "What meaning do they hold?"

"I suspect he was trying to fend you off," Mr. Lynch mused. "Some peasant folk believe that vampires are compelled to count things. By throwing a handful of small objects at you, Grigore hoped that he could confine you to this spot long enough to count all of them, giving him time to make good his escape."

Atticus sighed. "This must be brought to a halt. He might have done real damage to the mausoleum if we had not happened to notice the disturbance."

"Monuments can be mended," I exclaimed, "but think how gravely he might have injured you if he had chosen a more effective weapon. What if he had decided to use the axe against you, Atticus, or the scythe blade? This man has become a menace."

Mr. Lynch nodded heavily, rubbing his chin. His smile had vanished, and with it his mirth. His gentle voice was entirely serious when he said, "Your wife is quite right, Lord Telford. I'll take these objects into my custody for the night and will escort you to your room. In the morning we must speak to my guardian and tell him that he must take action. Grigore is too dangerous to remain at Thurnley Hall."

CHAPTER TWELVE

"My husband is not a vampire," I said. "Let us be clear on this."

My uncle's already red face flushed even deeper at my tone. "Naturally that goes without saying."

"Does it? Your manservant certainly seems to need clarification on that point."

Atticus and I, along with Mr. Lynch, had confronted my uncle the next morning in his study. At the time he had been conferring with the lawyer, but as soon as we had entered carrying the items Grigore had left behind at the burial grounds, my uncle had asked Durrington to leave. Now these objects were arrayed on the desk, sinister reminders that a subject that might otherwise have seemed silly in the light of day was all too real to at least one member of the household.

My uncle leaned across the desk toward us to emphasize his words, bracing himself on his hands. "And I say again that I am shocked and horrified that Grigore would act as he has. Please accept my apology, my lord."

"That isn't necessary, sir. Grigore did me no harm." Atticus was the only one of us to appear at ease. He stood by the fire with one elbow propped on the mantel, thoughtfully tapping his stick against the toe of his boot while I paced across the threadbare rug.

"But he might easily have done," Mr. Lynch pointed out. He stood by the desk, arms folded, his dark eyes grave. "It is terrifying to think how differently things might have happened if Grigore had chosen to attack instead of fleeing."

"I agree entirely," my uncle said. He stood behind his desk with his hands still braced on the blotter. Why did none of the men take a seat? Their restlessness was making mine worse.

Belatedly I realized that none of them would sit unless I did so. How ridiculous to conform to etiquette at a time like this! But I dropped into an armchair with a frustrated huff, and the men finally seated themselves as well.

My uncle settled into his chair with an expression of relief. "I will dismiss Grigore at once," he said.

Astonishingly, he and I were in agreement for once. "He may try to take revenge if he believes that Atticus caused him to lose his position," I warned. "How will you prevent that?"

He drummed his fingers on the cracked leather arm of his chair. The skin around his eyes was puffy, and I wondered if it was from lack of sleep. "The sooner he goes, the better," he said. "I'll have him put on the train to some destination far away. If necessary I'll set a watch on him until he leaves. I'll make certain he doesn't have the opportunity to take revenge, if that should be his aim."

"But how shall he live if he is stripped of his position?" Atticus asked.

"He might easily hire himself out for physical labor," Mr. Lynch said. "With his size and strength, he should have no difficulty finding work of that sort."

No one could have been more unwilling than I to argue against sending Grigore away, but I heard myself saying, "He may not find it as easy as that, since his English is far from fluent. And you said yourself that he is a little bit simple. He will need help to find an occupation."

"I agree," Atticus said. "I don't want any rash action on our part to cause the man's ruination and land him in the workhouse. We bear a responsibility to him."

Strictly speaking, it was my uncle who bore this responsibility, but it was like Atticus to share it—even when his own welfare was most at risk here.

"What happens if we find him a new position and he attacks someone else?" my uncle demanded. "Are we to take the risk that his mania may drive him to further violence? An asylum may be the best place for him."

Mr. Lynch's jaw tightened. "As much as I agree that we cannot allow him to continue to put Lord Telford in danger, I must protest against that. The only actual violence he has committed was against the chain that secures the mausoleum gates. Haven't you some acquaintance who needs a man of all work?"

He and his guardian continued to wrangle, but a startling idea had just occurred to me that made the discussion suddenly recede from my attention. What if Grigore had killed my grandmother? If Mr. Lynch was correct and the manservant had thought my grandmother might rise from her grave, perhaps he was the one who had put her there. If he feared she was a vampire, he might have believed he was protecting himself and the household by killing her. His appearance at the tomb the night before might have been an attempt to finish the job.

Why, then, had my uncle behaved so strangely upon her death? Had he suspected foul play but had no proof? In that case, though, he would have had every reason to insist upon the doctor's examining the body, which had not been the case. Had he feared that exposing the murderer would put himself at risk?

It was all quite troubling. And I did not even feel that I could ask him, because if my suspicions were unfounded, the suggestion that his mother had not died naturally might cause him great pain . . . and might cause an innocent man much trouble, if Grigore was in fact innocent.

"I shall speak to him," Mr. Lynch said now. "I've picked up a fair bit of Romanian, and Mrs. Antonescu and I between us should be able to convey the meaning."

"Why Cook?" I inquired.

"She is half Romanian. I'll do my best to convince him that his superstitions about the baron are misplaced, but if he proves obdurate, I'll lock him in his room until we can summon the constabulary to take him to the village jail and put him under guard."

"The constabulary?" my uncle interjected. "Do you really think that's necessary?"

"It does seem excessive," Atticus began, but I leaned over to take his hand. "I don't want this man to have another chance to hurt you, Atticus. Please let Mr. Lynch and my uncle take whatever precautions are necessary."

"We must insist, my lord," said Mr. Lynch. "My guardian would never forgive himself if you fell to harm when he could have prevented it. Would you, sir?"

My uncle cleared his throat. "As you say, we must take all necessary precautions. Victor, I would be grateful if you would speak to Grigore as you've suggested. Make certain he understands that if he cooperates no harm shall come to him, so there is no need for him to distress himself—and no need for us to involve the police."

His ward left a slight pause before replying. "As you think best, sir," he said politely.

As soon as he had left the room and the door had shut behind him, I said, "Atticus and I will be leaving today." Last night after returning to our room we had come to this decision.

My uncle gave me a swift, startled glance. "Today! That is very sudden."

He did not, I observed, ask us to delay our departure. "We only stayed for Grandmama's funeral," I said. "It is high time we returned home. We'll be able to catch an afternoon train if we don't tarry."

"Please don't concern yourself that this business with Grigore is hastening us away," Atticus added. "There are business matters that require our attention, and we've trespassed on your hospitality longer than any of us had expected."

Only my kindhearted husband would try to reassure this relative of mine that he should not take our abrupt departure personally. "If you'll just send Ann to help us pack," I said, rising.

"Of course, of course." My uncle rose, his expression carefully grave, but I suspected he was relieved that we were departing. "If you need anything else, don't hesitate to ask Mrs. Furness. My household is at your disposal."

"That reminds me," I said. "If you would be so good as to have Thomas bring me the trunk that was promised to me with my mother's belongings, I'd be obliged."

A change came over my uncle's face then, a flicker of evasion in his eyes. "Of course," he repeated. "You may find the contents a bit—ah—tumbled about. Durrington insisted upon going through it in case anything inside had been disposed otherwise by my mother's will."

"Naturally," I said. *And in case anything was incriminating for my uncle,* I thought.

Atticus rose and reached out to shake my uncle's hand. "In case we don't have a chance for a proper goodbye later," he said genially. "Thank you for having us to stay, sir. You must think about visiting Cornwall one of these days."

Bless him for those noncommittal words. If he had actually invited my uncle to Gravesend, I probably would have shot up to the ceiling like a rocket.

Following his gracious example, I stepped forward and extended my hand as well. I said, "I'm glad we were in time to meet my grandmother. Thank you for making us welcome."

But as I made to withdraw my hand and follow my husband to the door, my uncle gripped my hand all the tighter. He said quickly, "A word with you, niece?"

Atticus raised his eyebrows at me, wondering if I needed extricating, but I shook my head slightly and smiled to let him know that he could leave without me. When he had left us alone, my uncle released my hand. "It isn't my place to inquire into your private conversations with your grandmother," he said, to which I thought, *it certainly isn't.* "I shan't ask you what she told you in secrecy. But in case she said anything that—er—may have shocked you, or even frightened you, I beg you to remember that her life was much constrained by age and circumstances, and she sometimes took great pleasure in, well, drawing extreme responses out of visitors."

"I don't understand. Do you mean that she told deliberate falsehoods to distress or anger me?"

"I didn't say that." He scratched at his sparse gray fringe. "I'm expressing myself badly, and it is difficult when one doesn't wish to speak ill of the dead, especially one's own mother. But she might have led you to believe that she—that our family—devil take it!" He turned and paced away from me down the length of the room. Without turning his head, and in so low a voice that I could scarcely catch the words, he said, "She enjoyed creating a sensation. Best of all when it meant setting her family at loggerheads. She relished any opportunity where a slight exaggeration or a—a false implication might create excitement, even a quarrel."

All at once I thought of my late father-in-law, who had taken such delight in baiting me. "His chief delight nowadays is in sticking pins in people to see what makes them flinch," Atticus had told Vivi on the occasion of their first meeting. Certainly the late Lord Telford had enjoyed stirring up visitors and picking at them until their composure was in tatters. I could see a certain resemblance to my grandmother, now that I reflected on it.

"I've known one or two people like that," I admitted. "But if you mean that she deliberately misled me about anything, I should like very much to have you set the record straight."

The face he turned toward me was strained. "Please feel free to ask me anything about which you have doubts, niece."

But of course the one question I wanted to ask—*Did you murder my grandmother?*—was something I could not utter. If he was innocent, I would insult him past forgiveness, perhaps even to the point of violence; if he was guilty, my suspicions would put me in danger of being permanently silenced.

"Thank you," I said at last. "There is something I've wondered about. Why were you and my mother both forbidden to marry?"

It should not have been a difficult question, but his eyes widened, and he ran one finger around the inside of his high collar as he had done once before when uneasy. He cleared his throat. "We weren't *forbidden*, precisely. Is that what she told you? Mother did tend toward the melodramatic!"

"Oh? Then what is the truth?"

"Well, ah. We were expected to—ah—make very elevated marriages. Not to, as it were, throw ourselves away on lesser matches." He coughed into his hand and, avoiding my eyes, rummaged in his breast pocket for a handkerchief. "Our parents had very high expectations for us, and they were well aware that we might not find worthy partners for a very long time. Perhaps never."

I folded my arms and gave him a level look. "That is not at all what my grandmother told me."

Holding his handkerchief to his mouth, he coughed again and gestured vigorously with his free hand. "Terribly sorry," he gasped. "I have these spells. Must excuse me . . ."

It was so transparent that I could have laughed at him. "Very well," I said. "I'll not trouble you further." I withdrew from the room, closing the door behind me on the sound of my uncle's counterfeit coughing fit.

Suddenly he struck me as pathetic instead of sinister. Was this more manipulation, or was it the man himself? If he was truly so clumsy at subterfuge, perhaps I had been wrong in thinking him a murderer. He certainly was maladroit at hiding emotion. But if his own actions had not been haunting him since my grandmother's death, what had been?

~~∽⤙⤚∽~~

I had not made much headway in packing my trunks when Thomas arrived with the box that had been my mother's. In my excitement I grew clumsy and dropped a pair of earrings, and Ann had to scurry after them as they rolled away.

Atticus observed me with an indulgent smile. "Would you like some time alone?" he asked, and when I beamed at him gratefully he chuckled, kissed my cheek, and slipped his coat back on. "I shall be in the library," he said, making for the door. "Take all the time you need."

How fortunate I was that he was sensitive to the fact that I wanted privacy in which to make this first exploration of my mother's belongings. I told Ann I would ring for her when I needed her, but I stopped Thomas before he could follow her. I had meant for some time to question him, but the housekeeper had always made some excuse whenever I asked her to send him to me. It was as if my uncle had given orders that I should not have the opportunity to speak to him.

"Thomas, won't you have a seat?" I asked. "I'd like to talk to you for a moment."

He drew himself up to full height—or what would have been, had his shoulders not been stooped from age. "Now, miss," he said reproachfully, "as if I did not know my own place better than that! I can stand, thank thee, for all I'm no young man."

In truth, I cared little whether he stood or sat, so long as he could answer my questions. The *miss* worried me, though. Had he forgotten who I was? "You must have been at Thurnley Hall longer than anyone else," I said. "When did you first come here?"

If he had been attached to some other household forty years ago, he would be no help. But I was lucky, in this respect at least. He answered promptly, "Why, man an' boy, full sixty year. I still mind when Percival Burleigh brought home a bride from foreign parts."

"My grandmother?" This distracted me from my main interest. "How did old Mr. Burleigh's household and tenants feel about his foreign bride?"

He shook his head in disgust, and I had a feeling that if we had been outdoors he would have spat. "That foreign woman! It were she who turned everything awry."

"What do you mean?"

"I remember my father talkin' of it. The sheep began foamin' at the mouth and dyin', he said, an' the milk curdled overnight. It were a dark day when she became mistress of Thurnley Hall."

I restrained a sigh. Superstitious nonsense, and secondhand at that. Better to stick to my real interest. "You must have been here when my mother was growing up," I said.

His rheumy eyes were confused. "Tha' mother?"

"Miss Miriam, she would have been then."

He brightened. "Aye, she were a pretty thing. Such a pity she went away. The house were the gloomier for it, that's certain."

"Did you know my father as well? Robert Crofton. He was a farmer."

To my surprise, he gave me a reproachful look, and his voice grew stern. "Robbie Crofton again, is it? Tha' knows thy father and mother will have none o' those goin's-on. Be a good lass, an' let's have no more talk o' my carryin' messages from thee to the young farmer."

Could I possibly learn anything useful from him when his memory was so uncertain that he was confusing me with my mother? This was not encouraging. "Do you remember any of his messages to her—I mean, to me?" I asked.

But he actually wagged his finger at me. "I'll lose my place for certain sure, Miss Miriam. Does tha' want to break thy mother's heart? Best mind thy father, now, an' leave off this foolishness."

Before I could form a response he had begun to shuffle toward the door, and I could not think of a strong enough reason to detain him. All I had learned was that his mind was vague and that my mother had asked him to bear messages between her and my father.

Turning to the trunk, I hoped that my mother's actual belongings would be more enlightening, but it seemed there was little they could tell me. On top was the daguerreotype portrait, and I felt an unexpected rush of gratitude toward whoever had placed it there for me. The blue dress that I had seen before took up most of the space. It was a fine, heavy satin, so stiff that it could stand by itself, and it was not even faded from its years in storage. The lace at the wide neckline and along the hem was crumpled but not yellowed. I felt a pang for the young woman who had worn this extravagant dress. She had not expected the sorrow that was to come to her. This was a dress for dancing and flirting, for attracting the eyes of dashing young men across the length of a waxed ballroom floor. I could understand why my mother had left it behind; a farmer's wife would have no use for such a dress. Or had she left this and her other belongings because she thought that her parents would relent and welcome her back, along with her new husband?

Beneath the dress and matching pale blue slippers were other fripperies: a beaded reticule, embroidered handkerchiefs, stockings, lace mitts. None of them accorded with the mother I had known; I could hardly imagine her wearing such girlish things. She must have changed greatly after leaving her old life. Of more interest to me were the books. Each bore her name on the flyleaf in a precise hand, but that was the only evidence of her that I could see at first. She had not written anything else in them, and there were no letters or papers tucked between the pages. The books themselves told me little about her inner life: as well as the volumes of verse, I found a prayer book inscribed to her on a long-ago Christmas by her mother; a book on household management, evidently a precursor to Mrs. Beeton's guide; and volumes of popular poetry and essays.

A curious feeling came over me as I knelt before the empty trunk surrounded by these oddments from a life abandoned nearly forty years before. It was as if these objects belonged to a phantom. Not the ghost of my late mother, but a creature of pure fancy who had never lived. These were the things that a mother might assemble from wishful thinking of what her daughter might become. A hope chest for a child, not a bride-to-be.

Altogether I was not surprised that my mother had left this trunk behind. The only part of it that spoke at all to the life she ended up living was the book of household management, but even that must have felt at the time like a yoke she was throwing off as she left Thurnley Hall. That would explain, too, why there were no mementos of my father and their courtship here. If they had been precious to her, they would not have been left with these castoffs.

A knock at the open door made me look up. Mr. Lynch stood in the doorway gazing at me. "I apologize for disturbing you, Lady Telford," he said. "You seem so absorbed that I hesitated to knock."

"It's quite all right," I said, gathering my skirts to rise, and when he stepped forward and extended his hand to help me to my feet, I accepted it readily. Too readily, perhaps, for once I was on my feet he did not release me at once but continued to hold my hand with an expression so intent that my husband's caution came rushing to mind.

"Do you have news of Grigore?" I asked, withdrawing my hand and moving toward the door in what I hoped was an inconspicuous fashion. I didn't want to insult him by being pointed about his presence in my room, especially since he had not behaved inappropriately since the fitting, but it was probably best to abbreviate this tête-à-tête.

"Yes, I spoke to him. Rather, Cook and I did. He took it very well, considering, and agreed quite calmly to let Thomas stand watch over him until I return with a constable from the village."

"Well, I am glad to hear that he was so cooperative."

"Glad but not entirely convinced, I take it?" Amusement warmed the low, melodious voice. "Perhaps it will ease your mind to know that in addition to offering the fellow an attractive financial settlement I told him that I would spread salt across the threshold of his room so that the baron would not be able to enter and attack him." He gave me a conspiratorial smile. "That means that Grigore must stay in his room in order to be protected."

"That was clever of you. Thank you."

He must have seen my eyes flick back to the trunk and its contents, for he said in a different tone of voice, "Forgive me, but you seem troubled. Is it something besides this unhappy business with Grigore?"

I hesitated, but his voice was so warmly sympathetic, his eyes so touchingly concerned, that I found myself confiding in him. "I had hoped to learn more about my parents here at Thurnley Hall," I said. "Especially my mother. But my uncle had little to tell me, and Thomas is too confused to be relied upon. My last hope was this trunk that belonged to her. But nothing in it carries a sense of her spirit—nothing at all."

His brow furrowed. "You've found no letters or journals?"

"No. I think they were all burnt by her father. Still, I had hoped that something might remain. Even something as small as a painting or a sketch."

"That's right. I had forgotten that my guardian said she had an artistic bent." He mulled this, rubbing his chin with a studious air that he might have borrowed from an elder. "Have you looked through the portfolios in the library?" When I stared at him in confusion, he explained, "There are a great many stored away beneath one of the window seats, full of unframed pieces. From what I've seen, they are a jumble of different periods and different artists, so it's just possible that something of your mother's may have escaped notice there."

"How wonderful! I must go look at once."

"Of course you must." Despite his words, his hand fell on my arm to detain me. "Only wouldn't it be better to take your time? If you and Lord Telford would postpone your departure for just one day, you would be able to have a thorough look at everything. You wouldn't risk missing something because you were in a hurry to catch your train."

I looked away to hide a smile at the eagerness in his voice. He was so boyish in his transparency that it was touching. I could hardly blame him for wanting to detain Atticus and me as long as he could, since his guardian was his only other company . . . and hardly a kindred spirit. After our departure, the days might be lonely for him.

For a moment I felt protective of him, an impulse that might, I realized, be prompted as much by my approaching mother-hood as by my friendship with the young man. Or perhaps it was because he reminded me of a youthful Atticus, who had known loneliness too.

In any case, the decision was easy. Now that Grigore was not a threat, I could afford to be generous—and indeed, I would relish an unhurried examination of the artworks that might contain something of my mother's.

"I shall ask Atticus," I said, "but I expect he won't mind if we stay the night and leave tomorrow. Thank you for telling me about the portfolios."

A flush of pleasure warmed the ivory of his complexion. "I'm delighted to be of help," he said eagerly. "I'll show you where they are now, if you like, and help you go through them."

After he led me to the cache of unframed art, Atticus and I spent several hours sifting through all that the portfolios held. Although we could not be entirely certain, there were two watercolor moorland scenes initialed *MB* that might have been my mother's work. They were painted with a dash and energy that suggested a spirit too restless to be contained in a prison of domestic duties. Even if they had been painted by another artist, they evoked for me something of my mother, and I was pleased that my uncle was gracious enough to make me a gift of them.

Our last meal together at Thurnley Hall was a bittersweet one. Mr. Lynch was animated with, I believe, excitement that he had been able to do me a good turn, and my uncle exerted himself to be charming. While I could not summon up much familial warmth for him, I enjoyed listening to his anecdotes of Yorkshire history . . . all the more so, I admit, since we would be parting so soon.

~⤚◊⤙~

Sleep came swiftly that night. I think the knowledge that this would be our last night in Thurnley Hall gave me sufficient peace of mind to drop off easily. I did wake later in the night, but for a mercy it was not because of the nightmare.

At first I did not know what had disturbed my sleep. Perhaps I had sensed my husband's absence, for even before my eyes opened I was reaching out for him. My searching fingers encountered only the bedclothes.

"Atticus?" I mumbled when I could detect no presence of him beside me.

The curtain rings clattered as the drapery of the bed was drawn back, and in the soft light of a lamp I saw him standing there. He was dressed but for his coat, and he was knotting his cravat even as he said, "I'm here, my love."

"Why are you dressing at this hour?"

"There's something I need to see to." His voice was calm, unhurried, as if setting out on an expedition in the middle of the night were a perfectly reasonable thing for him to do.

My sleep-shrouded mind could not quite comprehend this. "It can't wait until morning?"

"I shouldn't be long—and it's nearly dawn, anyway."

"Wait. Let me straighten your cravat." I sat up, fighting back a yawn, and he seated himself on the edge of the bed obligingly. He watched with a smile as I tucked the ends of his cravat into his waistcoat, the one I had given him on his birthday, and smoothed it down. "There," I said. "Now you may go." But I slipped my arms around his neck, willing him to stay.

"You don't make it easy to leave you." He took my face in his hands and kissed me softly, lingeringly. All of my senses were filled with him, with the honeyed taste of his lips, the caressing touch of his hands, the scent of cedar and sandalwood that clung to his skin. When he raised his head, his blue eyes were luminous with love and wonder as he took me in.

"My God, but you're beautiful," he said half to himself. "With your hair all tumbled like that and your eyes soft with sleep . . . I doubt Venus herself was more alluring."

"Come back to bed, then." I made the invitation as tempting as I could, and he took another long kiss from my lips before reluctantly shaking his head.

"I won't be easy in my mind until I resolve this. And when I return to bed I want my thoughts to contain nothing but my bewitching wife." He stroked my cheek before standing to leave.

"Won't you tell me what is so important that I cannot compete with it?" I asked.

Laugh lines peeked out from the corners of his eyes when he smiled. "What a coquette you are, Clara. It's nothing I want to trouble you with. Go back to sleep, dearest, and I'll be with you again before you know it."

Nothing I said was going to shake him. Despite his relaxed demeanor, he was set on carrying out this mysterious mission, and I knew just how determined he could be when he set his mind on something. It occurred to me that his leg might be troubling him again and preventing him from sleeping, and perhaps he simply wanted a pretext to exercise it but was reluctant to say so.

Though I would curse myself for it later, I chose not to inquire further. I was drowsy, the bed was soft, and if I could not sink back into my husband's arms, then the arms of Morpheus were very nearly as inviting.

I believe I told him as he put on his coat and took up his walking stick that I loved him. Much later, when I thought back on this last conversation, I hoped that the knowledge of my love went with him as he stepped out the door . . . and out of all knowing.

CHAPTER THIRTEEN

When I next opened my eyes it was to a knock on the door. "My lady?" came the soft voice of Ann. "May I come in?"

The bed was still empty apart from myself. Sitting up, I pushed back the bed curtain and saw that the room was likewise empty. So Atticus had not yet returned.

"Come in, Ann," I called, and the little maid entered, walking carefully so as not to spill the jug of hot water she carried for my husband to shave with.

"Did my husband ring for you?" I asked her, but she shook her head as she carefully placed the jug on the washstand.

"No, my lady. I've not seen him this morning."

I told her that she could bring breakfast, and rather than put the hot water to waste I washed my face and hands. Atticus could always ring for more when he returned.

I dawdled over my breakfast porridge and ham, expecting that at any moment I would hear the tap of his stick in the hall and that the door would open on the sight of him, handsome and genial, ready to explain the perplexing errand that had summoned him away from me in the night. But the minutes ticked past on the mantel clock without any sign of him. Finally I rang for Ann to help me dress. Waiting here in our bedroom was accomplishing nothing.

The first place I looked was the library, and it was not until my heart sank at the sight of the empty room that I realized how completely I had assumed him to be here. There was no sign that anyone had entered since I had vacated it the day before, triumphantly bearing the two watercolors.

No doubt he was conferring with my uncle and the lawyer. But when I knocked at the door of my uncle's study, no answer came. Listening closely, I heard no voices from within, so I turned the handle and pushed the door open. Like the library, the room was empty.

It is early yet, I told myself. *Doubtless my uncle is still breakfasting, and Atticus went to seek him.* Swiftly I went to the dining room, in case my husband had taken it into his head to break his fast there instead of in the privacy of our room, but this room, like the others before it, had no occupant. I supposed the next step was to seek out my uncle, but I was not certain I knew exactly where his room was, so I tugged the bell pull to summon one of the servants to the dining room.

Mrs. Furness was the one who answered, considerably puzzled to be called to that room at this early hour of the day. "You've not seen my husband, have you?" I asked her before she could inquire as to my wishes.

"No, my lady. The last time I saw his lordship was yesterday evening, when I brought in the hock after dinner."

I bit my lip. "Will you show me to my uncle's room, then? Perhaps he'll know."

Taken aback, she said, "Mr. Burleigh has not yet risen, my lady."

"Take me to him anyway."

She looked as if she wanted to object, but something in my expression silenced her. I set a brisk pace in my impatience, and her chatelaine of keys clinked faintly as she lengthened her stride to match mine.

"Would any of the other servants have seen him?" I asked.

"I shall inquire and let you know, my lady," she said, stopping before a door that had to be my uncle's. She rapped smartly and withdrew with a curtsey as my uncle's voice boomed out a command to enter.

Despite the housekeeper's claim, he had in fact risen, and he even seemed to have finished his breakfast. Now he was sitting by his fire behind a table that bore the remnants of the meal and holding a newspaper before him. Without looking out from behind the paper, he said, "You may clear, Thomas."

"It isn't Thomas," I said, which made him lower the paper and regard me in surprise. He was wearing a dressing gown in a rather loud heliotrope.

"I did not expect to see you at this hour, niece," he said. "Does this mean that you and the baron are departing now?"

"I am trying to find him," I said. "You've not seen him this morning, have you?"

His surprise seemed genuine. "Neither hide nor hair, not since last night. Why, have you lost him?"

"I am beginning to think so," I said, and to my irritation this made him give one of his barking laughs.

"A baron is a substantial thing to lose! Well, I'm sure you'll find him again. Unless you quarreled. Is that it? Eh, niece? Perhaps you gave him the rough side of your tongue and he decided an airing-out would be welcome. Well, don't fret. No doubt he'll return in his own time, and next time you won't be so quick to play the virago."

His words had set my teeth on edge. I said shortly, "We did not quarrel. Is there any chance that he might be in conference with Mr. Durrington?"

This cut his mirth short. Evidently my urgency was beginning to communicate itself to him. "I'll ring for Thomas to ask him. You'd best not interview him in person, for he's likely to be in a state of undress."

"Of course," I said, embarrassed that I had been about to charge off to the lawyer's room without pausing to consider this. "I'll check our room again in case he returned during my absence."

"Yes, do so. I wouldn't be at all surprised if he is waiting there and getting out of temper that *you* are gone!"

I hoped fervently that he was right, but in the Cradle Room all was as I had left it. The water remaining in the jug had cooled on the washstand. I took a deep breath and told myself there was no reason to worry yet. Atticus might have been detained for a thousand harmless reasons. What had he said when he left me? That he needed to "see to" something. That made it difficult to narrow down his probable destination. Crossing to the window, I gazed through the leaded panes at the broad swathe of lawn below. There was no sign of him. The sky dripped with rain, so it was unlikely that he would be walking for the pleasure of the thing—or, after so long, to exercise his bad leg.

Despite my attempt to remain calm, my mind was beginning to dart about in anxiety. What if he had met with an accident or become trapped somewhere? I knew it was premature to picture such calamities, but they would not be vanquished. I almost ran back down the hall to the library, and the glimpse of a man standing before the shelves with his back to me made my heart take a joyful bound before I recognized him as Mr. Lynch. I stared, stricken, and sensing my presence he turned and saw me.

"A good morning to you, my lady," he said with a smile. Then his expression sobered as he observed me more closely. "Is something distressing you?"

"It's Atticus," I blurted. "Have you seen him? I can't find him anywhere."

Concern softened his dark eyes. "No, I've not seen him this morning. Is there something particular about his absence that worries you so?" And then, as I hesitated, he took my arm. "Come, sit down. You look quite faint. Tell me why you are so distraught and how I may help."

But I resisted the gentle pressure on my arm. "I can't stop looking until I find him," I said. "You're very kind, but the best way you can help is to search for him."

He would not be so easily diverted, though. He maintained the gentle but firm grip on my arm. "Tell me why his absence is so frightening to you. Did he go in search of something in particular? That may help us locate him."

Shutting my eyes, I took a deep breath and tried to bring order to my thoughts. Flying off in every direction was not an efficient or effective way to search. "I think we should summon my uncle," I said. "It makes more sense to inform you both at once."

"I shall fetch him," he said at once. "And I'll have Mrs. Furness send up some tea. I think a restorative would be beneficial to you."

I nodded, since it seemed the quickest way to send him on his errand. In truth, the idea of sitting down to tea while Atticus was missing was abhorrent, although I knew the young man was just trying to help. His imagination was probably constrained by his limited experience of women.

But here I did him an injustice. It was, in fact, my uncle who showed the greater ignorance. As he returned with his ward to the library, he announced, "This is simply hysteria, niece. There is no reason your husband is not simply taking a morning constitutional. What you need is some sal volatile and a nice long rest."

"Sir, the servants." Mr. Lynch shut the library door with a rebuking air. "I'm certain the baroness doesn't want this matter trumpeted to the entire household."

"As grateful as I am for your discretion," I said, "I think it may be best to inform all the servants and involve them in the search."

"Search!" My uncle snorted. "So you think he's unwilling to be found, do you? Tell the truth: you quarreled. He probably means to teach you a little lesson by making himself scarce. Wise fellow, the baron—nothing brings a wife to heel better than being ignored for a spell."

I was very tempted to reply with a pointed reminder that I had experience of married life and he had none, but descending to such childish one-upmanship would be of no use. Instead I briefly set forth the circumstances under which Atticus had left: the early hour, the mysterious errand, the fact that he had fully dressed. This rendered both men thoughtful.

"What do you think he meant by something he needed to see to?" my uncle asked, his manner much more subdued than before.

I stared straight at him as I said, "I can think of a few things he might have been curious about, or even suspicious." I had the satisfaction of seeing my uncle's beady eyes widen for one startled moment before darting away. He looked the very picture of guilt. "I want to summon a constable," I announced.

He vigorously waved his hands as if to expunge the idea. "Now, now, don't get in a pet, niece. There's no need for such dramatics. Ladies are so apt to work themselves into fits over the least little things!"

"On the contrary, sir," his ward said coolly, "Lady Telford has always struck me as a woman of great good sense. If she feels that this is an emergency, oughtn't we to take her concerns seriously?"

Sputtering, my uncle replied, "I never said this was not a serious situation. I merely think that introducing a police officer into the matter at this early stage is excessive and—and inconvenient."

"Inconvenient to whom, exactly?" I asked.

He heaved himself out of his chair and paced over to stare out of one of the mullioned windows. "If your husband has merely been taking the air and returns to find the house all at sixes and sevens and the police questioning everybody, he will be mightily embarrassed."

"That prospect does not strike fear into my heart, Mr. Burleigh," I said. Fear did, however, seem to be present in my uncle. Yesterday he had also been reluctant to involve the police in the matter of Grigore. My suspicions were redoubled. Why should an innocent man protest so vigorously against the presence of the police?

"I would be much easier in my mind if the authorities were to take a hand in the search," I told him. "We should also ask volunteers from the estate to help comb the countryside. What if you're correct and Atticus was merely taking a walk? That was many hours ago. He might have had an accident of some sort."

Mr. Lynch nodded gravely. "Yes, he may have struck his head, or had a fit of some sort, or even—I hate to say it—been set upon by footpads. Such things, alas, are not unknown even this far from the city. Sir, I don't see that we have any reason *not* to involve the authorities."

My uncle remained standing with his back to us. In a strangely solemn tone of voice, he said, "If you both insist upon it, I suppose we must. When Thomas returns from taking Durrington to the station I'll send him back to fetch a constable." Now he turned to face us, and the choleric flush had faded from his jowly face. "But before that," he continued, "we should search the house thoroughly to rule out what we can, because the constable is sure to ask us if we have. We can make a systematic sweep starting with the servants' quarters and moving through the whole house. If, as you suggest, your husband has fallen ill or somehow been wounded, he may be unable to call for help."

This resolve was a surprise, albeit a pleasant one. This threw my suspicions into confusion. I could not reconcile this decision with his earlier appearance of guilt.

My uncle's secret motives could wait until later for me to examine, however. At this moment it was vital to take advantage of his cooperation in searching for my husband. "That is an excellent idea," I said. "Mr. Lynch, perhaps you would search the grounds while we sweep the indoors?"

"Of course," he said. "There are plenty of places where he might have come to grief. I beg your pardon," he amended hastily. "I mean that there are many ditches and crevasses where he might have slipped and turned his ankle, or something of that sort." He bowed briefly. "I hope I shall return with good news, my lady."

"Thank you. I hope so."

There was a silence after he left us. Then my uncle said, still in his newly serious tone, "Niece, it may be wise to write to your friends and servants at Gravesend in case they have heard anything from the baron that might indicate where he intended to go. Even though he told you that his intention was to return soon, he may have changed his mind and decided to pursue his investigation farther afield."

I had to admit that there was wisdom to the suggestion. "I'll compose some telegrams," I said. "But I am curious as to what you meant by an investigation. What do *you* think drew my husband from my side and into the night?"

This time his eyes did not evade mine. "I wish I knew," he said quietly. "I truly wish I did."

After I had dashed off the necessary letters and telegrams, Mrs. Furness and I, accompanied at my insistence by my uncle, made a search of the house. With the housekeeper unlocking the unused rooms as we went, we began with the servants' quarters and moved upward through the common rooms and into the personal bedrooms. I hesitated not at all to rifle wardrobes, peer under beds, and prod tapestries, calling out for Atticus at frequent intervals in the ever more urgent hope that he might answer.

To my uncle's credit—and to my own surprise—he did not forbid me from entering anywhere. It may have embarrassed him for me to see the ruinous state of some of the chambers, with their broken furniture, flaking plaster, and cracked windows, but not once did he attempt to induce me to leave a room unsearched. By the time we descended from the attics, my black dress was almost gray with dust and accumulated cobwebs, and I was so agitated that my hands shook. I could not understand how a man could vanish so entirely unless something terrible had happened.

Mr. Lynch had reported no results from his search of the grounds, so I sent him with Thomas to send my telegrams and fetch a constable. But there was no reassuring figure in uniform accompanying him when he returned.

"It seems there is no longer a standing police force in Coley," he explained. "I was given to understand that the village has so diminished in the last year that it became unnecessary." He must have read my dismay on my face, for he added hastily, "I wired to Ilkley and Halifax to send an officer at their earliest convenience. If they can't oblige, I think Leeds will be our best hope."

Where the news had brought me nothing but distress, it seemed to cheer my uncle. "So we may be left to our own devices for days yet," he said with offensive heartiness. "Ah, well, we must make the best of it."

"You don't sound at all sorry," I burst out. "What is it that you're so desperately afraid will be discovered? Is that what happened to Atticus? When he spoke of looking into something, did he come too close to learning what you're trying to hide?" A terrible idea was forming in my mind. Perhaps the reason that my uncle had not discouraged my search of the house was that he knew that Atticus was not here to be found.

Mr. Lynch's voice was at its most soothing. "I'm sure my guardian only kept quiet about it so as not to worry you. If there had been any real danger, naturally he would have warned you."

"Warned me about what?" I demanded.

My uncle looked from me to his ward with a hunted expression, saying nothing. It was left to the younger man to say, "The fellow must have been long gone by the time the baron went missing. Probably leagues away, in fact. So you see there was no reason for your uncle to alarm you."

He clearly meant his words to soothe, but my heart was beating all the faster as their meaning sank in. I said, "Do you mean that Grigore has disappeared as well?"

The young man grimaced and spread his hands. "'Disappeared' is not the word I would use. It looks as though he did a bolt after I left him in his room. Grigore has never been intelligent, and he evidently felt it was better to leave of his own volition even though that meant forfeiting all that we could have done to help him."

The words were meaningless noise to me apart from the single point that Grigore, the madman who hated and feared my husband, was unaccounted for. "When?" I whispered.

Again my uncle did not reply, and his ward had to answer for him. "Last night," he said.

I stared at them, aghast. "Why did you not tell us?"

My uncle cleared his throat as if trying to summon up his usual bluster. "A man doesn't like to be thought incapable of handling his servants," he rumbled, and I could have flown at him. Was his vanity responsible for this disaster?

Mr. Lynch interposed, "Please don't worry, my lady. I'm certain Grigore's departure had nothing to do with the baron's disappearance."

"There is no possible way you can be certain of that!" My heart thudded beneath my ribs with the force of a hammer. Had Atticus been waylaid by the deluded giant? The thought made me feel so queasy that I was afraid I might faint. "If I had known Grigore had escaped, I would have done everything in my power to keep Atticus from going off by himself in the middle of the night." By now I was straining to keep my voice steady. "I hold you both responsible for this."

"Clara, please—"

"Don't pretend this isn't your fault! If he is injured or—or dead, his blood is on your hands." They stared at me with similar expressions of shock, and I longed to escape the sight of them. If Atticus had come to harm through their idiotic ideas of chivalry—or, worse, my uncle's desire to save face—I would never forgive them. Nor would I rest until I had made them regret their negligence.

"I am taking the carriage and going to send some wires of my own," I announced. "If I cannot raise the police quickly enough, I'll hire a private investigator. I'll summon my own servants from Gravesend. I'll—"

"These are excellent ideas," Mr. Lynch said in a placating tone. "But you oughtn't to go alone. Won't you let me accompany you? It is the least I can do after having failed to warn you about Grigore."

Grudgingly I agreed, for an argument would merely have delayed me. My uncle did not volunteer to accompany us, perhaps out of reluctance to be closed into the small space of a carriage with me and my anger.

Once at the station, I composed lengthy wires to Gravesend, to the Bertrams, to the authorities of several nearby towns, and to a firm of private investigators in London that I recalled had assisted Sybil Ingram when a valuable necklace of hers had gone missing. Mr. Lynch attended me patiently as I wrote these all out. At last I felt ready to return to Thurnley, but as he and I reached the threshold he paused, striking his forehead.

"I haven't sent word to my employer in Coventry," he exclaimed. "He'll be wondering what has kept me. Would you mind if I sent him a wire to let him know I've been detained?"

"As you think best," I said, with an ill grace. Now that my messages were in the hands of the telegraph operator I was eager to resume my search for Atticus.

"I shall be quick as a wink," he promised, putting his hand to his heart. "Do go ahead to the carriage; you needn't stand about here getting chilled. I'll be with you again before you know it."

It seemed to me that he took a considerable time, but in my state of anxiety the wait probably felt far longer than it truly was. I was glad I had taken his suggestion to wait in the carriage, where Thomas spread the rug over me before returning to his place at the reins. At last Mr. Lynch emerged.

"Is your employer likely to dismiss you for being absent for long?" I asked as he joined me in the carriage, although I cannot say that the answer mattered to me; I was merely making conversation to keep panic—and tears—at bay.

"Quite likely, I'm afraid, but that isn't important." He leaned across the carriage to take my gloved hand. "I shall do whatever I must to help you find him," he said gently. "I owe it to you, after having kept Grigore's disappearance from you."

"It is my fault more than yours." If only I had listened to my first instinct and ignored the summons to Thurnley Hall, none of this would have happened. I could try to throw the blame on others, but a great deal of it fell on my shoulders, and I knew that I would never stop regretting my actions unless I found Atticus safe and unharmed. I shut my eyes hard so that I would not embarrass myself by weeping before my companion.

Then I realized that there was one silver lining to the terrifying new knowledge about the Romanian: It gave me a potential clue as to where Atticus might be. If Grigore was involved in my husband's disappearance, perhaps it was something connected to the encounter at the mausoleum that Atticus had intended to pursue.

"Mr. Lynch, have you searched the burial grounds?" I asked.

"Not yet." Then his eyes widened as my meaning struck home. "You think Grigore may have forced an encounter with the baron there?"

"It seems possible, doesn't it?" Or else—though it was almost too horrible a thought to be endured—he might have disposed of Atticus there.

"We must search there at once," he began, but I shook my head.

"I shall do it. I need you to assist my uncle in his search. I'm afraid he is not very . . . effectual on his own." What I really meant was that I could not trust him not to practice some further deception if left unwatched. Even this short errand had taken us away from him too long for my liking.

"I understand," the young man said, and the gravity in his voice suggested that he had taken my unspoken meaning. "I will be vigilant."

As soon as we reached Thurnley, I summoned Mrs. Furness, who accompanied me to the burial grounds. Looking through the iron gates of the mausoleum, I saw nothing that seemed altered or out of place, and I was greatly comforted that the housekeeper had to use her key to unfasten the padlock and gain entrance. The fact that the chain and lock were unbroken made it unlikely that anyone had entered before us, and thus unlikely that there would be any shocking surprises within.

Nevertheless, we examined the interior scrupulously, looking for signs that anything had been tampered with. Until I found that all of the wall plaques were intact and undisturbed, I could not shake a horrifying vision of Atticus walled up alive in one of the niches in which the caskets were housed. To my great relief, there were no signs that anything inside had been tampered with, and as we stepped outside again I drew a breath of thankfulness. For the moment I felt reassured.

The burial ground likewise showed no signs of any violent activity. Even the smallest grave marker, a white marble lamb without inscription, was undisturbed.

"I suppose that must be a child's grave," I said to Mrs. Furness. "I wonder whose it was?" With no date, it was impossible to know whether it might have been another child of my grandmother's.

She snapped the padlock shut and tested that the gates were secure before replying. "That's hard to say, my lady. Naturally many of the family will have lost children before they were old enough to be named. It is all too common."

Something in the subdued tone of her voice gave the words a special poignancy, as if she were speaking not of the Burleighs but of herself. Or was she simply so attached to the family that she felt their sorrows as her own? Her face wore its usual expressionless mask, but the desolation she had hinted at spurred me to say, "Perhaps that is a pain that you have some knowledge of yourself."

My sympathy did not induce her to confide in me, however. She merely said, "The loss of a child is something we all must feel keenly, my lady. Do you wish to examine any of the outbuildings?"

I assented and let her lead the way out of the burial ground, but my thoughts were still tantalized by this unexpected puzzle. Mrs. Furness wore no wedding ring, and I wondered if the "Mrs." before her name was just the honorific bestowed on all housekeepers and not an indication of her actual marital status. If she had borne a child out of wedlock, I could well understand that she would not wish to tell me so. Yet I hoped I was mistaken. To be unable to speak of one's grief could render it even more painful. As a young woman, when I was mourning Richard in my heart, it seemed to make it all the harder that I could not wear black for him or even speak of him, since in the eyes of the world I had no claim on him.

Remembering this, I shook my head at my girlish folly. How much emotion I had wasted on that unworthy man . . . and how fervently I now hoped that I would not have cause to mourn Atticus.

Atticus, who was fifty times the man Richard had been, who was just beginning to do so much good in the world, who after his miserable youth deserved the longest and happiest life that anyone ever had. Atticus, who had brought the transformative radiance of love into my own life, and who had not yet had the chance to be a father or even to anticipate it.

Let him not be lost to me, I prayed silently as I continued the search for my husband. *Let Atticus be near—and safe.*

CHAPTER FOURTEEN

F our days passed.

How little those three brief words convey of the anguish, the urgent activity, the increasing fear that spurred our searching. The growing exhaustion and creeping sense of despair, which in their turn birthed a new anxiety—that in our weariness of body and mind we would miss some vital sign that would point us to my husband.

Inside the house and the outbuildings, outside in the pastures and on the moors, and even along the banks of the still-swollen river the searchers worked, as my uncle and Mr. Lynch tirelessly directed their activity. But even under their command it was impossible not to notice by the third day the dwindling energies of the searchers, their growing air of resignation, the encroaching carelessness.

I myself searched until I could no longer stand. When reminded to eat, I tried to do so; I needed my strength, as did the child growing inside me, but I felt too nauseated to eat much. Each bite also reminded me that Atticus might be starving somewhere, trapped or injured, and the thought robbed me of what little appetite I had. I subsisted largely on quantities of strong tea. When told to sleep, I lay down for a time, but I never felt refreshed. One day I emerged from a reverie to find Ann standing behind me working at my corset laces, and I did not know if she was dressing or undressing me, so detached was I from the usual rhythms of daily life.

Thurnley Hall itself came to take on an ominous aspect to me. Until now, if I had sometimes found my surroundings gloomy and timeworn, they nevertheless had held no actual menace. Now that it was the site of my husband's disappearance and possibly worse, the house's dark-paneled rooms and shadowy corridors held a sinister aspect. In every corner where darkness pooled I saw a malignant intelligence mocking me with its mysteries. It refused to give up its secrets, so they came to multiply and prey on my mind. The sad little drawing room with its ruined beauty whispered of moldering decay. The echoes of my footsteps through the vast stone vault of the great hall were like malevolent followers hovering just out of sight. At night, when the wan light of candles and lamps made the shadows dart and flicker at the corners of my eyes, I could almost imagine the darkness like a physical presence, a greasy fog that would smear my eyes blind and pour into my lungs until I choked.

I knew that my fancies were born of worry and exhaustion, but that knowledge did not banish them. Lying alone in bed at night, enclosed by the heavy curtains, I recalled how this had once been a cocoon of safety, but without Atticus it was desolate and barren. Lacking the warmth of his presence, it was as cold and comfortless as a bed of thorns on the bleak and windswept moor.

The moor had not escaped our search during this time. Just as men walked in rows through the overgrown meadows seeking a fallen form among the high grasses, so did they tread the slopes with an eye to the tangled growth of heather and gorse and bracken, climbing to rocky promontories and sifting the bushes beneath the cliffs. Many days of wind and rain had stripped the purple blossom, and the once-beautiful vista now seemed blighted and bereft of life. I even went to explore the long-abandoned lead mine on the property, in case Atticus had somehow stumbled into the trench that led to the low, arched opening.

Staring into the stone-lined archway, where I needed a lantern to supplement the thin gray daylight that penetrated only partially into the gloom, I felt my familiar nightmare rush to mind with smothering force. The dread of being trapped underground, of being surrounded on all sides by stone and darkness, made me shut my eyes for a moment and swallow hard, fighting dizziness.

"You needn't go inside," came the gentle voice of Mr. Lynch beside me. He had led me here at my insistence, and he stood ready with his own safety lantern. "Why don't you wait here in the open air?"

I shook my head vigorously, as much to dislodge the nightmare vision from my head as to answer his query. "I must see for myself," I said, as I had so many times in the past few days. I did not trust any other eyes to be as watchful for Atticus as my own, nor any ears but mine to be so sensitive to the sound of his voice.

As I descended into the trench, my foot dislodged a pebble, and the sound it made as it skittered down the path was so like my nightmare that I had to pause for a moment. *This is not your dream,* I told myself firmly, and stooped to enter the mine.

To my surprise, there was very little to see. The passage was a few feet wide and led over uneven, rocky ground to a wall where there must have once been a passage leading deeper underground. The opening was quite blocked by stones large and small, packed in tightly to completely seal it off. In the spirit of experiment I set my safety lantern down and tried to tug one of the rocks loose. It might have been set in cement, so firmly was it seated. When I cast the lantern's light directly on them I could see from the lichen and discoloration of the rocks that they must have gone undisturbed for many years. Clearly no one could have entered here.

"I am sorry to have wasted your time here," Mr. Lynch said when he joined me. "Old Fowler said that we'd be unlikely to find anything, but I was skeptical."

"It wasn't a waste to be able to rule it out," I said. What was more, it was heartening to learn that for my husband's sake I could conquer my fears and venture into the landscape of my nightmares.

Indeed, I needed every scrap of encouragement I could glean in these dark days. A telegram from Gravesend had related that Henriette's illness had spread to nearly the entire household, so the doctor had placed the house under quarantine and no one could come to our aid. No police had arrived; instead we received telegrams regretting their inability to spare men to assist us or promising to send aid when they could. Nor had George and Vivi responded. And as each day had ruled out more places where Atticus might be concealed, the process of elimination felt less reassuring. This latest failure brought home to me that if we did not find signs of him in any of the logical or nearby places, that opened up a dizzying number of possibilities—indeed, endless prospects. How could we comb them all? Each day that passed, moreover, made it less likely that we would find him whole and safe. Sometimes I felt that every minute that ticked by was a malicious conspirator against his welfare.

Startling me out of my gloomy thoughts came a shrill cry. It halted Mr. Lynch, who gripped my arm to draw me to a stop. "Did you hear that?" he exclaimed.

"It sounds like it came from the Hall," I said.

The cry came again, louder. It sounded like a child scream-ing out in pain—or fear. "Wait here," he said, and set out at a run down the path toward the house.

Disregarding his command, I picked up my skirts and ran after him. Even though the voice had not belonged to Atticus, I needed to know what had happened.

I soon lost sight of Mr. Lynch for, weakened as I was by days of little rest or nourishment, I found my pace flagging all too quickly. As I neared the house, the child's screams were renewed, and I dreaded what I might see.

Some of the searchers were gathering near the ruined wing, I saw, where high on the wreckage a boy of perhaps six years old was awkwardly sprawled. One leg seemed to be trapped amid the rubble, and Mr. Lynch was straining at a great chunk of masonry that must have been the cause of the child's distress.

"Fowler, hand me up a crowbar, a hammer—something to use as a lever!"

"I'll help thee," the older man offered, but Mr. Lynch's usually mild dark eyes flashed with anger.

"That just increases the danger, don't you see? If any more of these great blocks of stone are dislodged . . ."

He did not complete the thought but seized the pickaxe that another man handed up. "You must be very brave," Mr. Lynch told the boy, whose face had gone the color of paper. "The moment you feel the weight lift off your leg, you must draw away as swiftly as lightning. Can you do that?"

The boy gulped and nodded. My heart constricted in my breast to see the resolve in his round, sunburned face.

"Ready yourself," Mr. Lynch told him. Then he inserted the point of the pickaxe beneath the block of stone and levered it up a few inches.

The boy scrambled back, his hands clutching at the rubble for purchase, and a warning shout came from below as another block was dislodged and tumbled downward. Old Fowler reached up quickly to seize the child's arm and draw him to safety, and Mr. Lynch leapt to the ground. But the feared avalanche did not occur, and the gathered men visibly relaxed.

I darted over to the boy. His trouser leg was torn and bloody near the ankle, which was badly scraped and beginning to swell. I caught sight of my uncle among those gathered, and told him, "Summon Mrs. Furness to tend to the boy," as I crouched down to blot the boy's tear-stained face with my handkerchief.

"I'll carry him inside," Mr. Lynch said. "It will be quicker."

But the lad shrank from him. The terror that showed in the child's eyes baffled me for a moment before I realized its cause. I had grown so accustomed to the young man's hunched shoulder that I had ceased to notice it and had quite forgotten that for strangers, like the little boy, it could inspire disgust or fear.

"Sir, perhaps you'd better carry the little fellow," Mr. Lynch said quietly to his guardian, who hesitated but bent down to pick up the little boy, who willingly threw his arms around my uncle's neck. Rather awkwardly, my uncle hoisted him into his arms and started for the house. I started after them at once, but Mr. Lynch, mindful of his effect on the child, followed a few paces behind. I threw him an apologetic look, which was answered with a resigned smile. It was horribly unfair that his good deed should matter less to the boy he had rescued than his appearance.

"What is your name?" I asked the boy as I walked alongside.

"Ben, miss."

"'My lady,'" my uncle corrected.

"My lady, then." The child seemed to be recovering quickly, to judge by his matter-of-fact responses. "My father's the smith."

"What were you doing in the ruined part of the Hall? Didn't you know it's dangerous?"

"They said I could earn thruppence by lookin' for the gentleman what's gone missin'."

Horrified, I turned on my uncle. "You encouraged children to comb through the ruin?"

He put out a hand placatingly, but the child began to slip from his grasp, so he hastily withdrew it. "I understand your concern, but you will recall that we discussed the very real possibility that your husband might be trapped in the rubble. This very incident shows how easily it might have happened. And children can walk atop the wreckage with less likelihood of dislodging it."

"It stops now." I knew that, just as with every other likely location, searchers had visited the ruined wing at least once every day. But I had not known that those searchers included children. "If—if Atticus had been trapped among the wreckage, someone would have heard him calling for help sometime in the past few days," I forced myself to say. "We can't risk anyone else injuring themselves like Ben."

"What about my thruppence?" Ben piped.

"You'll have it, as well as something to eat, if you let Mrs. Furness see to your leg," I told him. "And I'll sew up the tear in your trousers."

The housekeeper clucked over the lad but assured him that his ankle would be fine. When I related what had happened, she shook her head rebukingly at the boy.

"There was no need to be frightened of Mr. Lynch's hunch," she told him. "Having a bent back does not make him a bad man."

Ben looked at the floor. "It isn't his hunch that frightens me," he mumbled.

He might have said more, but Mrs. Furness produced half a meat pasty for him, and he was far more interested in eating than in talking. I set about mending his trousers while the housekeeper tended to his injury, and soon the lad was ready, even eager, to leave.

I was on the point of departing myself when I remembered to ask Mrs. Furness if there had been any letters for me. There was the tiniest of pauses before her response of "No, my lady."

This made me pensive, and I continued to mull on it when I had retired to my room. The fact that I had not received a proper answer to any of my letters had begun to prey upon my mind. What if letters were being kept from me? It was possible that my mail was being detained, even if it was only to protect me from knowledge that might distress me . . . but it was more likely that my uncle was acting out of self-protection. Perhaps my own letters were not reaching their intended recipients.

The thought restored to me something of my former vigor, and I resolved to get to the bottom of the matter. The solution to this mystery, at least, might lie within my grasp. Swiftly I wrote another letter to George and Vivi. Then I rang for Ann.

"Please see that this goes out with the next post," I said. "It is urgent."

Her eyes were downcast, so I could not read her expression when she replied, "Yes, my lady."

It was impossible to know whether her demeanor was guilt, fear, or simply her usual shyness. I suppressed an impatient sigh and dismissed her. Then, after waiting what I judged would be a sufficient interval, I opened my door quietly. She was not in sight, but I guessed that she would make at once for the servants' quarters downstairs, and I darted down the hallway in that direction, moving as silently as I could.

I was just in time to catch sight of her skirt vanishing down the stair. I crept after her as far as I dared go for fear of being seen and halted on the staircase, listening with all my might.

Ann's soft voice barely reached my ears, too low for me to understand the words. But Mrs. Furness's reply came clearly. "Thank you, Ann. I'll see to Lady Telford's letter."

Brisk footsteps approached the stair, and I scampered up the steps and slipped around the corner, hoping the housekeeper would not choose the direction in which I had gone. Of course there was no reason to fear being discovered, I told myself. What could she do besides tell my uncle that I had taken to prowling about the servants' quarters? Nonetheless I breathed a silent sigh of relief when I heard her footsteps recede in the opposite direction. My chance of learning anything useful would be ruined if anyone realized that I was spying on the household staff.

Stealthily I left my hiding place and peered around the corner. Mrs. Furness was just in the act of knocking at a door. The voice that bade her enter was muffled, but I knew it was my uncle's.

No longer making any attempt at stealth, I strode down the hall and was in time to enter my uncle's study practically upon the woman's heels. She gave a start when I said firmly, "Mrs. Furness, my letter, if you please."

A flush crept into her round cheeks as she reached into her apron pocket and produced the letter I had written so short a time ago. "I'm sorry, my lady," she said.

"There's no need for you to apologize," I said, giving my uncle a hard look. "I'm sure you were just following orders."

My uncle rose from behind his desk. "See here, my girl, I won't have you throwing accusations around," he huffed.

"To my knowledge I have not yet thrown a single one, but I am on the very cusp of hurling a number of them," I said coolly. "Do you wish for Mrs. Furness to be present for this?"

My uncle gave me a hard look. Then he jerked his head at the housekeeper in a silent command. She withdrew without another word, and my uncle and I stared each other down.

He was the first to give in. "Very well, I've your precious letters," he snapped. Striding back to his desk, he jerked a drawer open. "Take 'em all if you wish."

Peering into the drawer, I was shocked by what I saw: a stack of correspondence too substantial to be merely from a few days. When I picked through them, I saw that these were all the letters that both Atticus and I had written since our first arrival at Thurnley Hall. "The seals aren't broken," I said, all the more mystified. "Why steal them if you weren't going to read them?"

His head rocked back as if he had smelled something foul. "I'm not a complete blackguard, whatever else I may be," he exclaimed. "I'd never do something as dishonorable as read your private letters."

A strange desire to laugh came to me. My uncle was offended at the idea that he might read my letters, when I suspected him of an infinitely worse crime. But at once the impulse died. My suspicion was too horrible to be laughed at.

"You have cut off all my communication beyond this house," I said, noting letters and telegrams addressed to Atticus and me as well. "It's a wonder that our friends have not been more alarmed at not having heard from us."

"I wired your friends in your names," he admitted. "I said you had decided to travel to Switzerland to visit a charitable institution there."

"I can only imagine that you must have sent telegrams to retract all of Mr. Lynch's requests for assistance also. The wires saying help was delayed or unavailable must have been your work as well. What can I possibly think except that you have contrived to abduct my husband, and now you are making every effort to cover your tracks?"

He drew himself up as if I had touched his pride again. "I should say not. I had nothing to do with the baron's disappearance."

"Then why are you acting like a guilty man?" I demanded. "Why do you not permit me to ask our friends for help? I cannot believe that you are guiltless. My husband clearly discovered something that you could not permit him to make known to the world. You needed to silence him." I held onto the edge of the desk to steady myself. "Did you kill Atticus? Or did you have him killed?"

He put a hand to his brow and rubbed it hard. "I had nothing to do with your husband's disappearance," he repeated. "I've no idea where he is."

He might have been telling the truth, but I knew now that he would split hairs to disavow anything unsavory if he could. I must pay close attention to his choice of words. "You did not say that you don't know what might have happened to him," I pointed out.

That seemed to dissolve the last ounce of strength remaining to him. He sank into his chair and buried his head in his hands. "The danger was there," he said, his voice muffled. "I saw it and I didn't act. But there is still time for you." He raised his face to me, and I was startled by the resolve in his bloodshot eyes. "You must leave immediately," he said.

"What is it you fear for me?" I asked warily.

"Don't you see? Grigore went missing before the baron did. We know the fool was terrified of your husband, with a superstitious fear beyond all reason. Isn't it obvious why we haven't found Lord Telford? Be honest, my girl. Haven't you known in your heart all along that Grigore must have killed him?"

I lowered myself into a chair. Hearing the words left me more shaken than I would have thought possible. "We . . . we would have found him." My lips were dry. "We would have found *them*."

That bark of laughter rang out derisively. "Grigore grew up on this estate, niece. He probably knows it better than I do—all the holes and corners where a person may hide. Nature often seems to grant idiots with a superior sense of cunning. No, I'm not surprised that he's eluded us."

"Then why not bring in the police in full force?" I shot at him. "Isn't that good reason to get help from every quarter that we can, and the most powerful help available to us? There is something you are keeping from me, uncle. You are too frightened to bring a constable to Thurnley Hall, even though it means compromising the search for my husband when his life may be at stake." My voice gave out on me, and I screwed my eyes tight shut as if that would blot out the horrible visions that had crowded the corners of my mind ever since Atticus had vanished. Visions of him dead or dying, walled up in some secret chamber, pinned into a coffin by the blade of a scythe . . .

A touch on my shoulder made me jump. My uncle had silently come to my side and now laid a hand on my arm in what must have been intended as a gesture of sympathy. "You should leave Thurnley Hall," he said quietly. "It isn't too late for you.

We will keep searching for your husband, but you should go."

He swallowed hard. "You *must* go."

"I can't," I said.

He wheeled around with sudden energy and strode to the sideboard to pour himself a drink from a crystal decanter. "Can't!" he mocked. "Idiotic female, can't you see that it's the only rational course? Listen to me and not your hysteria. Leave this place before something worse happens." He took a swig of the amber-colored liquor and carried both glass and decanter to his desk, where he flung himself into his chair again. "This is the best advice I'll ever give you, niece, so heed it well. Get away from here, as fast and as far as your money will take you."

I gripped the arms of my chair and took a breath to steady my voice, for I would not appear before him as the trembling, dithering creature he wanted to believe me. "I *have* listened to you," I said, "and now I must request that you do me the courtesy of hearing me. I say I can't leave Thurnley Hall, not yet. I am going to have a child. And if I left here without doing every single thing within my power to find my husband, I could not look my child in the eye when the day comes that he will ask me where his father is. For my future son or daughter's sake, as well as for my own, I must know what happened to Atticus—and I must do everything I can to save him."

The effect of my speech was shocking.

My uncle leapt to his feet with such haste and carelessness that his chair toppled over, and then he in turn almost fell over it in his hurry to back away from me. His normally ruddy face had turned pale, and his eyes had gone so wide that white showed all around the irises. As he scrambled to regain his balance, he thrust out a hand as if to fend me off.

"A child!" His whisper was stricken. Not, strangely enough, with sorrow or dismay. With fear. "God help us all," he groaned. "A child . . ."

"What is the matter?" I exclaimed. "What frightens you so?"

He had reached the far wall and, unable to put any more distance between us, he stared at me with the eyes of a doe cornered by hounds. "There is a curse," he said at last, and his voice was a croak. "When my mother left Romania to marry an Englishman, her father cursed her for flouting the aristocratic match he had arranged for her. He called on all the ancient magic of their bloodline and swore that . . . that the first son born to any of her line would be . . ."

"What?" I cried.

He shut his eyes and breathed the words. "A monster."

Silence seized the word and buried it, but its echoes rang in my head. My hand found its way to my belly, whether to reassure myself or the unborn babe I did not know.

"Superstitious nonsense," I said with more confidence than I felt. "Claptrap."

But the voice of Mathilde Munro whispered, *Are you not afraid of what your children might be?*

My uncle shook his head slowly, a motion as solemn as the swinging of a funeral bell. "I have lived to see it come true," he said. "I do not wish to see it fulfilled again. Your child must not be born here, Clara. It would be even safer if . . ."

"Not one word more," I said, my voice shaking with anger. "Not one."

After a long moment my uncle looked away and sighed. The worst of the fear seemed to drain away from him, leaving him a strangely diminished figure, and when next he turned his face to me the look he gave me was almost pleading. "Don't you see that you are now in even greater danger?" he said with a strange gentleness. "If Grigore is still in hiding nearby and comes to learn of your condition, what is to stop him from trying to rid the earth of the vampire's babe?"

What indeed, if my uncle was the monster he evidently believed himself to be? How surprising that he should think it of himself. I had not credited him with so much honesty or humility, but at least I knew with certainty, from his own lips, that I could rely on him for nothing now.

"You must swear to tell no one," I said. "My secret cannot leave this room."

He nodded heavily but said nothing. I wondered how far I could trust him. How much had he succumbed to this conviction that he was less than human? If he was resigned to what he believed to be his nature, I could not depend upon him—for anything.

"That is why you and my mother were both forbidden to marry," I said, as realization dawned. "So that neither of you would have sons and fulfill the curse." Now I knew why my grandmother had said that my mother and I would have been welcome at Thurnley had it been known that I was an only child.

"If only I had found you in time," he said in a voice of utter defeat. "If I had encountered you before your marriage . . ."

"It would have made no difference," I said. "I'd not have let a ghost story determine whether I married. Why were you so determined to prevent Grandmama from telling me about it?"

His eyes darted away from mine, suddenly wary. "She wished to unburden herself of a lifetime's worth of guilt," he mumbled. "It would have done no good to anyone living, and possibly much harm. That is why I could not let your letters go out into the world. They might have spread secrets that could still harm our family."

"It was more than that, wasn't it? You knew I had suspicions about my grandmother's death, and you didn't want them to leave this house."

He hung his head in a wordless confession. Whether he had had a hand in her death or merely feared being suspected of it, he had acted guilty in every way.

"I'm going to the train station to wire again for the police," I said. "If you've given Thomas orders not to drive me, I'll walk." I hesitated, feeling a strange pang of sympathy for him. He looked so broken. "I'm going to demand an investigation," I said, almost gently. "It's for the best."

I don't know if he would have replied if the sound of running footsteps had not forestalled it. The footfalls came pounding toward the door and ended in a fusillade of frantic knocking.

"Come in," I said, since my uncle showed no sign of answering.

The door flew open to reveal a hatless Victor Lynch, dripping with water, his clothes drenched and clinging to his body.

He must have run all the way, for he was panting for breath. His eyes were full of dread and a strange tenderness as they fixed on me.

"We've found something," he said. "At the river's edge."

He held out an object to me, and almost mechanically I reached out my hand to take it. It was a fragment of a walking stick, the shaft broken off roughly as if by some violent means. It was topped with an ivory eagle's head.

CHAPTER FIFTEEN

"Forgive my appearance," he said in a hushed voice. "I lost my footing in my hurry to bring this to you. Is it . . . ?" With my forefinger I traced the line of the eagle's beak, which was chipped. I could imagine a thousand dreadful ways that the stick could have been damaged so. When I looked closer, I saw a brownish red substance caked in a groove of the carving. I knew at once it must be dried blood.

"Yes," I said. "It's his. At the river's edge, you said? I want to see."

He hesitated, but my face must have told him I would not be deterred, for he stood back to let me pass.

At the bend in the river where it passed at the bottom of the front meadow men were clustered near the rocks, heads bent over something I could not see. As I drew near, their voices broke off, and those who were wearing caps touched them to me with the respect due a baroness. Or a widow.

"After Mr. Lynch went to fetch you, we spied somethin' else," said one of the men. "Do you know this, my lady?"

Old Mr. Fowler was at the center of the group, and something in his muddy hands was the focus of the group's attention. Silently I held out my hand, and he placed the new find in my palm. A scrap of royal blue melton with light blue piping still attached, torn from the waistcoat I had made Atticus for his birthday.

I could not speak, but my face must have shown what meaning this had for me.

"We reckon his lordship were walkin' along the bank," came a voice. It was hushed, deferential. "It's slippery after all the rain, and as he fell his stick must have caught between the rocks an' snapped. The river's flowin' so fast that he would have been swept away before he had time even to call for help."

Swept away and carried off by the current with such force that his clothes tore where they scraped against the rocks. The violence of it wrenched my stomach, but it was less horrible than imagining the other: that as my husband had walked by the river, the giant Grigore had set upon him. That the stick had been broken in the struggle and Atticus overpowered, as the great hands tore at him and ripped his waistcoat.

The ground tilted suddenly, and a commotion broke out as many hands snatched at me to keep me from falling. "Let me carry you back to the house," said a gentle voice that I knew must belong to Mr. Lynch. "You're in no fit state to walk."

"Don't carry me." My lips were so numb it was difficult to move them. "Just give me your arm."

"We're that sorry, my lady," came a whisper. Then the murmurs of condolence rose and broke over me like a wave, and I felt I would drown in them just as Atticus—

"Thank you," I said. "All of you, for—" But I could not remember what I meant to thank them for, and I stared at them dumbly until Mr. Lynch placed my hand on his arm and led me back up the hill to Thurnley Hall.

What followed remains vague to me. I remember stopping the mantel clock in my room because the tick of every second was a jeering reminder that time had stopped for Atticus. I recall

Ann tipping spoonfuls of broth between my lips as if I were an invalid or an infant.

She helped me out of my black dress and into my dressing gown, but I refused to go to bed. The great dark bed with its ominous carvings and heavy hangings would have been too desolate. When Atticus had lain with me there, it had been a cozy nest, a secure cocoon. Now it would feel like a coffin.

My thoughts were disjointed. An idea would flare to life like a spark only to die away in the next moment. I sat before the fire but did not see the flames. Instead I saw my husband's last moments in all their hideous possibilities. My mind flinched away from the knowledge of his death, yet the tormenting images would not cease.

Had he thought of me in his last moments? I wondered. If he had, did he know how much he had given me—how, in the truest sense, he had saved my life?

Before I married Atticus, I had been hard and untrusting, caring only about my own welfare. It was little wonder, for life as a woman with no protector was a hard one, and over the years I had learned to be wary and self-interested. Being his wife had changed me: made me kinder, slower to anger, more forgiving, better able to find humor and joy in life. Until Atticus, I sometimes thought I had never known laughter. I had certainly never known love in its deepest, richest, most profound sense.

Now scenes from my life with Atticus unspooled before my mind's eye. The night at the theater when he had first approached me to propose marriage; how wary and hostile I had been at his irruption into my life. The afternoon when he came to tea and made me laugh for the first time. Our wedding day, with all my dread and apprehension about taking so great a step with a near stranger. Dancing with him before the assembled company at Gravesend, not yet knowing I had fallen in love with him but feeling more powerfully drawn to him than I could explain. Overhearing him arguing with himself, as I thought, when I dreaded that he was losing his mind. Trysting with him in the folly such a short time ago, feeling the sunlight on my skin as we lay entwined on the grass.

I remembered, too, when I had truly become his wife. It was the night that Richard had attempted to kill Atticus and had himself perished in the attempt. We had not expected that night to end in loving, certainly not after the grueling questioning, which on top of the emotional and physical strain had rendered us nearly numb with exhaustion. When we sought each other's embrace, comfort was all we desired at first: the reassurance of each other's nearness after we had come so perilously close to losing each other. All I expected, at least, was to sleep peacefully in my husband's arms.

But then—but then.

Not since Adam and Eve left paradise, I believe, has any woman been loved as exquisitely as I was that night. With all the fervor and reverence of his loving heart, Atticus had at last given expression to the feelings he had stored up for me for almost twenty years. And what was just as great a marvel, his caresses awoke the same passion from me in return. Indeed, my body's response to his touch was so powerful that it frightened me. What if my ardency shocked him, repelled him? His words when I hesitantly voiced this fear I would never forget.

"I am your safe haven, Clara," he told me. "With me you may be as abandoned as you feel—or as shy. Give me all of yourself: your passion, your tenderness, even your ferocity. I will treasure them all, for they are all part of you."

And my haven Atticus became, both that night and in the future. Within the circle of his arms I always felt cherished, protected, held in safekeeping away from whatever fears or anxieties tried to plague me. Secure in that knowledge of his unwavering love, I was able to cast aside my protective shell. I had been able to open my heart, to let it soften and become susceptible, because Atticus kept it in his tender protection.

Without him, I was naked and vulnerable again, lacking the armor that had kept me safe in the years before our marriage. Would I have to build it around me again, toughen and immure my feelings? A fine mother that woman would be. No, I had to be true to the Clara that Atticus had helped me find in myself— had given me the courage to be.

For he had done more than make me feel loved. Even now, even if he was gone forever, his complete acceptance of me gave me the first glimmerings of faith that I could give our child a good life on my own. Atticus, the worthiest, most honorable, most compassionate person I had ever known, had loved and honored and believed in me, and that knowledge gave me new strength.

It also gave me new resolve: I must be worthy of the honor and trust he had placed in me. For our child's sake, for my husband's, for my own, I wanted to be the best woman I could be, one deserving of a man such as Atticus. Having been loved like that was a charge upon me to make my life worthwhile, to continue to be the woman he admired and was proud of.

It frightened me, all the same, that I would be solely responsible for raising our child. I wondered if my mother had been frightened when my father died, leaving me in her sole care. But she was strong and courageous and determined, and I reminded myself that I took after her. If she had been able to endure through loneliness and hardship to raise me safely, I must do no less for my and Atticus's son or daughter.

A wisp of superstitious fear in the back of my mind whispered, *You shall bear a monster.* But I thrust it aside. Son or daughter, my child would inherit all of the beautiful potential of Atticus, and I would nurture that promise with every ounce of my strength. Bloodlines alone did not make monsters; I knew that.

But how grievously unfair that Atticus would never know his child. He had been robbed of the happiness, the pride, the bittersweet pleasure of years of watching his baby grow to adulthood. Perhaps even worse, our child would never know the wonderful man who had been his father. And I too had been robbed, of my helpmeet and life's best companion. The prospect of all the lonely years that stretched before me made me shiver.

Now the grief pressed in upon me from all sides, boxing me in, suffocating, and it was like being in my nightmare once again. I realized now that the horror of the dream had not been about anything so literal as being trapped underground. It was no wonder that venturing into the old mine had not caused me distress. For the nightmare had always been about being separated from Atticus—longing to reach him but being trapped in solitude. The thing I feared most was losing Atticus, and now the worst had happened. Life had nothing more cruel to do to me.

With that realization came a kind of clarity. Death had torn him out of my future, but not out of my past. He still lived in the thousands of memories in my heart, and in that sense Atticus would always be with me. I would still have all the shared laughter, the intimate conversations, the kisses, the passionate embraces. I pictured his vivid blue eyes, remembered his velvet voice, recalled the joy of his smile. When I closed my eyes, I could almost even recapture the sensation of being held in his arms. Atticus would never truly leave me, and my bruised heart swelled with love and gratitude for that.

A faint disturbance of the air behind me alerted me that I was not alone, and almost in the same instant there came a touch on my hair. Then a brush was being drawn slowly down the length of it, creating a faint sibilance in the silence. The motion, slowly repeated, made me feel close to Atticus again for one beautiful instant, as if my love and longing and grief had summoned up his ghostly manifestation to visit me.

It was not Atticus, though, who stood behind the divan and drew the hairbrush through my curls with such a soothing motion. A foreboding prickle tightened my scalp as I turned to see who was behind me.

It was Victor Lynch.

The sight of him was like a torrent of cold water dashed over me. "What are you doing in my room?" I exclaimed, drawing away. He had observed me in this most vulnerable of states, had intruded upon my private grief, and the knowledge stung like salt in a raw wound. "Why did you not knock?"

His smile was as gentle as it always had been. He had changed his clothes for evening dress, and his hair was dry, with the ends just curling, telling me that many hours must have passed since he had burst into the study, soaked to the skin. "You were so distressed that I thought it would calm you if I brushed your hair," he said softly, and his dark eyes were tender. "I know you enjoy it."

"I enjoy it when *my husband* brushes my hair," I said, and then my indignation began to change to something more like apprehension. "How did you know that?" I asked.

He said, "I used to watch the two of you together."

For a moment I was too shocked to respond. The hand holding the hairbrush extended toward me again, and I drew back sharply. "You spied on us?" I demanded. Had he found a way to watch us in our private room? The thought that he might have been watching us during any of our intimate, private moments made my stomach squirm.

"You and the baron were in such perfect accord with each other. That is rare, do you know? It was quite poignant seeing you together when you thought no one was near. The thousand little tendernesses that passed between you that no one else saw . . . I relished those."

"It was very wrong of you," I said, but I was too shaken to give my words the severity I intended. "You should not have invaded our privacy."

"Don't be angry with me." His voice was almost dreamy, and he gazed into the distance as if contemplating who knew what vision of me and my husband. He placed the hairbrush back on my dressing table. "It was the only way I could taste such a joyous existence, since I was barred from any such domestic union myself . . . or so I thought at the time."

Unnerved, I retorted, "I don't care to hear your reasons, Mr. Lynch. Now please leave my room, or I shall be forced to summon my uncle."

His eyes returned to me, and they were no longer vague but all too intent. "Now, Clara, there's no need for such formality between us," he said. "We are cousins, after all."

"Cousins?" I echoed. So my earlier conjecture had been correct. My uncle, while obeying the letter of his parents' ban on marriage, had taken a mistress—and he had had the gall to condemn fallen women for bringing their ruin on themselves! To judge by the fraught interactions between him and the younger man, the fictional arrangement had not worked out well.

"Well may you be shocked," he said, misinterpreting my reaction. "So was I when our grandmother told me ten days ago. That dreadful old virago actually summoned me so that she might taunt me with the knowledge, saying that she and my guardian—my father, I should say—were so ashamed of me that they could not admit I was their kin. She told me that as a bastard I was worthless, that I had brought nothing but disaster to the family."

I felt a pang of sympathy for Victor in spite of everything. How could he know how to act properly when he had been treated as an inconvenience or a pariah by everyone in his life? "It was cruel of her to tax you with something over which you had no control," I said warmly.

His gaze had seemed to turn inward, and I was not certain he had even heard me. He said softly, "A deformed monstrosity, she called me. She even told me that it would have been better for me to have been drowned at birth." When I stared at him in horror, he put an unsteady hand to his eyes as if to shield them from my gaze. "I could not bear to listen to her spew her venom any longer," he said in a low voice. "The anger was like a scalding tide rushing through my veins. I wrapped my hands around her throat and . . . finally she was silent."

Now I was silent too—stricken dumb with shock.

After a moment he gathered himself. Taking a deep breath, he lowered his hand from his eyes and gave me a twisted smile that was probably meant to be reassuring. "I had never killed before," he told me almost casually. "Not a human being, that is. It . . . soothed me."

My head whirled with the import of his words. So this was why my uncle had been acting in such a peculiar way: he must have known of his son's deed and tried to shield him and hide his guilt. What I had interpreted as guilt at his own act was actually revulsion at a murder that he had not himself committed but certainly bore some responsibility for. This, too, was why he believed in the curse: he knew his son to be a murderer.

In desperation I wondered if anyone was in earshot. The house seemed terribly still. The bell pull, which would summon one of the servants, was across the room from me. If I ran for it, would he be able to stop me from reaching it? But even if I succeeded in ringing, that left heaven knew how long until anyone answered its summons. Time that Victor might employ in making me regret calling for help.

Unaware of my fevered thoughts, he continued. "I realized that all the years that I had resented being treated as a monster I should have embraced that destiny," he said. Now a new confidence infused him; he stood tall, and his voice took on strength and clarity. "Instead of studying folklore and fiction for ways to expunge or vanquish that corrupted side of myself, I should have been celebrating it and learning how to benefit from my power. Now I finally have. Now"—he took a deep breath that expanded his chest—"I am fully myself. The monstrous Victor . . . the monster victorious."

I tried to swallow my panic. He might still listen to reason. "Would you not rather be man than monster?" I ventured. "To feel the kinship with humankind that you would experience by—by doing good?"

The smile that had always seemed so gentle had taken on a chillingly detached air. "There is no kinship," he said. "From my earliest days I can remember only horror and revulsion. First at my deformity, then because word spread that I was the bastard son of unknown parents. Everywhere I heard the refrain: I was despicable, hideous, an abomination. Is it any wonder that I came to embody the words that were hurled at me? I took pleasure in avenging myself upon the schoolfellows who had been so quick to revile me, in devising for them the most finely tuned torments. Then it was the masters who began calling me monstrous." He spread his hands, gracefully indicating himself. "What point was there in continuing to resist my destiny?" he asked with an almost lighthearted air. "Words cannot express the exhilaration of accepting what I am, Clara."

My mouth had gone dry, and I had to make more than one attempt to ask my next question. Finally I managed to form the words, though they were little more than a whisper. "Did Atticus learn what you did to my grandmother? Was that what he was going to investigate on the night he vanished?" If Mr. Lynch had had something to do with his disappearance . . .

But he shook his head with a gentle regret. "I ought to have thought of that, but I didn't. Indeed, I had hoped to learn more from him about his mysterious supernatural qualities. I don't adhere to the narrow superstitions of peasants like Grigore, but I am convinced that the baron had some secret knowledge and arcane power, and I would dearly love to have learned it." He sighed. "Was he a vampire? I shall never have the chance to find out."

"I wish to God he were a vampire," I cried in despair, "so that he could come back to me." *And deal with you,* I finished silently.

Seating himself beside me on the divan, he patted my hand indulgently before I could snatch it away. "I know you must miss him," he said, his low, pleasant voice sounding genuinely regretful, "but his death, though unfortunate, is most convenient for me—or shall I say *us?*"

Dread flooded my heart in a cold rush. "How do you mean?" I whispered.

The soft brown eyes gazed into mine with an expression that was somehow almost tender. "I wish to make you my wife, Clara," he said.

My lips parted, but I could not form words, and he continued, "I admire you more than any woman I have ever met, and I can think of no one better suited to be my consort—or, what is most important, to continue our family line."

"What?" I gasped.

His eyes shone with excitement. "Imagine what a prodigy of strength and cunning our son will be, with the Burleigh bloodline doubled in him! He shall be our magnificent legacy, turning others to his own ends, becoming a scourge upon this miserable planet. Perhaps he may even come to rule England, or the empire itself. He shall be the epitome of ruthlessness, the apex of viciousness." He smiled. "The perfect monster."

My voice shook when I said, "I am not going to bear your son, Mr. Lynch."

"Come, Clara, there's no need for such hauteur between us," he said, with a kind of gentle reproach. "As much as I admire your dignity and reserve, you may admit the truth to me. I know you are fond of me." He leaned forward, as if, to my horror, he were about to kiss me. A wordless sound of protest struggled up from my throat, but all he did was lift a tendril of hair from my cheek and tuck it behind my ear, letting his fingertips linger on my hair. "Don't be afraid," he said with a chuckle. "I won't force myself upon you. I know that when you have had a few more days to reconcile yourself to the baron's death you will find that your heart has opened to me and that you will be ready to marry me."

"A few *days?*" The words burst from me. How could this man—this murderer—sit calmly beside me and act as though this were sane? "I can't possibly consider remarriage," I told him with as much force as I could muster. "No matter how much time passes, it is out of the question."

"And I would think less of you were you to say anything else when your loss is so fresh," he replied promptly.

"But I am too old to bear children," I said desperately, hoping with all my heart that he would believe me. "I'm at least ten years older than you. You must look to some other woman to wed."

He *tsk*ed at me. "You are in the prime of womanhood, Clara. I have complete confidence that our marriage will be fruitful." Then his eyes took on a roguish twinkle far more horrible than anger would have been. "Mind you, it would be unwise to dilly-dally. I can't promise as leisurely a courtship as a lady of your station might generally expect."

I did not think I could speak without being overcome with nausea, so I was silent as he rose as if to depart at long last. The room had darkened over the course of his stay, so that the fire was now the only source of light in the room. It threw his shadow onto the wall behind him, and in the way of shadows it changed and distorted his silhouette, exaggerating the slight unevenness of his shoulders and the curve of his upper back so that the minor imperfections of his body turned grotesque.

I had not thought him monstrous before. But now, having seen what distortions of his soul lay beneath his handsome face and courteous manner, I would never be able to think of him as a normal man again.

I had believed he was finally on the point of departure, but he remained standing over me where I sat on the divan. "As your suitor, I shall naturally take a close interest in everything that concerns your welfare," he said, "and I must insist that you take more nourishment, however much grief may have temporarily diminished your appetite. You mustn't compromise your health."

When I did not respond, he said softly, "I shall be a good husband to you, Clara. As I said before, I observed you and the baron closely, so I know all the little ways he showed his affection for you. Be assured that I am a quick study."

Before I realized what he intended, he had drawn my hair away from my neck and bent to put his lips to my throat where he had bared it. In just this way had Atticus kissed my neck that night we frightened Ann. A shudder of revulsion passed through me at the intimacy of the touch, but he seemed not to notice . . . or care. "I shall bid you good night," he said with what sounded like real affection. "We'll talk again tomorrow evening."

He moved unhurriedly to the doorway, and as soon as the latch clicked behind him I leapt from the divan intending to lock the door. The key was no longer in the lock, though. There was nothing for it but to push the bureau in front of the door. Panic gave me strength, however, and in moments it was done.

Hastily I gathered my few most necessary belongings, including all the money that Atticus and I had brought with us. I bundled everything into a shawl and knotted it. Best to be as unencumbered as possible, for if I had to walk all the way to the village, I did not want to be weighed down.

Then, as quietly as I could, I pushed the bureau away from the door. The process was still far noisier than I would have liked, though, so I waited a minute by the door, listening hard to the silence for any sign of life, before turning the knob.

The door did not budge.

First carefully, then desperately, I pulled at the door, hoping it was merely stuck. It was all too clear what had happened, though. Why had I not anticipated that he would lock me in?

Still, it would not detain me for long. I rang for one of the servants and paced back and forth before the door until I heard the sound of footsteps approaching. My freedom was at hand.

The footsteps came to a halt at the door, and there was a gentle knock. "My lady?" came the voice of Mrs. Furness. "Did you ring?"

"Yes! Mr. Lynch has locked me in. Please open the door at once."

There was a pause, during which I heard nothing. No jingling of keys came to my ears, nor did the sound of a key in the lock.

"Mr. Lynch locked you in?" she repeated then.

In my frustration I felt I could have beaten the door down with my fists. "That is what I said. Don't you have the key?" A dismaying thought came to me. "Did he take yours from you?" "No, my lady. He didn't take my key." "Then let me out, for heaven's sake! I need to get help." I grabbed the doorknob and rattled it as if that would hasten the woman.

The housekeeper's voice, when she spoke next, remained as courteous as ever. "I'm sorry, my lady," she said calmly. "If Mr. Lynch wishes you to stay, then stay you shall."

"What?" I cried, disbelieving. When she made no answer, I hammered at the door. "Mrs. Furness!" I almost shouted. "Let me out this instant!"

But there was no answer. When I stopped pounding at the door I could hear her footsteps receding down the hall, growing quieter and quieter until they faded entirely. I was a prisoner.

CHAPTER SIXTEEN

I snatched a hairpin from the dish on my dressing table and knelt before the door to see if I could pick the lock. After twenty minutes I was in tears of frustration. Either the lock could not be picked, or I needed better tools. Scissors, a button-hook, and a needle from my sewing kit also proved to be no use at all.

The windows were my next thought. They swung outward readily enough when I unfastened the catch, but when I scanned the sooty gray exterior of the house and felt the stone with my hands I found that I would not be able to get any purchase on the smooth surface, and there was no convenient trellis or gutter spout.

Just as climbing down was out of the question, so was leaping to freedom. The ground lay dauntingly far beneath, and it fell away so steeply that I might easily break a limb, and that would trap me just as surely as being locked inside the house. Worse, if I jumped I might injure the baby.

My eyes raked the view for a source of assistance, but no one was in sight in the deepening twilight. Moonlight glinted on the river, but all of the men who had thronged its banks earlier had clearly returned to their homes now that the need for them was past . . . now that we knew Atticus was dead.

Sudden grief swelled in me with a force that felt as if it would shatter my body. Fiercely I pushed it down. Later, when I was safely away from this wretched place, I could mourn my husband with all the reverent love he deserved. But now, as sickeningly unjust as it was, I knew I must focus my entire mind on escaping.

Leaning out the window, I shouted for help until my voice grew hoarse. But nothing happened. No voice called out in reply, and no one approached, either outside the house or within. Probably the only people in earshot were the household, and Mrs. Furness or my uncle—or both—had most likely told them to disregard my pleas.

What else remained? As I scanned the room in search of something I could turn to my use, I recalled Victor's revolting claim to have watched Atticus and me. When I went back over his exact words, I realized that he had not said that he had access to a peephole; he might simply have meant that he took advantage of all the ordinary opportunities of watching us. It was just possible that Ann had spoken about having seen Atticus bite my throat, as she thought, and Victor might have heard of this instead of witnessing it firsthand.

But it was also entirely possible that he had some secret means of watching us in the Cradle Room, and that meant that there might be another means of entering the room—and leaving it. The house was reputed to have a priest's hole, I recalled, although none had come to light during all our searching of the past few days, and if such a hiding place lay adjacent to this chamber, it might very likely have another exit. A secret passage, in fact. In other circumstances I would have smiled at the thought, for it reminded me of home.

For the next few hours I examined the dark oaken paneling of the walls, forcing myself to carefully trace every carved square with my fingertips in search of a crack that might reveal a hidden opening. As unlikely as it might have been, that wisp of hope was enough to prevent me from dissolving into complete despair. I found nothing to encourage me, but I resolved to go over the paneling again the next day with the assistance of daylight. Ann did not come to undress me for bed, nor would I have felt safe undressing any longer in this room, where I might be under observation. The only place where I felt I had any certainty of privacy was in the great four-poster bed with the curtains drawn all around me. When at last I crawled beneath the coverlet and huddled there waiting for the merciful oblivion of sleep, I realized that the distraction of Victor's machinations and my own search for a means of escape had prevented the worst of my grief from making itself felt. I had not yet determined whether that was something to be thankful for when I fell asleep.

~~~~~~

I was already awake and waiting the next morning when a knock at the door came.

"Your ladyship," called the voice of Mrs. Furness, "we've brought your breakfast. If you are thinking of trying to break out of the room when we unlock the door, I advise against it."

It was wise of her to anticipate this, for it was exactly what I had resolved to do. Nor did her warning alter my intention. As soon as the key turned in the lock and the door began to swing inward, I yanked it open and darted through the opening to freedom.

At least, that was my intention. Instead, I collided with a huge form and found myself seized about the waist by a grip of iron. When I looked up, I saw to my astonishment the implacable bearded face of Grigore.

For an instant, I was frozen with shock. Then I seized him by the front of his smock and shook him—or tried to, for it was like trying to shake a mountain. "What did you do to my husband?" I shouted. "Did you kill him?"

The man regarded me warily and said something I did not understand. I cried out in frustration and fury and beat my fists against his chest, but he disregarded this except to hold me at arm's length, so that I swiped at him in futile misery.

"There's no need to take on so, I'm sure," the housekeeper said rebukingly. Beside her stood the cook with a tray. "You'll feel better after you've eaten something."

"Does my uncle know you're holding me here against my will?" I demanded, struggling in the burly Romanian's grip as he carried me back into my room. It was useless to fight him; he might have been made of solid rock. Evidently growing annoyed with my struggles, he gave me a shake that practically rattled my teeth before plunking me down without ceremony on the divan. As he took a position behind me with his huge hands clamped on my upper arms, the cook placed the tray on the small table before me.

"My uncle won't permit this," I told Mrs. Furness, as my head spun from Grigore's rough treatment.

"On the contrary, he feels that Mr. Lynch's plan is the most sensible course of action." With a jerk of her head she indicated that the cook could leave, and she did not resume speaking until the door had closed behind her. "It would do the family no good if you were to run about spreading tales of what you have seen here—or what you think you have seen."

To my consternation she began to move about the room, fingering my belongings and placing some of them in a box. My sewing kit. A silver brooch. My husband's razor. "What are you doing with our things?" I asked.

She scarcely glanced at me as she opened the drawer of the dressing table and poked through its contents. "The whole household knows by now that your grief for your husband has unseated your reason, and you will do yourself a mischief if anything sharp or dangerous is left in your possession."

In other words, she was removing everything that I might be able to use as a tool—or a weapon. Even the meal on the tray before me, a meat pasty and bowl of broth, seemed to have been chosen so that it would not require implements. I had to concede that it was a wise precaution. But when she opened my mother's trunk and began to extract items from it, I made to rise and was only stopped by Grigore, who held me forcibly in place.

"What possible harm can I do with books?" I protested. "Leave those to me, at least."

"You might tear out the pages to write messages on them," she replied calmly.

"How, when you have taken the pen and ink? And who on earth would I give them to? Mrs. Furness, please listen. I won't cause any trouble for my uncle or Mr. Lynch. I only want to return home." At that moment I felt I would promise anything if only they would set me free. "Tell my uncle that I'll not do or say anything to throw suspicion on the family if he will only release me."

"I'm sorry, my lady, but you'll get no help from me."

Her placid stubbornness baffled me. "I can believe the others being taken in by lies about my going mad from grief, but I don't understand why you are helping my uncle hold me captive. You know how wrong this is! How is he forcing you to go along with his schemes?"

The housekeeper folded her hands at her waist, the very image of the obedient servant, even as she most strenuously defied the role. "You misunderstand, my lady," she said. "It is young Mr. Lynch's wishes that matter to me. Whatever he desires, I will do everything in my power to provide."

Bewildered, I asked, "Why?"

"He is my son."

"*Your* son?" I said in astonishment. I remembered her strange demeanor when we had discussed the lamb grave marker, which I had taken to mean that she had lost a child to death. But that did not seem to be the case after all. "You were my uncle's mistress?"

A tight little smile came and went on her round face. "That's putting a fine face on it. The fact is that many years ago I was a parlormaid in the London residence of an acquaintance of Mr. Burleigh's. I was a comely thing in those days, and during a visit to his friend Mr. Burleigh took a fancy to me. When I resisted, he told me that he would see that I lost my position unless I was . . . kind to him."

I stared at her, aghast. No wonder she had been so angered by my uncle's scathing comments on fallen women. Disgust filled me at what my uncle had done to her. I could see in her features traces of the pretty young girl she had once been—and also I could see a resemblance to her son, now that I knew to look for it. The delicacy of her nose and chin had been blunted somewhat by the years, but I could see now that Victor took after her.

Under my scrutiny she dropped her eyes to her apron and smoothed it down before speaking again. "When I found I was going to have a child, he offered me a good deal of money to go away, but I told him that I would do nothing of the sort. Unless he gave me a position where I would be able to earn my living and also stay near my child, I would go to his mother and tell her everything. I was surprised at how quickly he agreed. Later, when I came to Thurnley Hall and met his mother, it made more sense."

"So after you had the child he made you housekeeper here."

"He kept that much of his bargain, yes. But he sent Victor to be raised by a farm couple on the estate until the boy was old enough to be sent to school. And once Victor left university, he was sent to a position far away. Then another, when that did not suit his temperament. And so on." Her jaw set, and her plump, comfortable figure was suddenly infused with steel. "For nearly all of his life, I have never seen my son for more than a few weeks at a time—between school terms and the intervals between the different positions he has held. I have had to make do with those meager scraps to keep my heart whole. It is like keeping a starving man alive by feeding him a rusk twice a year."

It was a desolate picture, and now that I was approaching motherhood myself I could not help but feel pity for her. "But he doesn't know that you're his mother?" I asked. "You didn't tell him?"

She took control of herself once more, straightening her shoulders and making a visible effort to regain her composure. "No," she said more calmly. "The knowledge would bring him no happiness, and his happiness is all I desire." Then a great sigh escaped her. "If only he had been allowed to stay with me! He would have known love, not revulsion. I have never shrunk from him because of his defect. I would never have made him feel that he was flawed or freakish, as his foster parents and his schoolfellows did."

She might, in fact, have prevented him from becoming what he was now. The cruel injustice that had been done to her and then to her son was now being visited upon me, and some day, unless I could prevent it, upon my child. This chain of misery had to be broken.

"He told me that before she died my grandmother taunted him with the news that he was the son of Mr. Burleigh," I said. "How did she come to have that knowledge? Did you tell her?"

"I'm the last person who would have done that! I'd seen what malicious joy the old woman took in making those around her miserable. I knew no good would come of her learning Victor's parentage. But she must have worked it out of her son eventually." She shook her head. "And it was the death of her."

My eyes widened. She actually knew that her son had killed old Mrs. Burleigh—and yet her loyalty was still to him? That was possibly the most horrifying thing she had yet said, and dread tightened my breast. If she stood behind her son when he committed murder, was there any extremity in which she would not be his willing accomplice?

Apprehensively I asked, "Why are you telling me all this? Do you think that if I have pity for him, it will make me more willing to cooperate?"

"Doesn't it?" she returned. "It can't have escaped you that he is very like your late husband in many ways, my lady. He did not have the advantages of the late baron, but . . ."

"Advantages!" I burst out, outraged that she could compare the two. "My husband suffered every bit as cruelly as your son, or even more so, yet he did not let it turn him into a twisted maniac bent on exacting revenge for his wrongs. He became compassionate and selfless, not vindictive and selfish. The idea that I am to be made your son's broodmare to create more monsters like him is so loathsome—"

Before I could finish the thought she had stepped forward and slapped me hard across the face, first with one hand, then with the other. With my arms pinioned by Grigore I could neither fend off the blows nor return them.

"Do not call my son that," she said quietly.

My cheeks smarted with the sting of the blows, but the shock was almost sharper than the pain. "It is what he calls himself," I flared. "What he is resolved to be."

She was visibly breathing hard, and now she put a hand to her breast as if to quiet her agitation. "He is a better man that anyone knows him to be, even himself."

"Then you must help him to recognize that," I urged her. "You must help him along the way. A fine way to start would be to persuade him to release me."

Her quick astonished glance toward me showed how far this idea was from her thoughts. "Why should he listen to anything I have to say?" she asked in surprise. "I am only the housekeeper."

So she still did not intend that he should know he was her son. I wondered if there was a way I could turn that information to my own use. It seemed to me, however, that a man who was pleased with himself and the world would be less dangerous than a man who was greatly disappointed. Right now all he knew was that he was the natural son of a gentleman. To let him know that his mother was a servant might devastate or anger him, and in that mood he might be more of a threat to me than he already was.

As I was thinking this, the housekeeper nodded at Grigore to release me, and he did so. My arms ached as the blood flowed back into the places where he had gripped me, and I eyed him resentfully as he joined the housekeeper by the door. I knew better this time than to run at them. I must find a less obvious means of escaping.

In the very act of leaving, the housekeeper paused and turned back to me. "On behalf of the household," she said, "allow me to say how very sorry we are about the death of Lord Telford. You have our deepest sympathies, your ladyship."

For a moment I was unable to speak. Then I whispered, "Get out."

She curtseyed neatly and obeyed. Then came the sound of the key turning in the lock, and I was alone once more.

This time I nearly tore the room apart in my search for something that would help me break free. I would have reduced each stick of furniture to splinters, even the gargantuan bed and the famed cradle itself, if it would have helped me. I was still more angry than frightened, and my desolation at having lost Atticus, suppress it though I might, fueled the rage and made it burn all the brighter.

I hardly noticed the passage of time, but as the dinner hour struck, there came a knock at the door and the sound of a key in the lock. Cook entered carrying a tray, followed by Victor and Grigore.

Any wild thoughts I might have had of running for the door were thwarted when Grigore stepped into my path, reminding me of the shaking he had given me earlier. He looked as if he might not stop at shaking me this time.

He could not stop my mouth, though. I demanded of Victor, "How can you let Grigore go about freely when he almost certainly killed Atticus?"

"Now, Clara," he said, with a mildness that infuriated me. "You don't know that he did."

"Ask him, then! See if he can defend himself. He wouldn't answer me, but you speak his language. Make him tell me the truth."

He gave a slight sigh. He was dressed for dinner, and in his formal suit he struck a bizarre contrast with the burly servant in his peasant garb. In a tone of slightly strained patience, he said, "I don't think there is anything to be gained by my doing that. I trust Grigore, and you shall simply have to trust me."

For the moment I forgot that I was addressing a murderer and a madman, whose anger I did not want to awaken. "Trust you?" I burst out. "You have made me your prisoner. I could hardly trust you any less."

Shutting his eyes briefly, he drew in a deep breath, evidently in an effort to keep his temper. "You aren't my prisoner, Clara; you're my betrothed," he said evenly. "I fear you are working yourself into a state of nervous excitement. Please take control of yourself. I should hate to have to ask Mrs. Furness to administer laudanum to you."

This was so clearly a threat that I took myself in hand. The prospect of being drugged into submission made me repress a shudder, and I made myself say calmly, "That won't be necessary."

"I thought as much," he said, brightening. "You are a woman of sense, Clara; I admire that in you. As such, you can surely see that the best course of action is to look to the future, not the past."

Evidently he expected me to somehow put my husband's probable murder out of my mind and focus instead on the future that he was constructing for me. My precarious calm threatened to desert me, especially now that I noticed the cook was laying two places at the table by the fire. "Do you intend to dine with me?" I asked.

Gesturing for me to be seated, he drew a chair up for himself. "I plan to make it our habit each evening. It affords us an excellent opportunity to know each other better." He placed a linen napkin in his lap as the cook served our plates, adding, "By the time you accept me formally as your future husband, you shall have come to feel quite comfortable in my presence."

Comfortable! My hand itched to pick up my plate and throw it in his face. But Grigore took up a position behind him, ready, I was certain, to suppress me if I made any sudden motions. Perhaps I could learn something to my advantage if I stayed calm and minded my manners . . . if, in short, I became a model prisoner.

This evening was to set the pattern for all those to come. Playing the suitor, Victor was never anything but polite and considerate, except in refusing me the one thing that I desired—my freedom. Whether I tried to reason with him or sat in icy silence, he paid me compliments and made conversation about the life we would lead together. I felt like the girl in the fairy tale, held prisoner in an enchanted castle, who each night was forced to repeat her refusal to the Beast who asked her to marry him.

And behind him Grigore always stood, a looming promise that if I lost my head and attacked my captor or attempted to escape I would regret it.

The day after this memorable dinner, I grew more methodical in my search for a means of freeing myself. Carefully, slowly, I examined everything that remained in the room. Mrs. Furness's search had been brief, and she must surely have missed something that could be of use to me. I still believed in the possibility of a hidden entrance, and I retraced my steps in search of it despite Victor's having told me the night before, with a tolerant smile, that none existed.

Adding to my tension was the worry that soon it would become apparent that I was expecting a child. I had no idea whether my captor would find Atticus's child a boon or a threat, and I did not want to gamble on what he might do with that knowledge.

Without any occupation for my days except my search for an escape route, I began to feel as if the balance of my mind was at risk. It was a struggle to keep my grief for Atticus at bay, yet I knew that I had to do exactly that, to remain as calm and logical as possible, in order to thwart my captor's scheme. It occurred to me that Victor might have had Mrs. Furness remove my mother's books and all other forms of passing the time so that I would find his company more pleasing by contrast after hours of empty solitude.

On the fourth day of my captivity, as I had each previous day, I searched my room once again for anything that might be of use to me. Little enough remained; even the bed sheets had been removed after Mrs. Furness discovered that I was tying them into a rope so that I might climb down from the window. Even though I knew I had already thoroughly examined the contents of my mother's trunk, I opened it to search again. Besides the daguerreotype portrait, it now contained nothing but the blue satin dress and a few handkerchiefs.

I regarded the dress with a bittersweet smile as I drew it from the trunk, smoothing out the creases and trying to imagine how my mother would have looked in it.

Then I noticed a strange thing. Under my fingers, the bodice *crackled.*

It was sensation more than sound. Something stiff lay beneath the satin, something more crisp than the interlining generally used in ladies' clothing. When I unlaced the bodice and laid it flat so that I could examine the inside, nothing looked awry, but when I experimentally stroked my fingertips over the area, I felt the outline of something sewn between the layers of fabric. When I held it closer, I could see that in one area a seam had been ripped out and then sewn again in a slightly darker shade of thread.

Something was hidden in the dress.

Without my scissors, I had to bite the thread until it broke. Then I was easily able to pick the stitching out with a hairpin, and I thanked heaven that this dress had been made in the days before machine stitching. When I slipped my hand into the opening between lining and satin, I felt paper. I drew out a yellowed envelope on which *Miriam* was written in a hand that I knew had to be my grandmother's.

My heart gave a little leap of amazed anticipation, and I pulled the letter out of the envelope with a hand that shook with excitement. A letter that someone had gone to such pains to hide would not be a commonplace affair telling of weather and gossip. This was a missive of huge importance.

My dear daughter, it read,
I suspect that you will soon be eloping with Rob Crofton. Despite your father's attempts to force you to give him up, I know how determined you are, and I know how little a parent's prohibitions matter in the face of a love as deep as yours. You are only doing what I did before you—which is why I write to you now to warn you. You need to know the terrible risk that lies before you if you follow your heart, Miriam.

So my mother had married for love, after all. The knowledge brought a sweet measure of peace to my heart even in the midst of my turmoil. Why then, I wondered, had my grandmother painted me such a different picture? Had she found it less painful to endure her daughter's loss if she rewrote history in her mind and remembered my mother as the kind of woman who acted out of calculation instead of love?

Your father will not permit me to tell you why you are forbidden to marry, which is why I must write this letter to you in secret and hide it in the lining of your best dress on the pretext of mending it. I hope that when you run off to marry your young farmer you will take this dress with you. I think you will want it for your wedding dress, and I can only pray that I am right—and that you will find this letter in time to prevent disaster from happening.
I said that I defied my parents in making my marriage. They had arranged a match for me with a distinguished aristocrat, a worthy alliance for our ancient and venerated Romanian lineage. My father was so enraged by my choosing Percival Burleigh that he laid a curse on me and my descendants.

You may laugh, but in the country of my birth, curses are not taken lightly. My family has always claimed to have an uncanny gift, so when my father crafted this curse he did so with the full belief that powers beyond our understanding lay ready to obey his summons.

The curse was that the firstborn sons of my line shall all be monsters.

Now, at this moment you are thinking about your brother Horace, but he was not my first son. Before your birth, I was brought to bed with a son.

I caught my breath. Perhaps I was about to find an explanation for the nameless graveyard marker and the cameo of Niobe.

The delivery was difficult and I was very ill afterward, so I have no direct knowledge of what happened—and would have been powerless to stop it even so. When at last I grew strong enough to ask after my baby, my husband told me our son had been born with such severe deformities that he died of them.

My eyes squeezed shut as if I could unsee those terrible words. The poor woman. No matter what she had become later, I could not help but feel compassion for her and her child.

This threw me into a deep melancholy. Even though I do not know for certain that my husband was lying, my heart tells me that he was unwilling to rear a child so deformed and took steps to relieve himself of that burden. My unspoken fear has poisoned our marriage and has burdened me with dread that someday we may yet be charged with . . . I cannot bring myself to write the word.

My uncle must have shared her knowledge—and her fear. No wonder he had tried to prevent me from learning this chapter of the family history: charges of infanticide might still have been made while my grandmother lived, and even if no legal action took place, the rumor would have been sufficient to destroy their lives. Never mind that he was not culpable; the entire family would have been tainted by the shocking history once it became known.

This is our terrible secret, the reason we have insisted that you and Horace not marry—so that you will not be faced with a decision no parent should be forced to make. It has also caused us to isolate ourselves from society for fear that the world will come to know of the family curse and suspect that the most dreadful of crimes lies beneath the unmarked lamb gravestone in the burial ground.

I beg you to return home before it is too late to stop another monster from being born. Whether or not you return, I implore that you burn this letter, for it can bring nothing but notoriety and shame at best and criminal prosecution at worst, should any of what I have just related become known.

Your father and I have been strict parents, but it was so that you might have a happier life than ours. I pray that our efforts and sacrifices will not have been in vain. Leave your sweetheart before it is too late, and return home to

Your mother

How devastated my grandmother must have been that this trunk had been left behind, and with it her letter. I wondered, though, if my mother's life would have been different in any substantial way had she found this message. I could not imagine her throwing over the man she loved for the sake of what probably would have seemed a preposterous and even unbalanced tale.

Now I faced the question of what to do with the letter, for I could not sew it back into its hiding place. After a struggle with indecision, I tucked it into the bodice of my mourning dress so that it lay against my corset. I had heard it said that knowledge was power. If only there were some way that this tragic knowledge could endow me with the power to escape from Thurnley Hall.

CHAPTER SEVENTEEN

The jingling of keys outside my door seized my attention. I just had time to get to my feet and straighten my dress from sitting on the floor examining the paneling for the hundredth time when the key scraped in the lock and the door swung open. It was the afternoon of the fifth day of my captivity.

"Forgive the intrusion," Victor said, as Thomas carried in one of my trunks. This was not the hour at which he usually visited me. "Plans have changed. We're leaving Thurnley within the hour."

"Leaving Thurnley?" I echoed, as Mrs. Furness bustled in and set about opening drawers and removing their contents. "Why?"

"Never mind why," he said shortly. His manner was strangely agitated. For once he did not attempt to kiss my hand or make charming banter. His eyes darted about the room, and he strode restlessly about, snatching at the window curtains and bed hangings to look behind them, even prodding the bed-clothes and stooping down to peer beneath the bed.

"If it concerns me, I deserve an explanation," I said, speaking sharply to hide the uneasiness mounting within me. "Will you tell me where we are going, at least?"

"I haven't quite determined that. Some place far away, where we can have complete solitude—that is all I know just now." He must have seen my dismay, for he forced a smile and came to take my hand before I could prevent it. "Don't worry, my dear. I shall take good care of you. Soon no one will be able to part us."

That was the most horrifying thing he had yet said. At Thurnley Hall there was still some small chance that I might be found by my friends, since it was the last place I was known to be. It was still possible that George and Vivi or someone from Gravesend would seek me here. If Victor took me to some more obscure location, no one would know where to search for me. And what if it was some truly remote place, far from any village, where escape meant wandering a wasteland with no prospect of any aid at all? It was imperative to stay here.

"I must know why we are leaving," I said, feeling my heartbeat throb in my throat.

His jaw tightened just slightly. "Clara," he said with warning in his voice, "as your affianced husband, I do not have to explain myself to you. You must trust me to make the right decisions. Now please direct Mrs. Furness in packing whatever belongings you wish to take with you. Thomas, help me see to the carriage."

He bowed briefly to me and departed. Before the door shut behind him I glimpsed the inevitable Grigore in the hallway, ever keeping watch.

But despite the anxiety that the prospect of leaving Thurnley awoke in me, I had also seen something that made me take heart. Victor Lynch was frightened. That was why he was suddenly resolved to depart. And although I had no idea what had unsettled him so, anything that woke fear in my captor was almost certain to be a boon to me.

Nevertheless, in alarmingly short order Victor and Grigore arrived to escort me to the carriage. I pleaded for more time—to pack, to change my dress, to pay a final visit to my grandmother's tomb—but to no avail. All too soon I was being hustled out of the house toward the carriage that waited in the drive. Victor relinquished his grip on me to Grigore in order to direct Thomas in strapping the trunks onto the carriage, and the Romanian ignored my protests at his holding my arm so tightly. At my other side was Horace Burleigh. It was the first time we had come face to face in days, and I took a small satisfaction in how haggard he looked.

"Isn't it about time you put a stop to this ridiculous business?" I demanded. "You know this is wrong in the extreme. You have a duty not to allow Victor to proceed."

He refused to look at me. "He is my son, after all."

"No matter whose son he is, you cannot actually condone his kidnapping me and coercing me into marriage!" Despite my conviction, I hissed the words in an undertone so as not to be overheard.

My uncle rubbed his forehead with an unsteady hand. "I don't condone his actions, niece. But I must think of his welfare. It is possible that marriage to you will settle the boy, put an end to his—er—excesses."

"Excesses?" I repeated in disbelief. "Is murder what you call an excess?"

"Quiet!" he snapped, but Thomas and Victor seemed not to have heard; Grigore, though attached to me like a limpet, seemed to be only half aware of us at all, perhaps not understanding what we were saying. "He only needs a healthy occupation to focus his mind," my uncle hedged. "Once he has a child to raise, he shall settle down, I know it."

Could he possibly have convinced himself of this? Observing the man's wobbling stance and bloodshot eyes, which shifted to evade my scrutiny, I could only conclude that he had drowned himself in drink to shut out the reality confronting him. Once Victor and I were out of sight, I suspected, he would convince himself that none of this madness had ever happened, or that it had happened for the best. Contempt for him rose to my lips in the form of blistering words, but losing my temper would not help me. I must try to appeal to the basic human decency that I had to believe lay hidden under the layers of cowardice and self-interest, which he had convinced himself were paternal loyalty.

"You out of all people stand the best chance of stopping him," I whispered. Now Thomas had climbed to the driver's seat of the carriage, and Victor had paused to calm the restless horses; I had very little time. "Don't you owe it to any other innocent people who may fall victim to him? Be a real father to him at last and exercise your authority. Convince him that he must not follow this path."

He darted a glance at his son and moistened his lips nervously. "He wouldn't heed me. Besides, I confess it, I'm afraid to stand against him. After what he did to his own grandmother, why would he not do the same to me if I defied him?"

The rage of helpless frustration boiled in me, and I wished I could physically shake him until his wits awoke. "Can't you think of anyone besides yourself?" I demanded. "Do you really want to be responsible for unleashing a murderer on the world?"

Victor's reappearance at my side forestalled any reply he might have made. "It's time we were going," he said curtly, and my uncle released my arm with a gasp of relief, relinquishing his place to his son.

Now Victor grasped me by one arm, Grigore by the other, and they drew me across the gravel drive toward the carriage with alarming swiftness. My fierce struggles seemed not to delay us in the least. A few more paces, and they would be able to force me inside the carriage, and once inside, I knew with terrible conviction, I would find it nearly impossible to free myself.

"Help me!" I shouted over my shoulder to my uncle, twisting my body to try to break my captors' hold on me. "If you let them do this, I'll see you brought to trial as an accessory!"

He stood there, arms dangling ineffectually, while I writhed and fought. With a lucky blow I managed to bring one foot down hard on Grigore's, and the man growled and gave me a shake that made my hair tumble down around my shoulders.

"Oaf!" I snarled, struggling all the harder.

"I can put you over my shoulder if you prefer, Clara," Victor said. His polite manner seemed strained. "The more you struggle and delay us, the more you force me to be strict with you."

"Have a care!" my uncle called uncertainly. "Be gentle with her, son, for the child's sake."

For the space of three heartbeats Victor went still. Then he said, "Child?"

I knew it was dangerous to let him know of my pregnancy. But Grigore was the greater threat until I was confined within the carriage, and there was the possibility that his heart might be touched if he knew of my condition. These thoughts flew through my mind in an instant, and before I could change my mind, I said clearly, "Yes. I'm carrying my husband's child."

To make certain Grigore understood, I gestured toward my stomach and pantomimed rocking a baby in my arms. His eyes widened under his bushy eyebrows, and his grip on my arm relaxed enough for me to pull my arm from his grasp. Success!

But a ghastly smile was spreading over Victor's face, and he seized the arm that Grigore had let fall and held me even tighter. "A doubly monstrous child," he exclaimed. "Clara, what a prize you are."

"My husband," I gritted, trying to pry his fingers from my arm, "was not a monster."

A new determination seemed to infuse my captor, and he set off toward the carriage again. I dragged at him with my full weight, my feet churning the gravel, but I was only slowing him, not stopping him. "Grigore!" he called. "Assist me, if you please."

The big man hesitated. I had to act quickly, before he regained his resolve. As Victor pulled me closer to the carriage, out of the corner of my eye I glimpsed the restless tossing of the horses' heads, heard their pawing at the gravel. The tussle had made them uneasy, and old Thomas had dropped the reins, so absorbed was he in gaping at the scene unfolding before his eyes.

That gave me an idea. I pulled at Victor, drawing him as hard as I could toward the horses and away from the carriage door, which gaped open in menacing invitation. I needed only a foot or two, and then I was within reach. With the flat of my hand I slapped the hindquarters of the nearer horse as hard as I could, shouting, "Go!" at the top of my lungs.

There was a startled whinny, then the crunch of carriage wheels on the gravel as the horses bolted. Thomas gave a cry as he was almost unseated. The carriage went jolting down the drive and over the bridge that spanned the river, soon disappearing from sight.

"Why, Clara, you hellion," said Victor, almost pleasantly. "I do admire your spirit, but this is not a convenient time or place to exercise it. Time is pressing. Grigore!" he shouted. "What ails you, man? Come and subdue my bride for me. Father, go after the coach and help Thomas if he needs it."

The burly servant seemed to have overcome his scruples, for he began advancing on me with frightening resolve in his eyes. Frantic, I fought against Victor, trying to kick his shins and break his hold on me, but feeling the futility of my struggle increasing with every ponderous pace Grigore took toward us.

Then suddenly Grigore staggered, hunching over with a grunt of pain, and his hand went to his side as though he had been struck there. He caught his balance and turned, revealing a man who had advanced unseen behind him and who straightened now, drawing back his fist from the blow he had administered.

At the sight of his face, everything else seemed to fade into nothingness. All sensation and sound halted; all feeling of the earth under my feet fell away.

It could not be Atticus, of course. My dearest husband was dead. But he looked so much like him, albeit in a bedraggled state and with a week's growth of ginger beard.

Grigore recovered quickly and advanced on him, and the man dealt him a rapid succession of blows to the midsection that made the bigger man stagger back. Then the man with the ginger beard looked toward me.

"Lynch," he said, "I'll thank you to let go of my wife."

At the sound of that familiar husky voice I gasped, and at the same time I felt a shock jar Victor. It wasn't my imagination, then. Atticus was alive. It was impossible—but there he was.

"Baron?" my uncle exclaimed, as thunderstruck as I was. "How the devil—"

But Victor's voice, shrill with fear, cut him off. "What are you doing here?" he cried.

Atticus leveled a look at him that would have made any man quail. "I am here to stop you," he said.

Euphoria flooded my veins, tingling like starlight, warm as sunshine. Then I cried out a warning as Grigore swung a hamlike fist at him, and Atticus ducked it neatly before moving back in to pop the giant on the jaw with a well-placed punch. It was too soon to celebrate yet.

With renewed energy I fought against Victor. Fear seemed to have stunned him, and I was able to free one arm and jab backward with my elbow, feeling a fierce satisfaction when it made contact with his face. He gave a cry and released me, and I ran for the two struggling figures as fast as I could.

Atticus was holding his own against the giant, but I was not going to make him fight alone. I snatched up a handful of gravel and aimed a stone at Grigore's head as he advanced on Atticus, and when the bigger man turned his head to look for what had hit him, Atticus delivered a magnificent blow that made Grigore stagger back and lose his balance. He fell heavily to the ground, throwing a hand in front of him as he had done once before. Then he fumbled at the neck of his smock and drew out a cross on a leather thong, holding it up as if it would protect him.

"Heaven protect me!" he groaned in heavily accented English. "Begone, *strigoi!*"

Atticus was breathing hard with exertion, but his stance was confident and he scarcely limped at all as he advanced on the cowering figure. "You idiot," he said. "There are no such things as vampires."

Then, with one more swift blow, he leveled the giant. Grigore lay unconscious on the gravel.

With a sob of joy and disbelief I ran to Atticus. He caught me in his arms and held me tightly, burying his face in my hair. "Clara," he whispered. "My dearest love."

"I thought you were dead." I was desperate for the tangible reality of his body against mine, his hair under my hands, his rough beard against my cheek. I ran my hands over his shoulders and chest, reassuring myself that he was truly alive and whole, and gazed up into his face. There were lines of weariness etched in his face, as well as bruises and half-healed places where the skin had been broken, but his dazzling blue eyes and their tender expression were unchanged.

"You're really here?" I cried. "I'm not dreaming, I know it, but . . . if I am, please don't wake me, Atticus." I said it again because it gave me such delight to be able to speak his name. "Atticus. My love."

The smile that curved his expressive mouth was a sight I had believed I would never see again, and I found my vision blurring with tears as he took my face in his hands. "There's no need to cry," he said softly. "This is no dream. We'll never be parted again."

It was his kiss that at last fully convinced me that he was returned to me. At the touch of his lips on mine the grief and fear dissolved, and I was enveloped in a joy too profound for words. After feeling lost for all these dark days, I had found my home again . . . my haven.

The sound of voices brought me back to the present. "Don't try to run off," came the stern tones of my uncle. "It's futile to fight any longer, do you hear? Not now that the baron has returned."

"You've no call to treat me this way," said Victor petulantly. It was understandable for him to sound put out, for his father held him firmly by one ear, a grip both embarrassing and, to judge by the young man's fidgeting and glaring, more than a little uncomfortable. His nose streamed with blood where my elbow had struck it, I was gratified to observe. Seeing him so undignified, as if he were a schoolboy caught stealing apples, it was almost possible to forget how much power he had wielded over me and the entire household just minutes before. "I've done nothing wrong," he insisted. "You can't keep me here against my will."

"Until just a short time ago, I was saying much the same thing to you." My husband's eyes were steely as he regarded the younger man. "Burleigh, your son has held me prisoner now for more than a week. He slipped me a note to lure me out of the house in the night so that Grigore could abduct me."

So it had all been a smooth lie, Victor's supposed ignorance of what had happened to Atticus. He had even persuaded me to delay our departure from Thurnley so that he could carry out his despicable plan. I had actually pitied him for his loneliness, when he was manipulating me all the while. Even the broken walking stick and the fabric torn from my husband's waistcoat—which was otherwise intact—had been deliberately planted to make me believe he was dead.

Rage ignited within me, and I wanted to run at Victor and make him bleed afresh. Instead, I held Atticus close. No revenge was worth parting from him.

"When I regained consciousness," he continued, "I found that I was locked in a cellar room. I eventually learned it was located in the ruined wing of the house."

"So close by all this time?" I cried, stricken. "I had no idea any part of that wing was still intact. Atticus, I'll never forgive myself for not searching more thoroughly. To think of you, alone and suffering . . ."

"Don't torment yourself, my love. It was impossible for you to know. When I escaped, I found that the entrance was very carefully disguised with some quite convincing rubble. Besides, I'm certain that Lynch was careful to have Grigore or someone else in his employ guarding it so that he could draw off any searchers who came too close."

"The little boy who slipped," I remembered. "Victor, you sent him to search there deliberately, didn't you? You knew that if people were in danger of hurting themselves searching the ruins I would call a halt to it. And I played into your hands."

"I'm sure I don't know what you're talking about," said the young man calmly. "Grigore may have found a way to hide out on the property after I told him that my father was throwing him out with not a shilling to his name, and he may well have attacked the baron, but there's no way to prove that I had anything to do with that."

"So you manipulated him into going into hiding and working for you," I said. "What was the point of that?"

"He was already planning to take me prisoner," Atticus said grimly. "He remembered that I had been trained in bare-knuckle fighting, so he needed someone of Grigore's size and strength to overpower me. Of course, Grigore took some persuading, but armed with enough garlic and holy water, he seemed to find the courage he needed." He touched one of the scabbed places on his brow. "I owed Grigore a few blows in exchange for those he gave me," he said with rueful humor. "I daresay we're closer to even now."

"With all due respect, baron, your account makes no sense," said my uncle. He was looking more sickened and subdued as the plot unfolded, but he evidently felt driven to stand up for his son. "If the boy's purpose was to elope with your wife, he could have simply lured her away. Why go to the trouble of taking you prisoner and then waiting several days before taking her away from Thurnley?"

"To study Atticus," I said, as fragments of memory joined together and the dreadful answer took form in my mind. "Your son is fascinated by monsters, and he suspected that my husband might be one. If not a vampire, as Grigore believed, then something that he could observe and learn from. Is that right?"

Atticus nodded. "He persists in thinking that my brother actually came back from the dead, though I've done my best to disabuse him of the notion, and is obsessed with the idea that my family possesses some kind of secret to immortality. If I did have any kind of supernatural powers, I would certainly have used them to escape."

"How did you manage it?" I asked, tightening my arms around him. I felt I could not be sure enough that he was with me again, that he would not be taken from me once more. As if sensing my thoughts, he smiled down at me and pressed his lips to my forehead before he spoke again.

"Grigore was too cautious, in a way," he said. "Earlier today when he passed me bread and water through the aperture in the door, he placed a metal crucifix just inside the threshold—to keep me secure, as he thought. It was thin enough that I was able to use it to pry the hinges off the door. I kept out of sight and soon learned that you were a prisoner as well." He gave my uncle a hard look. "I'm still awaiting an explanation as to why you let that happen, Burleigh."

My uncle cleared his throat uncomfortably. "Well, my boy has a bit of a volatile temperament, don't you know. I thought a feminine influence might be healthy . . ."

"Don't listen to him," I said bitterly. "He's been too intimidated by Victor to stand up to him."

"As well he might be," said the young man. "None of you has yet seen the full extent of my power."

The menace in his tone gave me a flicker of doubt. As cowed as he had looked minutes ago, he seemed to be recovering his resolve—and it might be dangerous to be so confident that he was defeated. But before I could suggest placing him under restraints, he continued, "As for you, Telford, you've no proof of any of this. It's simply your word against mine."

"On the contrary," Atticus said, "I do have proof, which you kindly provided." Keeping one arm around me, with his other hand he reached into the pocket hidden under the lapel of his waistcoat. "This is the note he sent me," he said, holding it out for my uncle.

Victor's dark eyes flared. "So that's where you hid it. Only scoundrels have secret pockets, sir."

Whether or not that was true, I was thankful I had provided the waistcoat with that extra pocket. My uncle unfolded the paper. "'Lord Telford, I've stumbled upon something that Grigore and my guardian are trying to keep secret, and it may have terrible consequences for your wife,'" he read aloud. "'Their habit is to meet in the burial grounds in the hour before dawn so as to go unseen about their dark doings. I beg you to come see for yourself. Lynch.' Pretty clear, I'd say." Folding the paper, he made as if to place it in the breast pocket of his coat, but Atticus held out his hand for it. "I think it's time I brought in the authorities," my uncle said in a voice heavy with regret, yielding the note to him. "I've let you go unchecked too long, Victor. It's time you faced the consequences of your actions."

"You would see your own son hauled away in irons like some common criminal?" The young man's voice was more affronted than frightened, and I was filled with sudden anger that he should act the injured party when he had done so much damage.

"You *are* a criminal," I retorted. "I will make certain you are put on trial for what you've done. For the murder of our grandmother, for a start."

His dark eyes were reproachful. "You wouldn't do that to me, Clara," he said, and his voice had taken on that deceptively gentle quality that had disguised his true nature for so long. "How could you live with yourself if they hanged me because of your testimony?"

"If you are hanged," Atticus told him, "it will be no one's fault but your own. You are the one who killed her. The guilt is yours entirely."

A new voice said, "Victor did not kill Mrs. Burleigh."

Though the words were quiet, their unexpectedness made me jump. Unnoticed and unheard, Mrs. Furness had joined us. A parcel in her hands suggested that she had been preparing something for the journey that had detained her until now.

"But he confessed," I protested, recovering from my surprise. "He told me himself that he did it." The memory made me hold more tightly to Atticus, who had been at the mercy of that killer for more than a week.

Mrs. Furness set down the parcel and stood quietly with her hands folded in front of her in her usual docile demeanor, which made her words seem all the more grotesque by contrast. "Victor meant to kill her," she said calmly. "He choked her until she lost consciousness. I saw it all from the doorway to Mrs. Burleigh's sitting room, though he did not see me. But after he left the room, she came to."

"What?" Victor burst out. "Impossible!"

"She was hoarse and had difficulty speaking, but it was clear that she remembered what he had tried to do to her—and she was going to tell everyone about it." She lifted her chin proudly. "I finished the job that he had started. I couldn't see my boy put away for trying to kill a miserable old lady who was dying already."

We all stared, shocked into silence. That she had killed my grandmother with such calculation, and that she could speak so calmly of it, made me feel ill. My uncle's face had gone the color of putty, and he was regarding the housekeeper with a look so appalled that I knew he had had no knowledge of this.

Strangely, Victor looked most shaken of all of us. His already pale skin had gone even whiter. "What do you mean by *your boy?*" he asked in an unsteady voice.

The housekeeper's bosom rose as she took a deep breath. "I am your mother," she said in the same composed manner. "I never intended for you to know, but it seems that the time has come."

He recoiled from her. "But you're a servant!" he exclaimed, and the scorn in his voice made the housekeeper flinch.

"I can't change the circumstances of my birth," she said quietly, "or yours. But I want to help you in every way I can. You can call on me for anything, Victor. I only want your happiness."

For a moment he was entirely still except for the rapid rise and fall of his chest, the only sign of his turbulent feelings. Then, wrenching himself out of the grasp of his father, he advanced on her—but the look in his eyes was not gratitude. The housekeeper fell back as he stalked toward her, her first sign of uncertainty.

"You selfish old slut," he hissed at her. "You've taken everything from me. My identity, my destiny—I was going to be feared. To strike awe into people's hearts." He was forcing her down the drive toward where it bridged the river. I wondered if his intention was to scare her off or chivy her away from Thurnley. My uncle hurried after, and Atticus and I followed, with him leaning on me in the absence of his walking stick. "Do you have any idea of the power that was almost mine?" Victor continued, his voice growing shrill. "I was so close to being the complete and perfect monster."

"You aren't a monster, Victor," she said pleadingly, but his steps did not falter, and she backed away more rapidly. "Don't you see, that's what this means: you haven't committed murder. You don't have that crime on your soul."

"Crime!" His voice rose without warning to a near scream. His eyes were like charred holes in white paper. "That was my single greatest achievement, the apex of my power and magnificence, and you tell me that it was an illusion—that a woman had to finish my work for me because I was too weak to do the job myself!" Before any of us could stop him, his hands shot out and he seized her about the throat. "This time I won't need anyone to finish my work for me," he grated.

"Let her go!" Atticus shouted, and my uncle gave a startled, wavering cry, but it was Grigore who unexpectedly hurtled across the gap to seize Victor.

I did not know how much he had heard or understood about Victor's schemes, but he knew enough to recognize that the housekeeper was in danger. The momentum of the impact sent the three of them staggering toward the bridge. He shook Victor by the shoulder, but the young man's grip did not slacken, and I was horrified to see Mrs. Furness's face turning dark red and her hands plucking at his fingers in an attempt to loosen his hold.

"Stop him!" I cried, but Victor stepped back and away from Grigore's grasp. With a guttural, ominous sound Grigore advanced and brought down a big hand on the slighter man's shoulder. Victor twisted to throw his hand off.

If he had not been so determined upon his grisly work, he might have saved himself. If he had only reached out to regain his balance, to clutch Grigore's arm or hand. But instead, in that instant he lost his balance and fell backward off the bridge, carrying his mother with him. His head struck a rock, and I cried out as he and Mrs. Furness disappeared beneath the surface of the dark, churning water.

CHAPTER EIGHTEEN

My uncle gave a cry and ran for the riverbank, shouting his son's name. I could have told him it was futile, but if he had not seen what I had, it was probably more merciful not to tell him of it. But then, perhaps he already knew in his heart that his son was dead and simply wanted to thrust the belief away from him for as long as he could.

The sound of carriage wheels on the drive gave me all the reason I needed to look away from the swiftly running river. I had expected to see Thomas returning, but instead the coach drawing near was unknown to me. Scarcely had the driver reined in than the door opened and a familiar but unexpected figure came hurtling out.

"There you are!" Vivi cried, her arms opening wide. She wore a mantle over her traveling dress that disguised her figure, but there was no mistaking those Titian ringlets and wide blue eyes. "What is the meaning of that strange telegram you sent? And why have you answered none of my letters? I was so anxious that I insisted to George that we must come see you."

"Vivi, how glad I am to see you." I released Atticus long enough to hug my niece, and over her shoulder I saw George Bertram descend from the carriage. Behind him were two men in police uniform, a sight that filled me with relief so acute that my legs almost buckled beneath me.

"It is a relief to see the two of you as well," said George, who had overheard my words to Vivi. He reached out his hand, and Atticus shook it heartily. "We've been most perplexed about you."

"Perplexed and vexed," Vivi confirmed. "Why, Uncle Atticus, have you decided to grow a beard?" She wrinkled her nose. "It may take me some time to become accustomed to it."

Atticus's laugh sounded rusty, as if he had not used it lately. Indeed, neither of us had had much cause for amusement for many days. He took her by the shoulders and kissed her forehead. "It isn't a permanent addition," he said. "I'm touched that the two of you came to seek us out. If you had arrived just a few minutes earlier you could have helped us fight off our captors."

"Captors, my lord?" one of the constables inquired. "What exactly has been going on here, sir?"

Atticus started to speak, then changed his mind and shook his head. "The telling will take some time," he said. "Perhaps we can save the complete details of our report for tomorrow, after we have had a chance to rest. For now, be sure to take Grigore here into custody."

"He has a great deal to answer for," I confirmed. "In addition to attacking my husband, he conspired with Mr. Lynch to keep us both prisoner. As for my uncle—"

But an urgent plucking at my elbow stopped my words, and I found that my uncle himself, unobserved, had made his way to me. He drew me aside a few paces.

"Don't have them arrest me," he whispered piteously. "I beg you, niece."

"And why should I not?" I returned, but likewise in a whisper. "You deserve to be."

He clutched at my arm. "Be merciful. Give me a chance to change your mind. I am your kin, remember, and—"

"Oh, very well," I said, as much to put an end to his pleas as to be generous. "Come speak to me tomorrow, and we shall see. Mind you don't run off in the night, or I *will* have the constables pursue you."

He withdrew with hasty reassurances, which I scarcely heeded. He was not my chief concern now.

"This sounds like quite a nasty business," George was saying as I returned to Atticus's side. "There will need to be an investigation, I take it?" When Atticus confirmed it with a short nod, his earnest expression grew more concerned. "And it looks as though you've been involved in some fisticuffs, Telford. Neither of you has come to any harm, I hope?"

"I don't think so," I said, since the question seemed to be aimed at me. Perhaps Vivi had confided my news in him and he was concerned about the baby, but I did not give him a chance to ask. "Atticus, Grigore didn't injure you severely, did he?"

"He and Lynch did me no permanent damage, my love." Then he shifted his weight and grimaced. "I should be glad of a new walking stick, though."

Afterward Atticus and I spoke briefly with the police in a private room at the village inn. George had wired ahead for the constables to meet him and Vivi at Coley, so they knew as little as he about the events that had taken place at Thurnley. They were, to put it mildly, astonished at the tale we had to tell. They had taken Grigore into custody but agreed that we could give our full accounts the next day, after we had had a chance to recover.

We emerged to find that Vivi had appropriated the entire second floor of the inn for our use. Issuing orders with all the aplomb of a major general, she was overseeing the laying of a meal in the sitting room. "And mind you bring only the best wine!" she instructed a young footman, who bowed his way out of the room with as much deference as if she had been the queen.

The innkeeper's daughter showed Atticus and me to adjoining rooms, where fires already burned cozily and there was hot water ready for washing. As soon as Atticus had withdrawn to his room, leaving the door open a crack so that we could converse, I startled the girl by ripping my mourning dress off with such vigor that the buttons popped off. The thing had come to feel as much like a prison as my room at Thurnley.

"After I've finished changing, take this away and burn it," I told her. I would never be able to look at it again without thinking of the horrible days during which I had believed Atticus to be dead.

I washed quickly and bundled my hair into the simplest of chignons, for I did not want to be away from Atticus any longer than I absolutely had to be. My trunks had already arrived—Vivi's doing, no doubt—and the innkeeper's daughter helped me into a dinner dress. But when it came time to lace me up the back, I dismissed her and went to the door to Atticus's room.

He had finished washing and stood half dressed before the mirror, shaving. Such an inconsequential activity, or so I would have thought before his disappearance, but tonight it filled me with joy to watch him. My husband was alive and with me, and every moment together was a gift to be treasured.

When he saw me in the mirror, he smiled. "Just clearing away this foliage," he said. "I feel almost myself again."

Half of his chin was smooth already. I closed the door behind myself and came to stand at his side, so that when he set the razor aside I was ready to dab the last of the lather from his face with a linen towel. He began to slip his arms around me, but I put a hand to his chest to stop him.

"I need your assistance," I told him. "This dress laces up the back, you see."

His smile brought the familiar crinkles to the corners of his eyes. "And you trust me to lace you up, do you?"

I turned my back to him, but I could not resist peeking back over my shoulder. "I have it on good authority that you are rather handy with a lady's laces," I said demurely.

His chuckle was like a warm, cozy blanket settling over me, a sound that spoke of all that was comforting in my life—a sound I had once thought I would never hear again. Taking up the end of the cord that fastened my bodice, he worked at his task for a time. Presently he asked, "Do you remember the night of the ball, when you asked me to unlace you?"

"I shall never forget it. It was that night when you asked me to become your wife in more than name." And I had said yes—without even knowing why, out of some instinct deeper than reason, wiser than thought.

He tied off the cord and tucked the ends under my bodice. Then his hands glided across my back to my shoulders, and he turned me to face him. "Our marriage may have had a rocky start," he said softly, "thanks in large part to my blundering, but I'd say we've made a smashing success of it. Wouldn't you agree?"

I twined my arms around his neck. Looking into the endless blue of his eyes was like floating up into heaven, and only the touch of his hands kept me anchored here on earth. "A smashing success," I echoed. "Oh, my dearest—"

But he stopped my words with a kiss, then followed it with another. As with most of my husband's ideas, I found myself in complete agreement with him, and conversation ceased for a time.

Then came the sound of the door opening, and George's voice said, "Telford, are you nearly ready? Oh, I beg your pardon, my lady. I didn't know you were here."

"Just give me a moment to finish dressing," said Atticus, without taking his eyes from me. "My wanton wife here waylaid me."

"Atticus!" I exclaimed, half mortified, half delighted.

At the sound of my voice, Vivi joined her husband in the doorway. "Still not dressed, *au nom du ciel!*" she cried. "Your dinner will soon be cold. And more to the point, I am longing to hear about your adventures."

"That is not the word I would have chosen," I said darkly.

"Then you must come and disabuse me," said my niece, undaunted. "Do let Uncle Atticus finish dressing, Aunt Clara."

In truth, I saw no reason for him to do so when going shirtless suited him so very well. Nevertheless, he was able to complete the task swiftly when I ceased to detain him, and soon the four of us were gathered around the table. Roast hens with potatoes and turnips looked as tempting to me as any of the fine dinners we had ever served guests at Gravesend. My appetite had been poor during my imprisonment, but now that it had reawakened I was ravenous.

"Tell us first how the two of you came to be here," I said, taking up my fork to taste the chicken, which was sending up a beckoning finger of steam.

"Vivi and I thought it strange that we hadn't received any letters from you," George said. "Especially when we had written ourselves. Then came a telegram saying that your grandmother had died, Lady Telford, and that the two of you were staying for her funeral. Then nothing again for almost a week, and then a telegram saying that you had decided to travel to Switzerland to visit a home for distressed gentlewomen there in case it might offer any ideas for improvements to the Blackwood Homes."

"That would have been the work of my uncle," I said. "I found out after the fact that he had been detaining all our mail, both incoming and outgoing, as well as sending false messages. He sent the second telegram to assuage your suspicions."

"Well, it did rather the opposite. It seemed so extreme and sudden a change of plan, especially when you both knew how close the new Home is to completion and how vital your guidance is, Telford. So I wired back, and when there was no reply after several days, Vivi convinced me that we needed to investigate."

"Now, tell us what happened to you," Vivi commanded. "Is it true that you were held prisoner, uncle?"

"I was," he said quietly. "Lynch hoped that he could learn secrets of supernatural power from observing me."

"Supernatural power?" she exclaimed. She looked from him to me in search of a sign to indicate whether he was making a jest. "Did he believe that your nickname meant you were one of the ancient gods, Uncle Atlas?"

My husband's smile was a bit strained. "I'm not certain whether that would have been better or worse than being suspected of vampirism."

Her blue eyes widened in astonishment. "He thought you were a vampire? What could possibly have led him to think such a thing? That is absurd!"

This time Atticus's smile was closer to its normal self. "Believe me, I tried to tell him so. But he was convinced he could garner occult knowledge from studying me. He even drew some of my blood and took hair clippings so that he could perform experiments." When I exclaimed in horror, Atticus reached across the table to take my hand. "It's all right, my love. I'm no worse for wear."

"This is shocking, Telford," George exclaimed. His kind young face was stricken, as if this was the first time he had encountered such depravity . . . as perhaps it was. "Did no one hear you call for help? Or were you drugged?"

"Nothing could be heard from the habitable part of the house, or so Lynch said," Atticus replied. "That didn't prevent me from yelling at the top of my voice at first, but I soon found that Grigore had been given orders to make me stop. I was shackled, so he had the advantage of me."

Despite his oblique way of putting it, my heart constricted at the implication of the violence he had suffered. I felt a fierce satisfaction that Atticus had returned some of the blows tonight. "Were you not shackled today, then?" I asked.

"Grigore, as you know, is not terribly bright," he responded. "I soon found that I could slip the shackles when he wasn't looking. But until I had a way to escape the cell, it did me no good. The waiting was worse than any beating, especially with Lynch going on about the family he intended to raise with you, Clara." His icy blue eyes were haunted. "It was nightmarish to know that he could be mistreating you, without me to prevent him."

I shuddered. "I suppose I should be grateful that his peculiar code of honor held him in check. Believing as I did that he had killed my grandmother, I was afraid of awakening that murderous rage."

"Killed your grandmother?" Vivi burst out, and I had to go back and explain things from the beginning.

"Then, when he had kidnapped Atticus, he must have countermanded all of the telegrams I sent for assistance," I said. Looking back at that visit to the station, I realized that Victor had accompanied me and then lingered behind with just that aim in mind. "It is no wonder no one came to our aid, with both my uncle and Victor interfering with my every message. But I suppose he eventually realized that I wouldn't stop the search as long as I believed he was alive. So he planted evidence along the riverside to make it look as though Atticus had drowned or been murdered. And I believed it."

My voice gave out, and I had to shut my eyes to try to collect myself. His hand pressed mine reassuringly, and the touch seemed to infuse me with some of his strength. "I don't want to speak of it any more tonight," I said briskly, opening my eyes and smiling at the faces of those I loved. "Just now, all I want to do is celebrate that we are alive and that we have escaped that dreadful place."

"Hear, hear," George exclaimed, raising his glass. "I hope we never have cause to mount a rescue party for you again."

"That suits me quite well," Atticus returned, touching the rim of his glass to George's. "Now Clara and I want to hear all about your doings. Tell us everything that has happened in Cornwall since we left. Vivi, are you keeping healthy?"

How glorious it was to simply eat our dinner together and enjoy normal conversation again, to bring my mind back from the recent horrors to contemplate our real lives back at Gravesend. The cheerful talk of those I held most dear restored my spirits, just as the hearty meal replenished my body. A deep contentment filled me.

In a momentary lull in the conversation, Atticus said softly, "You're very quiet, my love."

I smiled to reassure him. "I'm just enjoying feeling peaceful. It seems like a long time since I've felt this way—and it must be even longer for you."

"Indeed. Having returned from the dead now myself, I can safely say I've had enough excitement for two lifetimes."

"Well, not *all* excitement is to be avoided," Vivi said. "Perhaps, Aunt Clara, there is another reason to celebrate?" She raised an inquiring eyebrow at me.

I had realized during our discussion with the police that Atticus had arrived at the scene of the fray too late to hear about my pregnancy. Now that I had been granted this miraculous second chance, I knew I did not want to delay any longer.

"If you and George wouldn't mind," I said, "may Atticus and I have a moment alone?"

George's baffled but polite expression as he pushed back his chair and stood made it clear that he had no idea what his wife meant, and I felt a rush of gratitude that he had not known sooner than Atticus. I ought to have known that Vivi could be relied upon.

"It's time Vivi and I left you in any case," he said. "After the day you've had—the week, I should say!—you two must be longing to recover in peace. We'll see you in the morning."

As Vivi passed behind Atticus and out of his range of vision she blew me a kiss. *"Dormez bien,"* she said archly.

When the door had closed behind them, Atticus turned an inquiring look toward me. "There is more good news?" he asked.

"Have you learned anything more of your father?"

"No," I said. "This is about us." Despite my resolve I found that there was a nervous fluttering beneath my ribs, and suddenly the width of the table that separated us was too great a distance. "Sit by the fire with me, won't you?"

Soon we were seated close together on the old-fashioned, high-backed settle. I took both his hands in mine and drew a deep breath.

"There is something I had intended to tell you on your birthday," I began, "but after we encountered that Munro woman I was afraid the news would be unwelcome. And then after we arrived at Thurnley Hall, when we discovered what dreadful people my family were . . ."

He squeezed my hands reassuringly. "As were mine, my love."

"Well, at any rate, I was afraid. It was cowardly of me, and I ought to have trusted in you, but I held back. So now, at last, I am telling you." Yet I was still finding ways to put off the telling. I looked into his brilliant eyes, gently quizzical now but nevertheless full of his love for me, and I said, "We're going to have a child, Atticus."

For a moment I could not tell whether he had even heard me, for he was completely still. Then he said quietly, "Are you certain?"

I nodded, feeling apprehension creeping back despite all my resolve as I waited for him to say something more. Why was he so quiet?

Then he pulled me into his arms, and he was laughing and kissing me and murmuring endearments, all at once, it seemed. "A child!" he exclaimed, and when he drew back to look at me the joy in his face was unmistakable. "My darling Clara, I should be horsewhipped for making you afraid to tell me. I didn't dare to dream this could come to pass, so I was trying to reconcile myself . . . I never realized I was causing you distress."

Relief and happiness were breaking over me like a wave, but I had to say something more. "I understand why it worries you not to know what we might pass on to our baby," I said. "But he'll have more than a blood inheritance, Atticus. His legacy shall also be all of the love and wisdom that we pass on to him."

"Of course it shall." He rested his hand gently on my abdomen, and even through my layers of clothing I felt the warmth of his touch, like a blessing bestowed on me and our baby. "I've no fear any longer, Clara."

"Then you are happy about it?" I asked unnecessarily, simply for the pleasure of hearing him confirm it.

For answer he took my face in his hands and kissed my lips with utmost tenderness. When he raised his head, the wondering love that shone in his eyes took my breath away. "More than I can possibly say," he whispered. "I wish I could show you just how happy you've made me."

The words awoke a distant echo, and a spirit of devilry suddenly took life in me. How could I let such a perfect opportunity pass, when I had vowed to turn the tables on my roguish husband?

I tried to look demure as I said, "There is one means that has proven quite effective in conveying that message."

An expression of astonished delight slowly broke over his face. "Why, baroness," he said huskily, "what a scandalous . . . shocking . . . irresistible suggestion."

"Not merely a suggestion, dearest. A request."

His laugh was so jubilant that I feared it would be overheard by the others many rooms away. As he rose and drew me to my feet to lead me to the bedchamber, I could not resist saying, "I told you I would astonish you one day."

He drew me close and whispered in my ear. What he said I shall not divulge, but suffice it to say that, once again, my husband made me blush.

Atticus and I were breakfasting alone the next morning when the innkeeper's daughter announced my uncle's arrival. Rather than have him invade our living space, temporary though it was, I told her I would receive him in the downstairs parlor.

"I'll accompany you," Atticus said, reaching for his suit coat. "I know you are more than equal to dealing with the man, but I'll be just outside the door if you wish for me—if he should need to be physically restrained, for example."

"I rather hope he shall," I said. "I think I would enjoy seeing that."

As soon as I stepped into the parlor and saw my uncle, however, I knew that no force would be required against him. He was much changed from when we had first met. The last traces of his abrasive heartiness and pomposity had vanished, and in their place was a subdued, even meek demeanor. His clothes were as rumpled as though he had slept in them—if he had slept at all. His eyes were bloodshot still, and he eyed me rather as the accused prisoner in the dock would regard the judge . . . which was apt, considering our relative positions.

He did not trouble with pleasantries. "What have you told the constables about me?" were his first words, blurted out in an anxious rush. "Am I to be jailed, as you promised?"

"I told the police what Victor and Grigore had done," I said, "and about Mrs. Furness's confession. I have not disclosed the part you played in the whole terrible business—not yet," I added repressively, as his face lit up. "Accessory to an attempt to kidnap is a serious business."

"I am sorry for that, niece." The words emerged stiffly, as though the act of apologizing was new to him. "I—I was not myself."

"You were very much yourself," I said dryly. "Circumstances and liquor notwithstanding, you maintained the self-interest you have shown throughout our acquaintance. What do you have to say for yourself? Why should I not tell the police everything that you did?"

"But what did I do, really?" he pleaded. "Apart from tampering with your letters and sending telegrams in your name, I can't actually be said to have *done* anything. I stayed out of Victor's way, that is all, as anyone would have."

"You did more than that. You lied for him when you thought he had committed murder. You actively thwarted my attempts to summon help. When Atticus vanished, you may not have known with complete certainty that Victor had abducted him, but you knew he was the most likely suspect—and yet you did nothing." The thought of Atticus shackled and beaten made my voice sharpen. "Then, for all the days of my imprisonment, you seem to have made no attempt to stop your son or to alert the authorities. What you call staying out of his way was abetting him. And then, when he decided to remove me to captivity somewhere else, you actually laid hands on me to try to force me into the carriage." My heart was beating more rapidly as the sickening feeling of horror and helplessness came back to me, and I fell silent, trying to calm myself.

He moistened his lips. "I don't know if I can make you understand," he said with unusual hesitancy, "for you aren't a parent—not yet. Even though Victor and I gave each other nothing but unhappiness, and even though there were times when I genuinely feared him, he was my son, and I could not see him treated as a criminal. It strained my loyalty almost past enduring to protect him when I believed he had killed my mother, but there was never a moment when another course seemed conceivable." His eyes were dull and defeated as he contemplated the past. "And yet he felt no such loyalty to me. It is a terrible thing to be frightened of one's own child, niece. Pray that you never know what that is like."

To fear the very person one loved best—that must be a terrible burden. At the same time, I wondered how much he recognized his own culpability in his son's actions. Bloodlines alone did not make monsters, I knew. It was not the circumstances of Victor's birth but everything that followed thereafter that had made him into the twisted, desperate creature he was. Had my uncle been a better parent, perhaps Victor would have been a better man.

"If you hadn't been so quick to protect him, perhaps you would have learned sooner that the real culprit was Mrs. Furness," I said, realizing that I had never learned her first name. "Did you ask the doctor to fill out my grandmother's death certificate in such a way as to protect Victor from suspicion?"

Some ruddy color crept into his cheeks. "I knew that he would be willing to stretch a point as a favor to me."

"So we can add conspiring on a fraudulent death certificate to the list of your crimes."

"I suppose so." After a moment, he added in a low voice, "He's been found, did you know? Both of them were retrieved from the river early this morning."

Despite all he had done—and, equally bad, all that he had permitted to be done through his passivity—I felt a flicker of compassion for him. "Identifying them must have been dreadful."

He shrugged and walked over to the fire, probably as much to escape the necessity of meeting my eyes as to enjoy its warmth. "At least I can bury my boy," he said without looking at me. "And mourn him."

"And Mrs. Furness? Does she have family to claim her, or shall you at last do right by her?"

"She'll have a plot near the boy's," he said grudgingly. "Perhaps an unmarked one, but devil take it, the woman wasn't a Burleigh and can't expect to be treated like one."

He found her an inconvenience, and yet her role in this sorry business was his fault alone. My voice was distinctly colder when I said, "Perhaps if you had not forced yourself upon her and then barred her from all but the briefest contact with her son, she would not have become unbalanced. The least you can do now is put her name on her gravestone."

After a hesitation, he shrugged and said gruffly, "I suppose so. Very well."

Silence fell. I was curious to see how he would end it, so I did not speak. For a time he stared down at the cuff of his coat and picked at a stain on it. Presently, without looking at me, he mumbled, "I suppose that when we next meet it will be in a court of law, with you bearing witness against me."

I had discussed it with Atticus, and even before I had left the breakfast table I had decided that there was little point in turning my uncle over to the law. Now that I saw how diminished he was, I knew that I had made the correct decision. Many of his actions had been motivated by love for Victor, who was now dead, and still more by fear—fear for his own skin, for his son, and even *of* his son. Without that goad, he seemed to lack the motivation to do further harm. Certainly, this broken husk of a man showed no sign of having the wherewithal to pit himself against anyone.

"When I speak to the constables today I shall confine my testimony to what I know about Victor's actions, and Grigore's," I said. "I'll not implicate you."

His body drooped as he gave a mighty sigh of relief.

"Of course, I have certain conditions—"

"I accept them all," he exclaimed before I could finish. Closing the distance between us in three strides, he seemed on the point of embracing me, but a look at my face stopped him. Instead he seized my right hand and shook it so vigorously that my earrings danced. "I am forever grateful, my girl—that is to say, my lady. Thank you one thousand times. You'll not regret your compassion."

I doubted he would be as cheerful once he heard the conditions. I had worried that they were too strict, but Atticus had told me that, if anything, they erred on the side of leniency.

"The first and most important condition," I said, "is that you sell your property, including Thurnley Hall."

He dropped my hand as if it had turned into red-hot iron and gaped at me. Before he could respond, I continued, "The second is that you leave England and never return."

"Leave England?" His voice was strangled. "And sell Thurnley! Do you mean to ruin me?"

"I mean for you to no longer exercise any power over others by virtue of being one of the landed gentry . . . and to go far away from those whom you have harmed, either directly or indirectly." As he struggled to come to grips with this vision of his future, I added sternly, "Be advised that Atticus and I shall set a watch on you to make certain that you abide by my terms. Don't think that it will escape our notice if you try to renege— or if anyone else ever comes to harm because of you, whether through action or inaction. And if that should happen, you may rest assured that before the next day dawns I shall be giving the authorities a detailed account of your doings during my stay at Thurnley Hall. Interfering with the mail, concealing a murder, assisting in the attempt to abduct me—all of it."

He had recovered from his initial shock, and although his expression was woebegone, he must have realized that it was futile to protest. His voice was almost meek when he said, "I shall do as you say. From now on I will be above reproach, niece. I swear it."

"I am glad to hear it," I replied, not troubling to hide my skepticism. "I don't know much about court procedure, but you may be asked to testify against Grigore. But I expect you to leave England as soon as your presence is no longer required."

"Haven't you heard, then?" he asked in surprise. When I stared at him in perplexity, he said, "Late last night when the constables looked in on him in the room where they had him confined, they found him dead. The doctor says that he must have had a weak heart, as do so many men of his size. He believes the physical and emotional strain of yesterday's events, followed by his arrest, must have been too much for him."

As shocking as the news was, I could not help but reflect that it might be for the best. Had Grigore lived, he would very likely have been sent to prison or an asylum, either of which would probably have been a kind of living death.

"Then you won't even be called upon to testify against him," I said. "You may begin preparing for your departure almost at once." Some stubborn remnant of pity forced me to ask, "Will you miss Yorkshire very dreadfully?"

He shrugged his shoulders. "I've never been liked hereabouts," he admitted, "and the ill feeling only grew during Victor's lifetime. Whenever he stayed at Thurnley he tended to . . . well, his pursuits were not such as would win the family any love from our tenants or in the village. I tried to hush things up, but sometimes it was difficult." His gaze had turned inward, and now he winced at whatever memory he had called up.

With a shudder I wondered if Victor had abducted others before Atticus and performed experiments on them, or if he had perpetrated other horrors. Looking back, I realized that the strange behavior I had seen in some of the townspeople had been catalyzed by the presence of Victor Lynch or the carriage in which he traveled, not by Atticus. They had not been superstitious people, just wary, and that gave me an idea of just how unpleasant Victor must have made himself outside the walls of Thurnley Hall.

"Perhaps I'll settle in Germany," my uncle continued, with the ghost of his old heartiness. "Find some quiet place with good hunting. Or possibly Styria; it is said to be beautiful."

It wasn't my concern that he find a place to his liking. "When you do relocate," I told him, "I want you to settle generous sums on Thomas, Ann, and Mrs. Antonescu. That is my final stipulation. They must be handsomely provided for when they leave your employ."

"Mrs.—? Oh, the cook. Yes, whatever you think best. You say that is the last of your conditions? Our business is at an end?"

Never had I imagined that my uncle, once so arrogant and bombastic, would speak to me in so plaintive and humble a tone. "Almost," I said, and handed him my grandmother's letter. "This is for you."

He drew it from the envelope and unfolded it, and his brow constricted in pain as he read the words. At length he said, "This is just what I feared Mother would tell you—what I tried so hard to prevent her from confiding."

"I can well understand why you tried to keep the story from me," I said. "But as she and your father are both gone now, there seems no need to disclose it to those outside the family. I shall keep her secret." In fact, I had decided not to share the letter with Atticus. It would serve little purpose that I could see to divulge my grandmother's tragedy.

"I thank you," my uncle said. "Where did you find it? I thought I had searched most carefully."

"She had sewn it into the lining of my mother's dress."

He nodded heavily. "Clever," he said. "She always was too smart for me."

I realized I did not know what else to say. I could hardly thank him for hosting Atticus and me. "Well, I suppose it's time we said goodbye, uncle."

"I suppose it is." Since I did not offer my hand, he bobbed his head in farewell and cast a look at my abdomen. "Er . . . good luck, niece. With the child."

I placed my hand over my womb, protecting it from his gaze. "I shan't need it," I said calmly. "Not in the way you mean."

When he opened the door, Atticus was poised at the threshold, and for a moment the two men eyed one another warily.

Then Atticus stepped aside, allowing my uncle to shuffle past him. As he passed down the hall I noticed how bowed his shoulders were, how shambling his walk. He had aged greatly over the time I had known him.

Atticus and I watched from a front window as my uncle made his way to his carriage, which had clearly been retrieved. Thomas sat in the driver's seat as before. When he caught sight of us in the window, he touched his cap. Then my uncle closed the carriage door, Thomas chirruped at the horses, and the carriage started down the street. Soon it turned a corner and was lost to view.

"He took my terms fairly well," I said. "I think he'll keep his word."

"He is a fortunate man indeed to be answerable to you," said Atticus, putting his left arm around me. In his right hand he held a borrowed walking stick. "I doubt anyone else would have been as generous to him."

"Let's not talk of him anymore," I said, resting my head against his shoulder. "There are so many things that are much pleasanter to contemplate."

"So there are," he said. "Like our daughter, for a start."

I gazed up at the handsome, beloved face I had believed such a short time ago I would never see again. "Oh, you wish me to have a girl?" I teased.

His smile brought crinkles to the corners of his eyes. "I shall be overjoyed with our child whether we have a girl or a boy . . . but I can't help thinking how charming it would be to have a miniature Clara about the house."

I laughed and slipped my arms around him. "What if I should be the only Clara? Am I not enough for you?"

"Never think it, my love," he said, drawing me closer. "I am still astonished that we are to be so fortunate as to have a child at all. It's as if a new life is beginning for us."

"So it is," I said. "A new life . . . and a new adventure."

EPILOGUE

Some months later, I was brought to bed of a fine boy child. Little Robert Atticus was blessed with a strong, healthy body, free of any obvious impairment that might cause him pain or draw unkind comment. Atticus could not make up his mind whether he was more delighted with me or with his infant son. Fortunately, as I pointed out, he did not need to choose between us.

Vivi, who was now thoroughly recovered from having borne her baby girl, Régine, bustled about Gravesend Lodge in the following days making certain that I was well looked after, although Atticus was even quicker to see to my comfort and grant my every wish. I believe that if I had expressed a desire for a banyan tree from India, he would have contrived to obtain one for me.

Seeing him hold our son in his arms was the pinnacle of happiness to me. The only thing approaching a flaw in my joy was that my mother was not present to see her grandson. But her photograph gazed at me from the bureau across the room, and I could almost believe that she observed and shared in my happiness.

"My love," said Atticus, sitting down beside me on the bed and carefully passing Rob to me, "I believe his hair is every bit as dark and curly as yours."

The satisfaction in his voice made me smile. "But he has your eyes," I pointed out, "and that is the important thing—to me, at least."

"What a heartbreaker the little fellow shall be!" Vivi said with a laugh as George and Sterry entered, carrying a crate.

"Another gift!" George announced. "If they don't stop soon, you'll be crowded out of the lodge and have to return to the Hall." He handed Atticus the accompanying envelope, which was addressed to us both in a hand that awakened a sense of foreboding in me. Atticus read the letter aloud.

Dear niece and nephew,

I understand that congratulations are due to you. Please accept this small token of my regret for what you suffered under my roof.

This gift shall soon be all that remains of the home of the Burleighs, for I understand that the new owner of Thurnley Hall has decided to have it torn down and replaced with a new edifice. Perhaps it is just as well, considering its unfortunate history.

I write to you from Styria, although I am considering spending the winter in Italy. My health is not as strong as before, and I believe the climate would do me good.

I pray that the Burleigh curse will spare your child, and I wish your family all the good fortune that was denied me.

Your uncle
Horace Burleigh

"It seems that he has kept his word to you, Clara," Atticus observed after he had finished reading. "I almost regret that he gives me no excuse to administer a drubbing."

"He isn't worth the trouble," I said. "But I have a terrible suspicion as to the gift he has sent us. George, would you mind opening the crate?"

When he had pried off the lid and lifted the contents out, my apprehension was confirmed: It was the antique cradle from Thurnley Hall. In our airy bedroom in the lodge the dark, bulky thing squatted like a malignant toad.

Vivi wrinkled her nose in distaste. "Well," she said doubtfully, "perhaps it is of great sentimental value."

"We can find room for it in the attic," Atticus said. "One question, though, my love. What is this Burleigh curse your uncle speaks of?"

I looked down at the adorable face of our son, who was waving his tiny fists as he lay in my arms, and felt a rush of thankfulness that I could put superstitious worries behind me. The Burleigh curse belonged to the past, not to our child's future.

"Nothing, dearest," I told Atticus, and kissed his cheek. "Nothing at all."

The End

Don't miss Clara's previous adventures in

WITH THIS CURSE

**Winner of the 2015 Daphne du Maurier Award
for historical mystery/suspense**

～⤙⤚～

Can a curse strike twice in a woman's life?

In 1854, seventeen-year-old chambermaid Clara Crofton was dismissed from Gravesend Hall for having fallen in love with Richard Blackwood, the younger son of the house. Alone in the world, Clara found a tenuous position as a seamstress, but she always blamed the Gravesend curse for the disaster that had befallen her—and for Richard's death soon after in the Crimean War.

Now, more than eighteen years later, Richard's twin, Atticus, seeks out Clara with a strange proposal: if she will marry him and live with him as his wife in name only to ease the mind of his dying father, Atticus will then endow her with a comfortable income for the rest of her life. Clara knows that he is not disclosing his true motives, but when she runs out of options for an independent life, she has no choice but to become Atticus's wife.

For Clara, returning to Gravesend as a bride brings some triumph . . . but also great unease. Not only must she pretend to be a wellborn lady and devoted wife to a man whose face is a constant reminder of the love she lost, but ominous portents whisper that her masquerade brings grave danger. "This house will take from you what you most treasure," her mother once warned her. But the curse has already taken the man Clara loved. Will it now demand her life?

Follow the adventures of actress Sybil Ingram, Clara's former employer, in

Nocturne for a Widow

Book one in the Sybil Ingram Victorian Mysteries series

❦

"DeWees offers up a win for gothic romance . . . sizzles with chemistry sure to please readers." *–Library Journal*

The ghost may be the least of her problems . . . Vivacious actress Sybil Ingram looks forward to a life of security when she leaves the theater in 1873 to marry a wealthy American. But when he dies on their wedding night, she finds herself a penniless widow. Her only legacy is Brooke House, a Gothic revival manor in the wilds of the Hudson River Valley. However, the eerie mansion comes with two tenants. One is a hostile ghost. The second, and far worse, is former violinist Roderick Brooke—the most insolent, dangerous, maddeningly gorgeous man she's ever met.

As Sybil and Roderick engage in a battle of wills—and wits—an even greater threat arises: the mysterious queen of local society, Mrs. Lavinia Dove. For reasons that Sybil can't imagine, Mrs. Dove is determined to have Brooke House and Roderick for herself . . . if necessary, by deadly means.

Available in ebook, paperback, and audiobook

Made in the USA
Las Vegas, NV
26 February 2021